THE BLIND SPOT

Judge Hammond, father of teenage Claire, marries his daughter's coach, attractive university student, Vale Rorke, twenty-five years his junior. Claire fiercely resents her father's autumn-spring second marriage.

When Claire and Guy Steele, her father's registrar, inadvertently discover that Vale is carrying on an *affaire* with American journalist, Jef Broome – with whom Claire had fancied herself in love – the battle is joined between the two young women.

It is this conflict which dominates the book, side by side with Vale's efforts to escape from the emotional entanglement which threatens to destroy her home and family and which eventually brings tragedy in its wake.

The story is set in the beautiful Cape Peninsula among the places and people South African Joy Packer knew best.

also by Joy Packer

The Blind Spot

a novel by
JOY PACKER

METHUEN

First published 1967 by
Eyre & Spottiswoode (Publishers) Ltd
© Joy Packer 1967, 1969
Reprinted 1977 by Eyre Methuen Ltd
and 1983 by Methuen London Ltd
11 New Fetter Lane, London EC4P 4EE
Printed in Great Britain by
Redwood Burn Limited, Trowbridge,
Wiltshire

ISBN 0 413 44210 1

AUTHOR'S NOTE

All the characters in this novel are entirely fictitious, except for the brief mention of the late Dr Verwoerd and his assassin, Tsafendas, and of the 'tokoloshe killer', Msomi.

Cape Peninsula   JOY PACKER

CONTENTS

I

CRY OF THE CURLEW

AFTERWARDS IT SEEMED TO CLAIRE HAMMOND THAT the scream – a strange lost cry – had altered the pattern of all their lives at Silverglade, for the scream had led to the discovery of the letter. Nothing was the same after that. Not for her or for her father, Judge Charles Hammond; or her young impetuous stepmother, Vale; or for Jefferson Broome, the stranger who had been in their midst last summer. Even Guy Steele, the law student who was her father's registrar and like one of the family, had been drawn in, and later the steadily growing web had netted every member of the household right down to jolly little four-year-old Micky, Claire's step-brother, and grizzled old Josiah, the Judge's Xhosa house-man.

Yet the hour before the scream had been steeped in peace and golden light, with the cobweb tide of a summer evening filling the southern ravines of Table Mountain and gradually engulfing the lower terrace of the garden where Claire lounged on the grass verge of the swimming-pool with Guy. Silverglade, the old house high on the ridge, built by Claire's maternal grandfather in a spacious age, was hidden from the pool by a blue haze of jacarandas and the grove of silver trees from which it took its name. From the stoep, still in sunshine, you could look down the valley across the Constantia vineyards to the Indian Ocean, a scene as lovely as any in the lovely Cape.

'Your old man was magnificent in court today,' Guy was

saying. 'He has a terrific sense of the dramatic. When he sums up it's like good theatre, full of curtains and surprises. He presents every aspect of the case. First you think the prisoner is bound to get off and then you think he's for the high jump, and in the end, whatever the sentence, you feel it was inevitable – that there could have been no other.'

'Makes him sound God-like.'

Claire sat up, dangling her feet in the blue water, the last of the sun on her bare back. Her hair, still wet from her recent dip, looked dark instead of ashen gold. She put up her thin long hands to disengage the clinging strands from her neck. She had a child's neck, he thought. A slender stem, defenceless and young. She was nineteen, only six years younger than her stepmother, but at first glance she looked less with her narrow hips and small enticing breasts; then you saw that her face was not childish. It was subtly sculpted with the smooth fair skin drawn tightly over the narrow patrician framework inherited from her father.

'Every judge should have a God-like quality,' said Guy, 'but few of them do. Your father is one of the few. He looks the part and he has the wisdom. He has compassion too. He understands the quality of mercy. But he's not soft. An innocent man would welcome your father on the Bench but a guilty man would fear him.'

As he spoke a shower of blue jacaranda flowers drifted gently to the surface of the pool. Guy kicked at the water and set them dancing towards a scum of pollen and a drowned spider at the deep end.

'We need Vale here with her beloved fishing-net. She'd have those off the water in no time.'

Claire jerked her head towards the changing-pavilion. 'Since she isn't here you might like to do her favourite job instead. The net's over there.'

She watched Guy as he sprang up – a lanky well-muscled

young man, with rather equine features, an aggressive nose, pushed a little askew in the course of a boxing match, a long determined jaw, a merry upturned mouth and thick dark hair, curling crisply after his swim. He brought the long pole with the little triangular net and began to skim the surface of the water. When Guy performed this task it was utilitarian, Claire thought, but, whenever her stepmother did it, it became an exercise in seduction.

Claire closed her eyes and recalled a day last summer when Vale had been languidly occupied with this chore. She saw again the attenuated figure in the white bikini, the provocative fall of full breasts as Vale leaned forward and drew back rhythmically, stretching a little from time to time to scoop up a drowned grasshopper or a spider with legs closely furled in death. She had netted a tiny frog that day and let it go hopping away among the banked blue hydrangeas. Vale's natural grace always heightened Claire's awareness of her own disability, a slight limp – the legacy of polio in infancy – no more than a hint of weakness in her right leg, a mere suggestion of certain muscles not withered but impaired. In her mind's eye she saw Jef Broome, their American house-guest, squatting on his heels at the water's edge, watching Vale, the sun glinting on his bright, fair hair and the golden down on his arms and legs, and she could hear his drawling husky voice.

'She's a poem, she's a Degas dream, but I can't write her and I can't draw her. I'll just have to remember a summer aquatint – long-legged girl with butterfly net.'

Claire had winced. She, at that time, would have given anything to be memorable to Jef Broome, but her stepmother had merely turned her dark boyish head and laughed over her shoulder. When she laughed that way her big black eyes brimmed as if the rising sap in her pliant body were on the brink of overflowing. And she had gone on quietly with her task, fishing for leaves, petals and admiration.

That had been last summer. Between then and now Claire had spent a year in Italy learning languages and the history of art and hoping that Jef Broome would come back into her life one day. But it was Guy who was beginning to monopolize her and Jef who was receding into the past. She had a secret store of memories of Jef, that challenging foreigner who had exploded into their lives with his disarming boyish candour and his controversial opinions. She had confided his effect on her own emotional development to her diary, seeking to impale on words sensations so elusive and poignant that they hovered moth-like between pain and pleasure. Some she had captured, and reading once more what she had written, the moths had fluttered again, soft and insistent. But gradually the magic had diminished and a few weeks ago she had closed the diary finally, with a snap. What was the good? He would come back – or he wouldn't – and, if he did, she'd get him! Meanwhile there was Guy.

'What about a last dip before we change?'

He was standing in front of her and she nodded and gave him her hands. He drew her up in one smooth movement and brought her into his arms, head flung back with her mane of pale hair hanging across his arm. They were finding their own special attitudes together, like dance steps, and she knew that now he would place his palm gently in the small of her back and hold her close against his body and that presently she'd melt with wanting him.

But the spell was broken by a cry – a terrible drawn-out shriek of fear and agony rising in an eerie crescendo from the hedge near the road.

'Oh, God,' she gasped. 'It can't be Micky! Micky's never cried like that.' Micky was Claire's four-year-old half-brother, Vale's son.

'It's not Micky. It's some wild thing caught in a trap. Come!'

They raced across the lawn to the thorn hedge, following the tormented fear-haunted cry which led them to the entrance of the drive. A wooden letter-box was attached to one of the wrought-iron gate-posts near a spot where the cotoneaster was thickest. Dart, the Judge's Alsatian, had heard the cry too and was already burrowing under the tangled thorns, whining as he did so. Guy knelt down and put his hands on the dog's neck.

'Steady – steady, Dart, old boy!'

The screaming had ceased as if the wounded creature waited in suspense. Guy peered into the dense thicket. The tiny biscuit-coloured flowers were almost over and the first orange berries clustered here and there among the thick foliage. The sun's last rays were on his broad tanned shoulders as he leaned forward tensely with the dog jostling against him.

'It's a bird,' he said. 'Trapped by the wing. You hold Dart, Claire!'

She crouched and grasped the Alsatian's collar and he strained against her, barking aggressively. Guy began to ease his hand through the prickly wall of cotoneaster.

'Damn! I could do with a glove.'

There was silence now except for the spasmodic barking of the dog. Both Guy's hands were working feverishly, pressing the cruel stems apart, forcing a tunnel through which he could reach the terrified creature snared between the thorns and the strands of rusty barbed wire that had once marked the Silverglade boundary.

'Got him! Poor devil, his heart's going like a sledge-hammer.'

Gradually and patiently he released the trapped wing and withdrew the prisoner. He stood up holding the bird high out of Dart's reach.

'Get that darn dog away!'

Claire dragged Dart a few yards, and then, from the house, they heard the loud sing-song of Harmonia, the cook. 'Dart-dog! Dart-dog! Dart-dog!'

Like all Bantu, Harmonia had melody in her blood and the two high-low notes with which she summoned the dog to his supper were as irresistible to the animal as the bugle call of 'come to the cookhouse door' would be to a hungry soldier. Dart stiffened and cocked an ear. He had stopped barking and in a moment Claire knew that she could let him go. As he bounded off in the direction of the yard, Guy lowered his hands with the bird in them. They were scratched and smeared with blood and he cherished the creature against his bare chest. Claire was suddenly glad that he had good hands, nervous, long-fingered and gentle.

'Feel its heart,' he said. 'Poor thing.'

She touched it tentatively, feeling the soft ruffled breast feathers and the wildly palpitating heart. The bird had a flat head, a long straight beak and round prominent scared eyes. It was biggish, fairly long in the leg.

'It's a young stone curlew,' said Guy. 'A dikkop – a night bird – the one with that weird cry —'

'Is it all right?'

'Yes, only frightened. It was caught between that old barbed-wire fence and the thorns. If it had gone on struggling it would have broken a wing – probably died.'

'Lucky we were near.'

He set the curlew on the ground and it swayed, shaky and dazed, recovering itself.

'I wonder if there's a nest in the hedge?' Claire bent to peer into the tunnel Guy had made pushing his arm through the thorns. There was no visible nest, but the gleam of paper attracted her attention.

'Paper,' she exclaimed indignantly. 'So untidy! Some beastly litter-bug! Oh, wait a bit, it could be a letter.'

She withdrew it easily and stood staring at the letter in her hand, puzzled and half annoyed.

'Now, how on earth did this get there?'

It was a fat American airmail letter with the stamps torn roughly off the long envelope.

The bird had moved unsteadily into the shelter of the low-growing branches. Neither Guy nor Claire noticed it now. Guy was standing next to her staring at the letter.

'Your postman evidently collects foreign stamps. He's pinched them and pushed the letter into the hedge instead of the letter-box.'

She was silent turning the letter over and over, studying it. The name and address of the sender was on the flap. Her face had blanched and her hands were ice cold as Guy took it from her. Her head drooped and she became aware of the curlew, standing near their feet, swaying a little. She wondered if the bird felt faint as she did at this moment – faint and shocked, as if she too had stumbled painfully into an entanglement that would inevitably enmesh those closest to her.

Guy was frowning – and she braced herself.

'This letter is for Vale. It's addressed to Mrs Charles Hammond —' He broke off as he saw the words starkly revealed in the gap left by the stolen stamps. ' . . . *honey love, if only you were free . . .*' A level ray of sunlight fell upon them like the beam of a torch in the darkening garden.

'Yes, it's for Vale,' repeated Claire tonelessly. 'From Jef Broome. Remember?'

'Of course. But I thought he and you —'

'No!' she cried sharply. As he looked at her he saw her face freeze in disillusion and disdain. Not for the first time, Guy thought that she possessed her own sort of beauty. Proud, almost ageless. Why did she care so terribly? Had Jef Broome really meant so much to her? Or was she distressed on her father's account, afraid that Vale was going to hurt him? She put out her chilly fingers to take the letter back.

'I'll see that my stepmother gets this when she comes home.'

She turned away without another glance at the rescued curlew immobile in the deepening shadows. He noticed that her left foot dragged a little as she mooched across the lawn. She held her shoulders well, but she was a moocher, one leg never quite carrying its full weight. He wanted to put his arm round her and give her a hug and tell her not to dramatize this business of a love-letter to Vale, but her attitude was deliberately aloof, warning him to mind his own business.

'You're staying to dinner, Guy?' she threw across her shoulder.

'I'd like to.'

'Good, we must change. Daddy and Vale will be back any time now. They're at a silver-wedding party. Daddy never stays late. He hates all cocktail parties.' She picked up her towel from the verge of the pool.

'I'm going on up to the house. See you later.'

He nodded and went thoughtfully into the changing-pavilion.

2

THE LETTER

WHEN CLAIRE CAME DOWN TO DINNER IN TAN slacks and a decorative tunic, her father, her stepmother and Guy were already on the wide stoep outside the dining-room. The shadows of the vine and the heavy bunches of grapes depending from the pergola were splashed against the white walls in the windless night. Below the stoep glimmered banks of hydrangeas and a rambling garden, beyond which the sleeping valley stretched away to the sea and the twinkling clusters of coastal lights. Behind the house ran the dark spine of mountains that split the Cape Peninsula from north to south, and the delicate grove of silvers from which Silverglade took its name. Most of the silver trees grew in strange appealing shapes, warped by the winter north-westers, but here and there one rose tall and straight, spear-bright and shining among its fellows.

The Judge, spare and aquiline, stood talking to Guy about some case that was coming on in the following week, and Vale, still in her printed silk cocktail dress, sat on a low cushioned garden chair with her hand on Dart's head. The light of an old wrought-iron coach lantern fell on to her short dark hair and the curve of her long neck and sloping shoulders. She looked fragile tonight, young and endangered. Like the curlew, Guy thought.

'Sorry I'm late,' said Claire to her stepmother. 'You were back earlier than I'd expected.'

Vale looked up and laughed.

'Surely you know your father at a party! It was all I could do to make him stay for the speeches. He goes to put in an appearance – but I admit he does that beautifully.'

Her glance and her tone mocked and flattered her husband at the same time. Charles Hammond grinned at her, the tiny wrinkles deepening around his eyes. He was perfectly well aware of his own physical presence and the stir it never failed to create in a room full of people. He was singled out by his height, by that noble head with the greying fair hair beginning to recede at the temples, and by a manner both easy and assured. At fifty he still had the athletic figure and fluid movements of a man as much at home on the golf course as on the Bench. Among his colleagues at the Bar, he was respected as a just and tolerant judge, one who picked the human marrow from the contentious bones of legal quibbles and technicalities. After the protracted death of his wife from an incurable disease his friends had been anxious to see him marry again, but he had been in no hurry. When he finally took twenty-year-old Vale Rorke to the altar eyebrows had risen, and for the first time in years his wisdom had been in question.

Claire's expression did not reflect the amusement in her stepmother's face as she stood, hands in the big flap pockets of her tunic, looking down at Vale.

'Did you enjoy the party?' she asked.

Vale shrugged. 'As silver weddings go, it was very well done. Honestly though, I didn't know half the people.'

Her voice – soft and furry – was bored.

'Always out of your age-group, aren't you, Vale?'

Claire's words fell into a brief silence between Hammond and Guy, and suddenly the warm stillness of the night was electric.

'Oh, I wouldn't say that.' Vale glanced at her tall husband. 'But we do have a good many duty parties, don't we, Charles?'

'I suppose we do.'

Claire had drawn something from her pocket.

'Guy and I rescued an injured bird this evening. It was trapped in the hedge near the letter-box. We found this. It's for you.'

She tossed the letter carelessly into Vale's lap and watched her stepmother frankly and intently. My God! thought Guy. She might have been throwing down the gauntlet!

Vale stared at the letter in her lap aghast. The colour drained from her face as her long fingers grasped it.

'A letter – with the stamps torn off. How extraordinary!' she said faintly. 'What's our postman up to?'

The Judge put on his spectacles. 'May I see it?'

Vale hesitated but her husband had already put out his hand for the letter and there was nothing she could reasonably do except surrender it. He examined it under the lantern.

'Shall I get you a sherry, Claire?' Guy asked. Anything to ease the tension.

'Yes, medium please, not the dry.' She spoke without turning her head, her eyes riveted on her father.

Charles Hammond did not know how long he had stood under the light. So this was it? He hoped that his face was blank. In fact, he had managed a twisted smile that lent him a faintly scornful look. He braced his broad shoulders as he turned to his wife and dropped the letter back into her lap.

'Give me the envelope later and I'll have a word with the postman.'

'It's from Jef Broome,' remarked Claire casually. 'I saw his name on the flap. I wonder if he wants to come and stay with us again?'

Vale's large dark eyes flashed lightning at Claire. 'If he does I'll let you know.'

She put the letter into her handbag and closed it with a

decisive snap. 'Josiah announced dinner before you came down, Claire. We'll go in.'

She rose and Guy moved to one side to allow her to go past him through the french doors into the dining-room. Josiah in his white drill suit and red sash was standing behind her chair and she sat down with the confidence of the mistress of the house – and of the situation too.

The tall candelabra, the flames of its branches scarcely wavering in the calm night, isolated the four at the polished mahogany table with its gleam of cut glass and silver. Presently the Judge rose to carve the chicken at the side table and Josiah, true to the ritual of years and the mistress before Vale, immediately switched on the light above it. Guy observed the bent head with the light gleaming on vigorous hair and glinting off horn-rimmed spectacles.

'A wing for you, Vale. Breast for Claire. A bit of everything, Guy?'

It was the usual patter. What was he really thinking? Impossible to tell. Guy's glance shifted to Claire. Physically she resembled her father, the same chiselled features and deep blue eyes, the same tapering hands. But in character she was entirely different. Where Hammond was tolerant and penetrating, his daughter was emotional and harsh in her criticisms, capable of making terrible mistakes – as she had done tonight when she had given her antagonism full rein and flung the letter in Vale's lap. She'd looked vicious then, but she had herself in hand now, her face blank and cold. Hammond put down the carvers and resumed his seat as if nothing had happened. Conversation at dinner was sustained by the host and Guy with an occasional remark from Vale. Claire was silent and withdrawn. No one referred to the letter. It might never have existed, yet it was a living question mark in the minds of all four of them. It was a relief when they went out on to the stoep for coffee. Josiah brought the tray and set it on the marble table. As soon as she had swallowed her small cup of black coffee, Vale rose.

'Micky's restless and fretful tonight, Charles. I'm going up to him. In case I don't see you later, Guy, I'll say good night.'

It was clear that she didn't intend to come down again. Now she'll go and read her letter by herself, thought Claire. That'll shake her. She's got to go back or forward. She can't stand still now that Daddy has been alerted. She'll know that as soon as she has a chance to examine that envelope properly. And Daddy? What about him? What can he do? He can't just ignore it. Or can he? And wait for the next move? He's capable of that.

The Judge was standing looking towards the mountain. 'There's a fire over there – to the right of Constantia Nek – seems to be moving towards the gum plantations.'

'Shall I get your binoculars, Daddy?' Claire asked.

'Yes, do.'

Through the powerful glasses they were able to see the mobile water tankers and the beaters, little black figures performing their wild antics on the fringe of the inferno.

'Shall we go up there and have a look at close quarters?' said Guy. Claire jumped at the suggestion.

'I'd love to.' Anything to get away from the atmosphere she had created. 'I'll change into old slacks and shoes.'

'And tie back your hair if you want to help beat,' advised her father.

'Will you come with us, sir?' asked Guy.

'No thanks. I'd say that fire was well under control even though it looks dramatic. But keep an eye on Claire. She shows off.' His grin was an effort. Guy laughed.

'I'll watch it.'

Hammond did not move when they had gone. He settled

himself on the chaise-longue and lit his pipe as the roar and throb of Guy's little Mini-Cooper faded. There was a hole in the silencer. Why did the young always have to make such a damn noise about everything these days? He shook his head. That was the wrong way to think. He couldn't afford to patronize the younger generation – or even to criticize it over much. He must keep his outlook flexible if he was to keep his young wife happy – or keep her at all.

He turned his head as Josiah came on to the terrace to take the coffee cups.

'Master want whisky?'

The sturdy old Bantu's rumbling voice was soothing. Josiah had been part of Hammond's life for twenty-five years – before Vale was born, before his marriage to Claire's mother. For every year in his employ Josiah had received a steadily increasing bonus. He must have saved a very reasonable nest-egg by now. Quite soon he would have to leave the Cape and return to the Transkei in conformity with the Government policy of sending urban Bantu back to their native homelands. The Judge did not wish to lose Josiah and Josiah did not wish to go, for, although he had a wife and family in the Transkei, the source of his income was here with his master to whom he frequently referred as his 'father'. The fact that the Judge was at least ten years his junior did not detract at all from Josiah's filial attitude, for, according to him, a man was as old as his wisdom, which would make Judge Hammond venerable. So, one way and another, both master and man were doing all in their power to postpone the necessity of parting.

'You can bring the whisky' said the Judge. 'And I'll help myself if I want any. There's no need to wait up. Miss Claire will lock the door when she comes in.'

'Yes, master. I go fetch whisky and iced water.'

Josiah removed the coffee tray with the dignity that

characterized every task he performed. Hammond was aware of the pride the Xhosa felt in their close association. We've learned a great deal from one another down the years, he thought. We appreciate each other. I wonder if he guesses at my problems? In his tribe it's customary for a Chief to take a 'little wife'. That's what I've done. He probably approves. His manner to Vale is respectful but paternal. What beautiful manners the Bantu have, even if they do practise some fearful customs. Hammond had tried cases of ritual murder in his time. Murder for *muti* – medicine. Could you fairly blame the murderers? You were compelled to condemn them, of course, but the principle was not so unreasonable. Human sacrifice for the good of the tribe. Christian teaching had the same sad basic theme. Human sacrifice for the sake of all mankind. Sometimes he wondered if he were really a good judge. He saw so many sides of every case, especially when he was dealing with the Bantu whose place in the white civilization was precarious. Many of them still thought as tribesmen despite their veneer of city sophistication. In the tribal territories they were subject to the tribal law of their own black courts. It was here in the cities that they were judged by white standards. He sighed as he heard Josiah pad into the house on the immaculate white tennis shoes he always wore on duty.

Upstairs in the main bedroom the light went on. Vale called down from the sleeping-porch over the terrace.

'I'm tired, Charles. I'm going to bed.'

He looked up at the pale anonymous face. 'I may be late. I have some work to do. How's Micky?'

'Micky, why, he's fine. Dead to the world.' So the child hadn't really been restless at all.

'I'll try not to disturb you when I come up,' he said. 'Sleep well.'

Soon there was only the orange glow of her reading-lamp

through the curtains dividing the sleeping-porch from their bedroom.

Hammond glanced up as Josiah padded on to the stoep once more bearing a silver salver with a decanter, a thermos jug of iced water and a glass.

'You make it too easy,' he smiled. 'Good night, Josiah.'

The Xhosa flashed his splendid teeth. 'Good night, master.'

The Judge seldom took a nightcap, but Josiah had an uncanny instinct for producing that silver salver when it was likely to be welcome. He knew his master's ups and downs, he understood the depression that followed a case involving a capital charge, and the nights when the Judge would be working late in his study, and tonight he sensed a disturbance in the atmosphere of the household. The young women were cross with each other and that meant trouble for the master. Josiah had known Miss Claire all her life and he was devoted to her, but that one could make a person shudder as if he had bitten into a sour fruit. The Proud One, they called her, from the way she tossed her head with the long straight fair hair and gave orders. She said 'Please' because she'd been brought up to do so, but she didn't *think* please. She hadn't liked it when her father had brought a young wife to Silverglade, even though the young wife had been her friend. She loved her father too much – especially after the death of her mother. Suffering had matured her too young. She had suffered the long sickness of her mother and before that her own polio sickness that had crippled her for a time. These things had made her lonely. As a child she had not played enough with other children of her own age, and later her slowly dying mother had been as sad as a wilted flower. Miss Claire and Josiah had always been good friends. He had helped teach her to walk again after her sickness and he knew her courage. She was a fighter. She could fight like a cat in a corner and she had fought against the coming of a new wife. But the Wise One was strong. He had brought the young wife home and Miss Claire had ceased her spitting because the only way to keep the love of her father had been to accept the new mistress of Silverglade. She had spoken to Josiah about it and he had advised her.

'How can somebody so young take my mother's place? How can she be a mother to me?'

He had answered in the respectful third person.

'Miss Claire is fifteen years old. A woman. My master does not seek a new mother for his daughter. He seeks a little wife to make him young again.'

'*I* keep him young,' she had announced in her arrogant way.

Josiah's expansive grin had broken the darkness of his face and suddenly Claire had laughed. When she laughed it was like a sunburst, warming to the heart.

'How will you take orders from my stepmother, Josiah?' she had asked.

'The new madam will leave the old ways,' he said. 'I can tell. That one is easy-going.'

He had been right, the new madam had indeed been content to let things ride. Harmonia had continued to rule the kitchen and after the son, Micky, was born, her cousin, Fedora, had come to help with the baby. But it was Harmonia who had comforted the little fellow when he was teething. She had put him in a sling on her massive back as if he were a Xhosa baby and he had lolled there against her warm cushioned mobile body as she went about her tasks in the kitchen in the leisurely way of her people. His crying would cease then and he would fall asleep. The Easy-Going One had no objections. She would come into the kitchen, her large dark eyes amused.

'I must try it, Harmonia,' she said. 'You must lend me

your sling.' But she didn't mean it. Her slim straight body with its brisk movements was not the right *muti* for a child with sore gums, and she knew it.

Miss Claire had gone away to Italy then for a year after leaving school. It had been easier in Silverglade without Miss Claire. There were often storms in the air these days like the dry storms of Josiah's own country when the lightning flashed before the rain came down.

He left the small light burning in the hall for Miss Claire and then he went to his own quarters across the yard. He tapped lightly on the door of Harmonia's room. There were times when he too found great comfort in the ample curves of the Xhosa cook. She was neither his tribal wife nor his town woman and she could be a proper virago in the kitchen when the mood took her, for, like all cooks, she was a woman of highly spiced temperament, but he and she found much to laugh about together and where there was laughter there was friendship and friendship was an all-embracing term. He heard the key turn and the door opened a fraction. She stood in her Victorian white nightdress, a fine well-cushioned figure of a woman, and without a word she made way for him. He gave a deep sigh of contentment.

'Ammonia,' he said. 'There are things wrong in this house tonight. Let it be right with you and me.'

'It is right,' she answered.

A little breeze sprang up and cooled the parched garden. It was not enough to fan the flames of the mountain fire. Hammond helped himself to whisky, water and ice without moving from his chair. He gazed across the valley at the jagged flickering red scar on the berg but he scarcely saw it. He was seeing his young wife and his daughter, Claire, in the days when he had first met and fallen in love with Vale. That was five years ago when Claire was still a schoolgirl and Vale a university student of twenty.

3

THE JUDGE'S WIFE

IT WAS CLAIRE WHO HAD INADVERTENTLY BROUGHT them together.

After his wife's death Hammond, suffering from profound mental and emotional exhaustion, was ordered a complete change. 'A sea voyage,' his doctor prescribed. 'If you don't take a holiday you'll crack up.'

Claire had insisted upon accompanying him.

'You need me, Daddy.'

'What about your schooling?'

'I'll miss one term. I can catch up, I promise you. If I need a coach later on you can get me one. Let me come, Daddy.'

He believed that she too needed a change of scene and willingly allowed himself to be persuaded. Claire was all he had left. He found his adolescent daughter good company with a keen intellect, a vivid interest in new places, and highly developed, slightly malicious powers of observation where people were concerned. She was inclined to seek hidden motives behind simple friendliness and it was something of a shock to him to discover that, like her mother, she viewed every attractive unattached woman with only lightly veiled suspicion. He had no thought of re-marriage then. All he wanted was a period of respite.

They left the stormy winter Cape and cruised through the islands of the Indian Ocean, winding up with three sunny weeks in Lourenço Marques on the coast of Portuguese East Africa. Claire sat with her father in sophisticated restaurants under the flame trees and watched the multi-racial world about her. She learned to enjoy a glass of dry Dao wine with her chicken piri-piri or the giant prawns for which Lourenço Marques is famous, she swam in the hotel pool, walked round the golf course high above the ocean with her father, and even went with him to a bullfight, where she displayed intense excitement rather than horror. She was fourteen but she conducted herself with adult poise. When she went out to dinner with him she wore very pale pink lipstick and nail varnish to match, accentuating her long nervous hands so like his own. She was conscious of her clothes and of the swell of her small round breasts; conscious too of the slight drag of her left leg when she was tired, but she fought that. Hammond came to realize, with a queer mixture of delight and dismay, that his daughter was, in fact, a woman.

They returned to Silverglade refreshed. But catching up a term's work was not altogether easy for Claire, and her class mistress suggested that she be coached in certain subjects. She gave Hammond the name of Vale Rorke, a scholarship student at the University of Cape Town who was helping to pay her way by coaching in her spare time.

Vale came to Silverglade two evenings a week and Sunday mornings. She came on her second-hand moped wearing stretchy slacks and a crash helmet. Because her legs were long and shapely and her hips narrow she looked good in the stretchies and when she swept off her crash-helmet the soft dark curls tumbled carelessly about her head and framed a heart-shaped face of dreamy-eyed but lively charm.

'Claire is spoilt and precocious,' the Judge told Vale at their first interview. 'She's had a difficult life – polio in childhood and its after-effects – luckily very slight – and then her mother's long illness during her most formative years. She may give you trouble.'

'Does she want to pass her exams?' asked Vale, going straight to the root of the matter as far as she was concerned.

'Oh, yes. That's a question of pride.'

'Then we'll get along all right.'

He noted with pleasure that she had an agreeable voice. Velvet. In fact, there was a bloom all over her – her skin, her voice, her whole personality – like certain fruit, and the wings of moths. Be gentle lest the bloom brush off, he had thought, and grinned wrily at the notion. Today's generation were tough, bloom or no bloom.

Claire approved of her new coach. Vale treated her pupil as an equal and she taught well. She was also prepared to discuss Claire's most intimate problems. At fourteen Claire was much preoccupied with boy-friends. 'I don't want to go steady,' she confided in Vale, 'but, if you don't, you get left in the cold, biting your nails.'

'You've got to keep switching,' said Vale. 'You've got to be the one who breaks it up, or you're trapped with one boy having a sole monopoly. You've got to keep your mind and your heart free against the time when you suddenly meet the one person you know you really want.'

She'd spoken with intensity, for she had recently done just that, and the one person she knew she really wanted happened to be Claire's father.

Sometimes Vale stayed on to Sunday midday dinner and in the afternoon she'd make up a four at tennis or just laze at the edge of the pool. They learned that her mother was a widow, and that she had one brother, John, an accountant in Johannesburg.

'My home isn't beautiful like this,' she said. 'Mother lives in a flat with a view of the mine dumps.'

'The mine dumps have their own sort of beauty,' said Hammond.

'So has machinery, if you're attuned to it. I'm not. I need

trees and mountains and the sea not too far away. I adore the Cape.'

They had been swimming and Vale rolled over on her back and spread her arms as if inviting the sweet spring air of the Cape to possess her and become her lover. Or was the invitation intended for the Judge? Like most of her contemporaries she was a sun-worshipper and her bikini was scanty. That day Charles Hammond found himself stirred by impulses long dormant, and the passive peace of mind that had become habitual was shattered finally and for ever. For once, Claire was imperceptive. Vale was her teacher and her friend, only six years older than herself, Vale was *hers*, and Claire had no inkling of the forces entering her life and preparing to change its pattern.

One evening Vale came to Silverglade without her moped. 'It's being serviced. So I came by bus.'

Hammond raised his eyebrows. 'It's quite a walk from the bus-stop.'

She laughed. 'It's a lovely walk. Shady, under the trees.'

'Too lonely at night,' he said. 'I'll drive you home.'

It had long since become understood that she stayed for supper after her bi-weekly sessions with Claire, and after the meal, while the schoolgirl tackled her homework, Hammond and Vale often chatted for a while before she returned to the bare little flat she shared with two other girls. He was growing accustomed to seeing her in his home and it seemed to him that she belonged there.

That night when they reached the hairpin bend of the high road with its view of Cape Town, a dazzling dancing maze of lights spreading from the mountainside to the sea and far across the Flats to the distant range of the Hottentots-Holland, Vale put her hand over his.

'Stop here a moment, Charles. Let's draw in off the roadside and just look at all that magic.'

He was only too glad to accede to her request. Presently he said:

'You must have a special boy-friend. Doesn't he resent the time you spend at Silverglade?'

She laughed with an undertone of bitterness.

'I haven't a special boy-friend.'

'How's that?'

'Because I won't go steady.'

'Why not?'

'Why should I?'

'Most young people do these days, as far as I can gather.'

'And what happens? Somebody stakes a claim and the others lay off. He thinks he owns you, body and soul.'

'You feel very strongly about it.'

'I know what I'm talking about. Your boy-friend expects to be your lover and no strings attached. He's committed to nothing. It's all experimentation. You contribute to each other's sexual experience. You can't call it love. There's no tenderness in it, no unselfishness. Only hunger and urgency.'

'No wonder! You inspire hunger and urgency, damn you, my beautiful!'

He drew her into his arms and his hand slid gently down her round smooth throat into the opening of her shirt. Her fierce response set him on fire.

'For God's sake, Vale, you'd drive any man mad —'

Her arms were round his neck and her lips were parted.

'Go mad, darling.' She breathed. 'Let me drive you mad!'

He felt the years of sanity and repression, the severe self-discipline and continence imposed by his wife's illness, rip away, leaving him prey to the ardent passion of youth. The scent and heat of her flesh, the young bursting curves beneath his hands transported him. He had never wanted any woman as he wanted this girl, who was less than half his age. He heard himself mutter:

'I love you – I loved you from the first moment I saw you.'

'And I love you, Charles.'

Later, when she had combed her fingers helplessly through her tumbled curls, he took her face between his hands. He could not see it clearly in the darkness, just the pale sweet heart-shaped blur.

'Listen, my love,' he said in a low voice. 'This sort of thing won't do. I'd better find me a wife – someone nearer my own age —'

'You won't like that.' She'd laughed, her arms winding round his neck. 'It's me you want. Me, me, me —'

'It's you I want – but I'm not crazy enough to ask you to be my wife.'

'Why not, Charles, my darling?'

'And spend the rest of my life in a torment of blistering jealousy —'

'There'll be no cause for that.'

'One day there will —'

But her mouth had stifled the words in his, and he had believed what he wanted most desperately to believe – that it would work out.

Before speaking to Claire he had consulted his widowed sister, Mrs Terblanche. Helen had always been very close to him and he valued her opinion. In her pretty flat overlooking Table Bay and the forests of Lion's Head he had smoked his pipe while she watched him with penetrating blue eyes in a humorous face.

'Helen,' he began, 'there's something I want to tell you.'

'Who is she?'

'Claire's coach, Vale Rorke. You've met her at Silverglade.'

Her half smile had faded.

'Charles! I was afraid of that – but I couldn't take my fears seriously.'

'You must take them seriously. I've asked her to marry me and she has said she will.'

'Then you're not here to ask my advice.'

'No, Helen. To enlist your support. A lot of my friends will think I've taken leave of my senses.'

'Well, haven't you?'

'I don't think so.'

'Have you told Claire?'

'Not yet. I wanted to get your reaction first.'

'My dear, if you want an honest opinion, I can only say I think it's a middle-aged man's infatuation for the glamour of youth. Monkey gland nonsense. There are plenty of attractive widows in our own social circle —'

'You're wasting your breath, Helen. I understand how you feel, and you could be right, but I hope – Vale and I both hope – to prove you wrong. In the meantime we need your backing. Keep your doubts to yourself and be an ally. Especially where Claire is concerned.'

There was a vase of strelitzias in the corner of the room, and, as she rose and stood near the flowers, it seemed to Hammond that his sister had the same character – hard, sharp and brilliant. Her fair hair rose in a crest from her handsome head and her profile was that of a powerful heraldic bird. She resembled him more closely than he realized.

'I've known you all my life,' she said, 'and most of yours, and I know when I can't influence you, no matter what I say or do. You and this girl have made up your minds. I'll do what I can to help. As for Claire, she's as obstinate as you are and she'll certainly resent Vale. All I can promise is negative – not to fan the flame.'

Telling Claire had proved more difficult than he had expected. In spite of his sister's warning, he had foolishly dared to hope that his daughter might welcome his decision to marry her friend. He told her in the library the following evening. She perched on the window-sill, silhouetted against the silver trees and the evening sky, so that her expression was indistinct, but her tone and the sudden stiffening of her pose were shocked and hostile.

'Marry Vale! But you're a quarter of a century older than she is!'

'We've considered that.'

'Daddy, how could it last? In ten, twenty years time Vale will regret it, if you don't.'

He found he was shaking with rage. How dared this child presume to put into words all his own private misgivings?

'I'm not asking your permission, Claire.' He had tried to keep his voice steady. 'I'm telling you of our decision.'

She was frozen against the window, staring at him dumbly.

'Vale is your friend,' he'd said at last.

'How can she stay that way?'

'Why can't she?'

'You'd be between us.'

So that was it. Jealousy. Her mother had always been jealous. Claire's position as first in his life was threatened. Relief and pity gushed through him in a warm tide. This was the true reason for her opposition. She was not prepared to concede her place to Vale. He grasped her rigid shoulders.

'Don't be silly, Claire. There are many ways of loving. You are my only child —'

'At present,' she cut in with sharp foresight.

She freed herself from his grip and slid from the window-sill, facing him. 'If you want to do this mad thing I can't stop you. Nobody can. I hope you'll be happy.'

She'd turned and dashed from the room, leaving him angry and upset. But not as angry and upset as she'd made him tonight. He'd never forget the way she'd tossed that damnable letter into Vale's lap, deliberately provoking a situation. She'd put him on the spot, forced an issue – *'Honey love, if only you were free . . .'* She'd meant him to see those words and draw some abominable conclusion. She was out to make trouble between him and Vale and she'd found a weapon. What the hell did she expect him to do? Demand the right to read Vale's letter? Ignore the whole thing and appear complacent? What did it all amount to anyway? Another instance of Claire's jealousy. He remembered now that she'd been attracted to that young American. And all the time he'd been making passes at Vale, no doubt.

The Judge frowned as he tried to recall that fortnight last summer. Vale's brother had swung the fellow on to them, ringing up from Johannesburg to tell her his American friend was going to be in Cape Town on holiday and didn't know a soul. Could they put him up? He'd come for a week and stayed for two.

Now he came to think of it, he had noticed the growing antagonism between his wife and daughter during the fortnight that Jef Broome had been at Silverglade, but he had closed his eyes to it for he had been professionally engrossed at that period in a distressing sabotage case. Three young Xhosas were on trial for causing the derailment of a goods train. The white engine driver had been killed and the fireman had lost a leg and an arm. It was treason and homicide. If the crime could be pinned on the accused they were guilty on both counts. But he could not help feeling that the prisoners before him were as much victims of circumstance as those they had been instrumental in killing and maiming. They saw themselves as soldiers in a freedom force, committed to carrying out their orders at any price. The organization to which they belonged was Communist inspired, trained and financed. They were the merest expendable pawns. It was the sort of case that particularly disturbed him, and so he had missed the overtones that had been singing for attention in his own home.

He frowned as he made an effort to visualize Jef Broome, the man out there in Virginia. The American had looked less than his thirty years, a slight fit figure, fair crew-cut hair, a snub nose, a broad boyish grin, and grey eyes that could be warm and naïve or cold as a dawn sky. His lazy rather diffident way of speaking could speed up suddenly into brusque dialogue, or he might relapse into silences weighty with implied criticism. His movements were quick and restless and his charm was mercurial. It all added up to vitality. Hammond remembered that he had been unduly irritated when the young man had expressed a wish to attend the trial. The Judge never allowed Vale in court when he sat on the Bench, and it was Claire who slipped in with Broome at her side. After it was over they had all gone to his farm, Leopard Bush in the Hex River mountains, for the week-end. To his annoyance, young Broome had shown an inclination to discuss the case.

'There are Communist-financed sabotage and terrorist schools all over Africa and outside it,' Hammond had explained defensively. 'These people are taught to infiltrate and they do their jobs regardless of the consequences to human life.'

The American had stared straight at him with that damned steely opiniated look.

'One has to seek the cause,' he'd said. 'Sabotage schools and the crimes they engender are only effects. The cause is surely your way of life in South Africa. If a people feel themselves to be oppressed, they go for violent measures. They're wide open to subversion.'

Hammond had said sharply, 'Our way of life is not intended to be oppressive. It's a great experiment in ethnic development, each race developing along its own cultural and traditional lines. Left to itself, without outside interference, it might possibly succeed. Even the African extremists themselves recognize a certain type of apartheid. Degrees of racial discrimination. The most militant subversive black groups refuse to allow any person of other blood in their ranks – no coloureds, no Indians, no Malays. Only Africans. Africa for the African.'

Guy, who had been with them at Leopard Bush that weekend, had supported him, counter-attacking, pushing the argument into Broome's field.

'How do you account for your American race riots and your forms of black-white terrorism? Your way of life is the reverse of ours. You strive honestly for integration, yet you don't get peaceful racial co-operation.'

'We haven't gone far enough along the road to equality of opportunity,' Broome had said candidly. 'We make good laws – and try to enforce them – but true economic and social equality is still an ideal. So far, our efforts spring too much from the head and the conscience and not sufficiently from the heart.'

Now, in the solitude of the summer night, Hammond recalled that week-end with growing indignation. He had fiercely resented Broome but he had bluffed himself into believing that his reasons were logical and not emotional. True, he had wanted to get away from racial tragedies and problems and the American had been an irritant, egged on by Claire to express his radical views, and Vale had done little to discourage the contentious disputes that she knew disrupted the peace of Leopard Bush for her husband. Disgruntled, Hammond had deliberately withdrawn into himself that week-end, and he realized now that he had left the coast clear for youth. What madness! Broome, Guy, Vale and Claire had ridden in the valleys and climbed the Hex River peaks while he had tried to relax in the sparkling mountain air and wild lonely setting that he loved. He had behaved like a surly old dog. So what had gone on while his back was turned? Had the wretched fellow become infatuated with Vale? And, if so, what did it mean to her? Had it simply flattered her feminine vanity while leaving her intrinsically untouched – or was that plain wishful thinking? But why the devil was Broome writing to her after all these months?

It had been clear to Hammond that his wife had been surprised only at the condition of the letter. She had obviously not been astonished that Broome should have written to her. She had been put on the wrong foot by Claire, and her attitude had suggested that there might be something to conceal. Damn Claire! Her manner towards her stepmother had been inexcusable. No wonder Vale had closed up like a clam and refused to play it Claire's way and open her letter there and then and read it aloud. That was what Claire's action had challenged her to do, and she had refused the challenge. He tried to calm himself. Vale had never given him the slightest reason to suspect her – till now. Surely when he went upstairs she'd show him the letter and explain everything and that would be the end of the matter. She might let off a few fireworks about Claire, and he sympathized. The whole thing had been most embarrassing, especially for Guy. Something must be done about Claire. After tonight Silverglade could never again hold both Vale and Claire.

Suddenly he longed for Vale to settle the whole business of the letter with a few simple words and a laugh. He lingered on in the night watching the fire across the valley, unseeing, while dread crept in on him. If only I didn't love her, he thought. But she is my life. Beneath a scarlet thread of pain ran a sombre strand of wounded self-esteem, for the failure of his marriage would humiliate him in the eyes of his sister, Helen, and of his friends who had felt all along that he was making a fool of himself. Charles Hammond was a

proud man, not accustomed to failure. His marriage must
not fail.

Upstairs Vale refolded her letter from America and fed it
carefully back into the long envelope through the gash left
by the stamps. She had not broken the seal. She looked carefully at the revealing tear. '... *honey love, if only you were
free* ...' What had her husband read into those words? As
for Claire, it would have been easy enough to withdraw the
letter, read it and put it back, leaving the envelope untouched
except for the postman's theft. Could Claire have done
that? There was no knowing. Claire had her own code. She
worshipped her father and would do anything she fancied
might protect him. And she was jealous – twice over – jealous of Vale's influence over her father, and, poor child, she
had undoubtedly had a 'thing' about Jef Broome.

She sat on her bed in her flimsy dressing-gown, frowning
down at the spoiled envelope. Charles had asked her to let
him have it. She took the letter and read it once more, her
heart pounding. What should she do? She started as she
heard her husband's step on the stair, and suddenly she was
shaking.

'Charles!' she called, as he entered his dressing-room.
'Charles!'

He did not answer her call. But after a few moments she
saw him standing in the doorway in his thin summer
pyjamas, a spare figure, lean as a young man's, his face arrogant, giving nothing away. Suddenly she wondered how well
she really knew him. How strong could his anger be? Would
he be capable of throwing her out? Never, with Micky so
vulnerable. And he loved her. But he respected himself too.
If she wounded him deeply enough – shamed him – she
might kill his love. What would he do then? Did any one
person ever know another well enough to answer such a

question? What am *I* capable of? she wondered. What would *I* do if I were pushed far enough?

She was staring up at him, her eyes wide and dark, her hair a living aura against the light of her bedside lamp.

'I thought you'd be asleep,' he said evenly.

She shook her head. 'Here is the envelope.'

He came and took it from her. It was empty.

'I'll talk to the postman tomorrow.'

'The letter,' she said, desperately. 'Do you want to read it?'

She was holding it out to him – the three thin folded sheets of airmail paper covered with small slanting writing. He looked down at her steadily.

'Do you want me to?'

She shrugged her shoulders. The sheets of paper trembled in her outstretched hand. He took them from her and she was hot and cold as if with fever. Claire, she thought, through you he is going to be hurt. I would have spared him this!

Hammond took the letter from her with distaste. He walked away from her to the wastepaper basket by her dressing-table. There were two bluebirds on it to match the blue magnolias on her white curtains. He tore the letter into small pieces and watched them flutter into the basket on to her used face tissues and the stubs of the cigarettes she had been smoking. So much for Claire and her intrigues! Vale was still sitting on her bed when he turned round, but her arms were held out to him as he had so often seen her hold them out to her little son in love and comfort. He went to her and felt the warm softness of her body in his embrace.

'Charles,' she whispered, 'darling, darling Charles.'

As he turned out the light he knew that tonight he would take her as never before. He made love to her selfishly, without tenderness, wanting to hurt her as she had hurt him. Once, when she might have cried out, he covered her mouth harshly with his as if he feared to hear a name not his own.

4

THE JUDGE'S DAUGHTER

'WE'VE DONE OUR STUFF,' SHOUTED GUY. 'WE aren't needed any more.'

Claire straightened up and waved across the burnt-out grass verge to where he stood with the foresters who had been beating on the fringe of the woods. The long canvas hoses from the mobile water-tanks were playing on the dying flames and on the smouldering swathe of bush that an hour ago had threatened the gum plantations of the mountainside.

A few cars were still parked at the side of the road to Constantia Nek, their occupants drawn by the lurid drama and infernal beauty of a mountain fire at night, and a group of coloured children scampered past, singing and flourishing the pine branches with which they had been beating at the blaze. What little wind there was had changed and blown the fire back upon itself, and the bush, already devoured, had yielded nothing more to feed upon.

Claire whipped the scarf off her head and shook out her hair as Guy rejoined her and they strolled back to his car.

'Let's go down to Hout Bay,' he said.

'Let's. We could paddle. My hair's singed and my feet are hot.'

In a few minutes they had reached Constantia Nek, the gap which divides the spine of mountains running the length of the Cape Peninsula between the Atlantic and Indian Ocean. From the Nek they could see the wide fertile

Constantia Valley with its farms and vineyards sloping away down to the Indian Ocean. There they turned west towards Hout Bay and the Atlantic, driving down the Kloof through the green tunnels of the ancient oaks, their branches meeting overhead to shut out the starry sky. Moonlight lay pale upon the dunes of Little Lion's Head and silvered the granite boulders of cliff and peak. The formidable profile of the Sentinel loomed across the Bay, forming its western wall and plunging sheer into the sea to be pounded eternally by the tireless waves.

'Such a pity – that fire,' said Claire. 'It'll leave a horrible black scar among those lovely woods.'

'Only for a while. Then there'll be new growth. It was lucky the wind changed. It could have been a really bad one if it had got out of control.'

'I'm afraid of fire, but it excites me. All the noise and heat and awful beauty of an elemental force consuming everything in its path.'

'Devastation, followed by germination,' he said. 'Life is like that. Everywhere, all the time.'

She thought of her father after her mother's death – his spirit lifeless and burnt out, and of the slow process of recovery speeded at last by the advent of Vale. She had come into his life like the spring and there had been the birth of Micky. How well she remembered that night. Her father returning from the nursing-home in the small hours of the morning. She had heard his car and run downstairs in her shorty-pyjamas to meet him. It had been a summer night like this, cool and balmy. He had come up the steps to the front door and she had let him in eagerly, waiting for news.

He had entered and paused under the hall light, his face weary and drawn but triumphant, and he'd put his hands on her shoulders.

'A son,' he'd said. 'Both doing well.'

Claire had felt his relief and exaltation pulsing through her as if his fingers transmitted strong electric currents.

'A son, Daddy! That's what you've always wanted.'

Perhaps some sense of exclusion, of no longer being part of this complete and perfect family had shown in her face as she looked up at him, for he had tightened his grasp on her shoulders.

'You are my first-born,' he had said. 'Never forget that! The first-born is very special – son or daughter.'

'You're very quiet,' said Guy.

'I was thinking of my father,' she said. 'And Vale, and Micky.'

He stopped the car by the beach and they got out and rolled up their slacks and took off their shoes and socks. They strolled along the shore in the shallows with the wavelets of the ebb tide washing over their feet and ankles. The lights of fishing-boats bobbed in the harbour and out at sea, and the straggling village and pretty houses on the mountainside were picked out in occasional winking gold. Hout Bay was once a tiny fishing village famed for its rock-lobsters and mussels. Now, like so many Cape beauty spots, it was growing rapidly, but it still retained its special Bohemian character. It was the home of a colony of artists, writers and a few philosophers seeking peace, and its uncrowned king was a famous entomologist who lived up the steep mountainside with his termites and bees, his wife's tame lizards, their blue crane with a broken wing, and a host of other birds, beasts and insects. But tonight his house, like most others, was in darkness, for it was past midnight.

'There's something I don't understand,' said Guy. 'Why did you throw that letter at Vale in front of your father and me? It could have waited.'

'You mean I should have given it to Vale secretly? Conspired with my stepmother against my father?'

'It would have been kinder.'

'Would it – in the long run?'

'I think so. You can't read a whole betrayal into a few words taken out of their context.'

'Perhaps not.'

Something in her tone made him glance at her sharply. Her face was remote in the pallid light and he did not then pursue the thought that crossed his mind.

'Well, it's your business,' he said. 'But I didn't like it.'

'Nor did Vale.'

'It's not going to make a very happy atmosphere between you.'

'I know.'

'Do you? Have you had time to realize just how difficult you've made things for Vale and your father – and yourself?'

'Exactly what do you mean?'

'You must know quite well that Vale is your father's blind spot. He's not going to believe a thing against her unless she wants him to, but he's going to hate you for trying to open his eyes.'

'I had to,' she said urgently. 'It's only fair.'

'How can you possibly know what significance to give those words – unless —'

Her arm was linked lightly in his and he felt her stiffen.

'Unless what?'

'Oh, forget it.'

She withdrew her arm and stood facing him.

'Isn't it significant that he's still writing to her? Would he be doing that if it was all over between them?'

'You talk as if you knew there *had* been something. I was with you at Leopard Bush that week-end, and, to tell you the truth, I thought you were the one.'

'Maybe he meant you, and anybody else – except Vale, of course – to think just that.'

He chuckled. 'To tell you the truth, that's what first made me sit up and take notice.'

'Of me?'

'Of you, yes.'

'History repeats itself.'

'You sound acid. I don't like you when you're acid.'

'You looked at Vale tonight as if you'd never seen her before, as if Jef Broome had just brought her to your notice.'

He was silent. He knew that it was true. He had seen Vale with that ripe apricot bloom on her skin, eyes shining, supple, graceful, a woman any man would want; he had visualized her in Broome's arms, he had even envied that jaunty American and had suspected that under the boyish charm there was ruthlessness, the determination to get what he wanted. How much had he wanted Vale? ' . . . *if only you were free* . . .' Had it really gone that far?

'Well?'

Claire had moved on. She was walking apart from him now, mooching with her hands buried in the pockets of her slacks, her head down.

'*Well*,' he echoed. 'If you want to know what I think, I think Vale is impetuous and she likes a scalp or two – all you women do – and maybe she's even had a bit of a tumble with Broome, and perhaps there've been a few silly letters, but that's all there is to it. I think the whole thing is best left and forgotten and it's a great pity you saw fit to underline it the way you did.'

'I think differently. My stepmother isn't really so impetuous. She's a schemer. She got Daddy although Aunt Helen and I were both against it. Daddy cares what Aunt Helen thinks. She's his only sister and they've always been very close. But he didn't want to know what she thought about him marrying Vale – a girl of twenty when he was forty-five. And he was furious with me when I said he was too old for Vale. But she's strong. She meant to have Daddy and she put a spell on him.'

'It's still on him,' said Guy. 'He's mad about her. And I believe she loves him, whatever she may have done on the side.'

'How can a woman love two men at the same time – I mean, how can she belong to both?'

'You tell me. You should know the emotional mechanism of your sex. All I know is that a man can love a wife and a mistress at the same time. One comes across it constantly.'

'It's not my idea of marriage,' she said heatedly.

'Nor mine. But human beings are fairly promiscuous animals by nature. We see plenty of love and jealousy and revenge dramas in the courts. As for a passing *affaire* – it should never be allowed to disrupt a marriage.'

'But if the *affaire* isn't passing – if it continues. What then?'

'That's a hypothetical question. We've been talking about Vale. Broome is thousands of miles away in America. Why worry till he shows up here – if he ever does again.'

'Ah,' she sighed. 'There you have it. Where will he show up? And when?'

They had reached the car, and she opened the door and sat on the floor, pulling on her shoes and rolling down her slacks. Guy did the same and then drew his long legs in behind the wheel.

Within twenty minutes they were back at Silverglade.

'Thank goodness the bedrooms are on the other side of the house,' he said. 'I must get this silencer mended. That's the trouble with buying a second-hand car, there's always something to be done.'

He sprang out and waited while she found the front door key in its hiding-place under the leaves of a dwarf lemon tree growing in a decorative Ali Baba jar. Before she could fit it into the lock he took her in his arms and held her with fierce possessiveness.

'There are times when I hate you,' he whispered. 'But I still want you.'

She felt the fire run through her veins and the melting that left her slack in his embrace. It was terrible to say good night, terrible to tear themselves apart. Guy was different tonight, more importunate, everything was different and her desire was heightened by the angry heat of his kisses and the fever of her own. And by something else – the memory of Jef Broome, her first real awakening.

5

JEF BROOME

WHEN HE HAD GONE AND CLAIRE STOOD ALONE IN the hall, leaning against the mahogany door with the graceful fanlight, she felt deathly tired. Her weak foot dragged as she went upstairs. When at last she crept into bed a swarm of re-collections of Jef Broome banished sleep. They buzzed like summer bees about her head and at last she gave up the attempt to disregard them.

Tennis with Jef – he played a dashing and intelligent game and didn't like to lose; swimming and surfing with Jef, brown-skinned, bright-haired, compact and vigorous; dancing with Jef, his chin touching her hair (when he danced with Vale his cheek was against hers for they were much of a height); then that day in the Botanical Gardens after the trial; and that Sunday morning in the little cemetery among the wild lonely mountains.

Her father, she remembered, had been violently irritated when Vale's brother, John Rorke, had landed them with this unexpected guest just when the sabotage trial was approaching its climax.

'You girls will have to look after him,' he had told Claire and Vale. 'Take him to Kelvin Grove, do anything you like, but leave me in peace to concentrate on this case. Guy can make up your four. At twenty-five he's young enough to work by day and play by night.'

So the four of them had gone to the informal Wednesday night dinner-dance at the country club and Vale had sparkled with new shimmering life and merriment. Claire had hated her that night. It wasn't fair. She was always up against this competition – a stepmother who was more fascinating to her boy-friends than she was herself. Claire had been strongly attracted to the young man from Virginia. When he'd talked to her there might have been no one else in the room, and when they'd danced they had moved in a charmed circle, but she saw now that it had been the same with Vale. They had discovered new night-haunts among the fairy lights of fashionable Sea Point and had come home to find her father still in his library, haggard with strain.

Jef had said to Vale one evening in Claire's presence:

'Guy says the summing up and sentence will be pronounced tomorrow. I'd like to be there.'

'I'm sorry,' she said firmly. 'Charles won't allow me in court when he's on the Bench – I can't take you, much as I'd like to go myself.'

Claire had chipped in.

'I'll take Jef. I've never seen Daddy in action.'

'Your father will be furious. You know that.'

'We can slip in at the back. We won't even be noticed.'

'I can't stop you.'

So Jef and Claire had gone to the Law Courts early on Thursday morning and found inconspicuous seats in one of the shiny pews. The court was not particularly crowded, but when they looked up at the gallery the dark faces of the non-Europeans glowered down, close-packed and attentive. Sombre men and sullen women with *doeks* (kerchiefs) tied round their heads or berets covering their crimpy hair.

The courtroom was not large; it was windowless, sound-proofed and air-conditioned, insulated completely from the outside world while justice took its course.

It's like a small theatre, she thought, with my father enthroned centre-stage in his robes of scarlet and slate-blue and his two assessors, one on either side of him, sitting rather straight on their high-backed chairs. His profile was often towards them as he listened to the evidence of the witnesses. She was glad South African judges wore no wigs. Her father looked superb with his thick grey-fair hair receding over his temples and springing in a peak from that broad brow. He was perfectly cast. From time to time his long fingers thoughtfully stroked the side of his high-bridged nose. There, immediately below him in the 'orchestra pit', was Guy wearing his academic gown, taking careful notes of the proceedings. A girl clerk operated a tape-recorder next to the witness-box and, behind the bench occupied by the prosecutor and the defence, the three accused stood in the dock with a policeman in attendance. As she saw Jef's eyes upon them Claire felt suddenly deflated, almost ashamed.

They were young and shabby, their dark faces were impassive. The ringleader was the last to give evidence and he elected to speak in his own language with an interpreter. The white interpreter was eloquent and sympathetic and Claire was sure that the young Bantu's testimony lost nothing in the translation. His grey jacket was threadbare but the corner of a clean white handkerchief protruded from the pocket. The faded open sweatshirt under it revealed the taut muscles working in his throat and his frequent gestures showed the livid palms of the hands responsible for wrecking a train, killing the driver, and maiming the fireman.

'I was obeying my orders,' he protested. 'I did not want to kill a man, but for our cause many must die on both sides. We are not to blame.'

We are watching a man on his way to the gallows, she thought. A young man. She shuddered in the potted air grown suddenly cold.

When the court adjourned for lunch she and Jef strolled across Queen Victoria Street into the Public Gardens where they ate a light lunch under the trees. Squirrels sat up expectantly near their table, undisturbed by the come and go of the coloured waitresses, and doves and sparrows pecked at the bread Claire crumbled for them.

'Treason and homicide,' Jef had said. 'The ringleader hasn't a hope. He spoke of killing as if it were an unfortunate necessity.'

'Perhaps the other two will get a lighter sentence.'

'Perhaps. But it's all so tragic, isn't it? According to their lights they had no alternative – any more than a soldier has when he is commanded to fire on the enemy.'

'But here there isn't a war —'

'Oh, yes, there is – a war against oppression. And violence seems the only answer.'

'If it *is* a war, then it's a war of aggression. Africa for the African. Nothing less than total victory and the annihilation of the whites will do.'

'Down the centuries the African has been driven by the white man to this final phase. We see it in our country as much as you do in yours. There's a black – white war there too.'

When he was serious, as he was then, his grey eyes held a brooding compassion and he looked older. This was a side of him very different from the gay boyish companion in holiday mood.

The south-easter cloud was tumbling over the face of Table Mountain as they returned to take their places in the quiet courtroom.

The prisoners were already in the dock and the dark faces in the gallery were gravely impassive, awaiting the summing up and the sentence. The courtroom was crowded and the tension palpable. Claire had never before witnessed a trial which might involve a death sentence and her hands were damp and tightly clasped as she listened to her father tell the court why and how he and the two assessors had reached their decision. He'll never do it, she thought. He'll never condemn a man to death. He'll find extenuating circumstances somehow. But as the summing up reached its climax she knew that, for the ringleader – the man who had declared that 'for our cause many must die on both sides' – there was no hope.

The moment came when the usher called for silence in court for the passing of the sentence. No black cap was donned but the words of the dread sentence were uttered in the even voice of her father, relentless and final, as he looked straight at the young Bantu ringleader.

'The sentence of the Court is that you be returned to custody and thereafter be hanged by the neck until you are dead.'

Nor was there any pious plea: 'May the Lord have mercy on your soul.' But Guy rose and asked the prisoner if he had anything to say.

The young man's hands gripped the rail of the dock, sweat shone on his face, and his Adam's apple leapt as he spoke in English.

'I die for my cause. I do not complain.'

His henchmen received their sentence of a period at Robben Island without expression, their feelings hidden by dark stubborn masks.

As she watched them Claire was seized by a sensation of physical nausea and a frozen heaviness in the region of her heart, as if the guilt of the condemned man and his accomplices had passed into the very core of her own being. She longed to cry out 'Forgive them! They knew not what they did!' The prisoners had been escorted from the dock, down the stairway to the cells, the three high-backed chairs on the dais were no longer occupied, the court was emptying and the drama was at an end. She felt Jef Broome's hand on her arm.

'Come, Claire.'

He had driven her home in Vale's little car.

'I was sorry for your father,' he said, after a while. 'That wasn't easy for him.'

'It won't be easy for the prisoners either,' she said. 'But it was dreadful for Daddy. He leans over backwards to find extenuating circumstances, and he always tries to avoid cases that may require a death sentence. He takes it hard.'

The woods of Devil's Peak and the nature reserve with the zebras and wildebeeste grazing near the fence fell behind them. They passed the Rhodes Memorial like a small Greek temple high on the mountainside, and the University with its incomparable view to the distant hinterland, and on through the sylvan magnificence of Kirstenbosch up to the high ridge where Silverglade looked down the far side over the valley of the vines. They parked Vale's car in the garage and entered the spacious house together. Josiah had put the drinks in the enclosed porch leading on to the stoep.

'Help yourself,' Claire had said. 'I'll see you later.'

He had watched her go upstairs and she had been conscious of his eyes following her, inimical yet half expectant as they met hers for an instant at the turn of the stair. For the first time in her life she had felt the luxury and lavish comfort of her home as a reproach.

Vale met her on the landing.

'Well?' she had said. 'How did it go?'

'Ask Jef about it,' Claire had answered abruptly. 'He's downstairs.'

Somehow, Vale's appearance just then had been a shock. Claire had felt very close to Jef Broome. That day she had taken a small step towards deeper human understanding and Jef Broome had given her a little push in the right direction. One remark had stuck in her mind.

'In life it's always the effect we see – often evil. We have to probe more deeply to find the hidden cause.'

It was then that he had established himself so firmly in her mind – in her imagination, perhaps – that she had wondered, with a spasm of disloyalty, whether this man could, if he wished, wean her from her father's views. Jef, with his progressive ideas, his snub boyish face and quick active body, made her father seem outdated, the symbol of an era of vanished dignity, essentially and unmistakably a master in a century when masters, as a race or as individuals, were being trampled in the mire of a gigantic worldwide black – white revolution.

That day in court she had been so proud of her father. He had looked splendid and arrogant in his robes. Now, as she lay in the dark of the night pierced by a dagger of moonlight reaching into the corner of her room, she wondered how he had felt when first he had worn the scarlet and slate blue, symbol of ultimate human power, of a man considered wise and just enough to pass judgement on his fellows, entitled to condemn another human being to death. The enormity of the responsibility hit her for the first time with its full impact. It was the sort of thing a man would pray about. Tears stung her eyes behind the closed lids. Was such a man to be humiliated and brought low by one intimate, irrevocable act of unwisdom in his own private life? Marrying Vale. Of all people, why had *he* placed himself in such a vulnerable position? If Vale wanted Jef enough she would get him just as she had got Charles Hammond. She would not hesitate to break her husband's heart and humble his pride. Yet none of them had suspected anything. Claire looked back, trying to divine when it had really begun – this infatuation.

The week-end after the trial they had all gone to Leopard Bush, the Hammond farm in the Hex River mountains about a hundred miles from Cape Town between the fruit-growing coastal belt and the arid semi-desert of the sheep-breeding Karoo.

Guy had travelled in his own car, giving Josiah a lift, and the Judge had driven the station-wagon with Vale next to him, and Claire, Jef, Micky and his nurse Fedora, behind with Dart and the bags and provisions. On a family week-end Vale usually cooked and Claire and Fedora managed the housework, but, when they had guests they took Josiah along and he performed most of the chores including cooking, which he did with the enthusiasm and expertise of an inspired amateur.

Claire and her father loved Leopard Bush more than anywhere else in the world. She sensed that to him it symbolized sanctuary, a place of rest and recreation. Whenever a case had exhausted him he recovered his peace of mind amid the saw-toothed peaks that rose, lavender and snow-capped, against a sky of pure fierce blue. Leopard Bush, which had been in the Hammond family for generations, lay in a tenderly folded valley watered by the swift golden Hex River. Fruit orchards surrounded the simple single-storeyed homestead which was built in the style of an up-country farmhouse. The slightly sloping roof was galvanized iron and a long passage ran straight from the front door to the back with the rooms leading off it. French doors opened from these rooms on to the two side stoeps flanking the house. At the end of one of these was a glass-enclosed sun-porch commanding a magnificent view of both mountains and river. The floors and rafters, more than a hundred and fifty years old, were of yellow wood the colour of autumn birch leaves. Sometimes, when the wind was from the north, you could hear the baboons barking up in the kloof, and if they were noisy at night it meant a leopard was raiding their sleeping-place.

The unenclosed section of the stoep was covered by wisteria and golden-shower. The wisteria's brief season was over but the golden-shower sprays were still abundant. Mrs Steyn, the manager's wife, grew vegetables and ran her own dairy and poultry farm, so Leopard Bush was well supplied, and so, for that matter, was Silverglade.

Claire's mood that week-end was one of elation. She had felt almost fey. She turned her head uneasily on her pillow as she thought about it now, opening her eyes wide and staring at the shaft of moonlight that had shifted and diminished since last she had observed it. But it was only an abstract background for the reality she saw at last for what it was. That week-end she had believed herself to be really in love for the first time in her life. She had believed that the quality of her love for Jef Broome was total – a thing of the mind and heart as well as the body – and there was a moment when she had been convinced that he returned her feeling with equal intensity. What an illusion!

All right, face it! she told herself. That Sunday afternoon meant nothing to him except a mask for the reality. I simply read my dreams into it. More fool me! The air had been fresh and bright. Her father, Vale and Guy had gone fishing some miles down-river in the hope of returning with fresh trout for supper. Jef had elected to go for a ramble with Claire.

'Would you like me to show you our family burial place?' she had asked. He was taken aback.

'Why, sure.'

'It's not morbid,' she smiled. 'We love it – at least Daddy and I do. It's the most peaceful place on earth.'

'So it should be,' he grinned.

It was in the foothills, half an hour's walk from the homestead, a place of sun and shade and the song of birds with tall cypresses standing sentinel over simple urns and headstones engraved with the names and dates of members of the Hammond family. Proteas and other mountain shrubs bloomed here and the dry earth rippled with the dance of fragile grasses bowing in the breeze. They sat on a rough wooden bench and listened to the voices of the kloof, bird calls, the hum of insects, the distant bark of a baboon, the chuckle of the river. The summer was nearly over and the early autumn heath mingled its scent with that of aromatic shrubs. He had taken a deep breath.

'To rest here at the end of the long journey – that would be good.'

'My mother's ashes were scattered here,' she said. 'Perhaps that's why Vale never comes here.'

He answered nothing to that. He followed a different thought – after a short silence. It was easy to be silent with him, the test of true companionship.

Then he had begun to tell her about the Smoky Mountains in his own Virginia – densely wooded above the soft green valleys that had known such bitter warfare – the War of Independence against England and the Civil War that had had its roots in the emancipation of the black man, the war that was still continuing in its final phase in the hot river valleys of the Deep South and the great industrial cities of America.

After a while they had risen and Jef had said: 'I can understand why you love this place where your ancestors sleep. One doesn't think of death here, one thinks of life.'

They were standing in the shadow of a cypress. He wore an open throated T-shirt and khaki shorts and his skin appeared to Claire to glow with the pink and gold of copper; his eyes on hers were brilliant under the thick tangled lashes and the unruly corn-coloured hair.

'You're lovely,' he said. 'Young, sweet, adorable.'

He kissed her, gently at first and then with passion.

The following night he had flown back to Johannesburg on his way home to America and for Claire the world had been emptied of a certain vibrance.

'You'll come back?' she had said at the last, as she and Vale bade him good-bye at the airport.

'I surely will,' he had answered, and they had watched him stride across the apron to the Viscount under the stars.

Soon after that she'd gone to Italy for a year's study and Jef had not come back. Not to her, at all events. Nor had he ever written to her. He had simply forgotten her. Only now did she know whom he had really remembered.

All the pieces of the jigsaw fell into place that night as she lay in bed in the summer darkness, wakeful, recalling, with so much hurt, a fortnight in which she had experienced the ecstasy of first love. She had been the decoy for her lovely stepmother. All the time it had been Vale Jef wanted.

Claire got up and went restlessly to the window where she stood looking out at the sleeping valley. The fire was out and the long shoulder of the mountain was pale and mystic beneath the sinking moon.

She was shaken by anger and humiliation – for herself and for her father – and deep down in the roots of her being she felt an ugly painful flowering of hate. For Jef. For Vale.

6

A NEW BEGINNING

THE JUDGE FOUND HIS DAUGHTER UNDER THE BIG plane tree in a secluded part of the garden. She was outside the perimeter of shade, sitting on the grass leaning against a folding canvas back-rest with a scribble-book on her lap and her bare legs stretched out in front of her. It was the first time he had seen her that day and he was determined to tackle an unpleasant task provoked by her action and her attitude the night before. Many years of riding his emotions on a curb had taught him to take it easy and keep his feelings under control.

Claire glanced up as his shadow fell across her. He observed that she was very pale.

'Hallo, Daddy. You looking for me?'

'As a matter of fact, yes.'

She scrambled out of her batwing seat and offered it to him, sprawling on the grass beside him as he moved the seat into the shade and let himself down.

'You're supple for your age, aren't you?'

He grinned. 'I can still beat you at tennis,' he reminded her. 'Am I interrupting the flow of genius?'

'No. It wasn't going very well.'

His manner reassured her. She had feared that he would give her the glacial treatment, and he could be very arctic indeed when he felt like it. He looked lean and ropy in his short-sleeved sports vest and shorts, his long limbs brown and sinewy. But his face was drawn and the little lines raying out from the corners of his eyes were deeply etched.

'Where's Vale?' Claire asked.

'Doing the week-end shopping. She's taken Micky and Fedora.'

'Horrible. Saturday morning in the village is my idea of purgatory.'

'Mine too.'

His gaze travelled to the scribble-book near his daughter's hand. Claire had literary aspirations. One day she intended to be a novelist, meanwhile she wrote short stories and articles in the mood and vernacular of her generation, and they had proved surprisingly saleable.

'What do you make on that sort of tripe?' he asked.

'Short stories, you mean? Boy meets girl etcetera. About forty rand a time. They're not worth more – yet.'

'You really do mean to be a writer, don't you?'

She warmed to his interest. 'It's my great ambition. I'm longing to try a novel.'

'At nineteen?'

'Why not?'

'My child, you haven't begun to live.'

'I'm very observant.'

'You're certainly that.' An acid note sharpened his voice. 'But novels need more than observation. They need experience of life.'

'Perhaps my experience of life isn't all that limited.' She tossed her head.

'I dare say not. You have a year in Italy behind you and what you got up to there – outside your lessons – I wouldn't know. I always hoped you studied Italian, the history of art, an appreciation of culture, old and new, a civilized way of life and an outlook more sophisticated than ours is.'

'All that. Italians too – especially Italian men – up to a point, of course.'

His eyes narrowed in laughter and the lines multiplied and lengthened, yet the effect was young.

'If your emotions were lacerated in the course of your studies you carry the scars well.'

'There were a few emotional lacerations, as you put it. Mere trifles.'

He said lightly: 'All the same, I expect those trifles felt like mortal wounds at the time.'

She considered this, a faint frown creasing the wide smoothness of her brow. Suddenly she too laughed.

'Not really. You see, one doesn't take Italian boys seriously. Making love is so completely their favourite pastime.'

'You're quite a realist.'

'I try to be.'

'So do I. And it occurs to me that you'd do better to give up this dilatory scribbling and get yourself a full-time job.'

All at once she was aware of the trend and hardening of his purpose and her own will prepared to resist his. He went on.

'It's only by doing a job – working with other people, getting new slants on unfamiliar aspects of life – that you can really widen your scope. If you want to write about human beings you must work with them as well as play with them.'

'I have a project,' she said with naïve self-importance. 'I need to work on it right here.'

'Indeed? May I know more about this – project?'

'I'm studying this valley. I want to write about Constantia – the people and the vineyards and the way the green belt is being eaten up by so-called progress.'

'Aiming high for a beginner, aren't you?'

'Perhaps. Why not?'

'It might be a pity to expend so good a theme before you've learned to handle characters and situations. In any case, you've a lot to learn besides problems of the valley before you can present them intelligently. People in the valley don't all cultivate vines or carve up their inherited holdings to show a quick profit. Many of them commute to and from offices in Cape Town and lead ordinary business lives. A great percentage of those who dwell in the shrinking green belt work outside it and only come home after five p.m. See? My advice to you is to go and learn what they work at. Then, when you really have the know-how, tackle your big novel. Most of your friends have jobs, haven't they? The unmarried girls, I mean.'

'Yes,' she admitted, reluctantly. 'But I'd hate to work in an office – nine to six – and have a boss dictating dreary letters, expecting me to go out and buy his sandwiches and make his tea and ring his silly wife and take her silly messages —'

His spontaneous amusement broke into his voice as he interrupted her vicarious complaints. 'So your friends have briefed you on the tribulations of private secretaries! But there are other jobs. Sarah Verity, for instance, I should say she's happy in her work.'

'Sarah Verity! She's not a contemporary of mine and she's very exceptional.'

Sarah Verity was a household name. She was responsible for the daily broadcasting of women's features and her programmes were enjoyed by housewives all over South Africa.

'It's her job I was thinking about. She might be able to put you in the way of something creative. I could have a word with Helen. She's a great friend of Helen's.'

Claire lay on her back and gazed up through the branches at the chequered design of leaves and sky. Her aunt Helen Terblanche had urged her to get herself a job for quite a while, ever since her return from Italy. 'You two young women – Vale and you – are going to find Silverglade too small to hold you both.' She was being proved right. Claire had considerable respect for her father's sister, but she was in the mood for voicing objections.

'Look, Daddy, just for argument's sake, let's suppose Aunt Helen could persuade Sarah Verity to take me on at the

S.A.B.C., how on earth would I commute all that way? Sea Point and back and through Cape Town in the peak hour every day.'

'You could probably P.G. with somebody over that side of the Peninsula – or you might even get yourself a tiny flat and share it with a friend.'

'How could I afford such luxuries?'

'You come into the interest on your mother's money when you're twenty-one, and I'm sure the trustees would give you an advance till your earnings can support you. I'm one of those trustees, after all.'

'You want to get rid of me – get me out of Silverglade?'

He rose with the alacrity she admired – no rheumatic moans and groans like so many men of his age – and he stood looking down at her with a crooked rather unhappy smile.

'I didn't say so.'

She sprang to her feet and confronted him, eyes hard and bright.

'I can take a hint delivered with a hatchet. I'll go and see Aunt Helen tomorrow.'

'Why not today?' he asked mildly. 'She'll be in this afternoon.'

Scarlet flamed on her high cheek-bones. 'Did you cook this up with Vale?'

'Vale is in the village. She had no idea I meant to talk to you. This – suggestion – is entirely between you and me.'

'And Aunt Helen?'

'Helen will help. She's very fond of you.'

He turned on his heel and she watched him stroll across the grass, unhurried, stopping here and there to inspect a flower-bed or border. So he'd talked to Aunt Helen already. He must have. All that stuff about Sarah Verity had come out very pat. Claire didn't fancy being managed and the idea of being thrown out to suit Vale rubbed her up the wrong way. But a job with interest and variety was tempting, worth considering. She would certainly telephone her aunt later.

After half an hour's reflection she wandered up to the house. It might be as well to ring Aunt Helen while Vale was out in the village. Claire curled up on the big chair by the telephone extension in the library and dialled her aunt's flat. Mrs Terblanche answered.

'Aunt Helen, Daddy wants me to get a job. He's come round to your way of thinking. I'll bet he's been on to you this morning.'

'You're wrong. It was I who rang him. I told him that Sarah Verity was looking for an assistant, someone who can learn to write radio scripts, among other things, and I thought of you. Your father was interested.'

Claire had a sudden vivid picture of her aunt, tall and angular, bird-featured like Isis, potent for good.

'I'm interested too,' she said.

'Then make an appointment with Sarah – and don't waste time.'

'Thanks,' said Claire. 'I will.'

Sarah Verity interviewed Claire after work on the roof of her Sea Point pent-house flat. Her flat-mate, the well-known artist, Katrina Westhuizen, had made it into rather a charming roof-garden and the raised studio skylight afforded shade and shelter for over-cooked sun worshippers.

Sarah had met Claire often with Mrs Terblanche, but she had never paid the girl much attention except to note automatically that she had a low sympathetic voice that might record well. She assessed her now with a long candid look. She saw a young strong face with intelligent eyes, a determined chin and a warm smile. Would she learn to interview people and make them feel at home with the unfamiliar self-conscious medium of the microphone? She had a pleasant positive personality. She would soon learn to give cues and throw leads. It was just a question of technique, and, of course, of liking people, being genuinely interested in how the other half lives. Sarah ran her hand through her coarse black hair, cut in a fringe that was not unattractive with her pronounced features and shrewd brown eyes. She was small and wiry, and might have been anywhere between thirty and forty. She was wearing slacks and a candy-striped over-blouse. At the office she was always very neat and tailored, but at home she was most herself in slacks.

'I need an assistant,' she said. 'Someone with initiative and a flair for writing – not essays, but dialogue with situations. You know the sort of thing. I've read your short stories. They're not too bad.'

'I'd love to give it a go,' Claire said. 'I haven't a clue, but I could learn.'

'You'd have to turn your hand to anything, editing material, being a disc jockey, typing correspondence – you type of course?'.

'Of course. Self-taught, though.'

'That's your headache, so long as you can tap away reasonably efficiently.'

'I can't do shorthand. But I've evolved my own abbreviations. I could take dictation at a pinch.'

'Useful, but I have a secretary. Your job would be more creative. I want ideas. You'll need to interview people – get their stories from them. Do you like the human race? Are you interested in other people's lives and problems?'

Claire's eyes kindled. 'I want to be a writer one day. I have to learn everything I can about people – good and bad. What makes them happy or sad, what makes them tick.'

'In that case you have the right idea. But it's important to have the sympathetic approach – to love your victim.'

'I'll remember.'

'Your salary won't be much at first but it'll rise when you prove your worth.'

'Could you give me any idea what it would be to start with?'

Sarah made an airy gesture. 'We'll have to discuss it with the English Section Manager. Come in to the S.A.B.C. building on Monday morning at ten and I'll introduce you around.'

'There's something else,' said Claire, frowning. 'If I land this job I'll need to move over to this side of the Peninsula. Is it easy to find somewhere to P.G. or someone who might care to share a small flat?'

Sarah stood up and shouted through the studio skylight.

'Katrina! Can you spare us a few minutes?'

'Sure,' came the answer, and a very tall young woman emerged on to the roof. Her untidy straw-coloured hair was wound in plaits round her head and she wore a paint-daubed smock over stove-pipe stretchies. She still held her palette and waved a paint-brush at Claire.

'Hullo, nice to see you.'

'We want your advice,' said Sarah. 'What can we do about this child here? She needs somewhere to live not too far from the S.A.B.C. I'm giving her a job.'

Katrina Westhuizen was, like her friend, Sarah Verity, a personality in her own right. In advanced artistic circles her abstracts had attracted favourable attention. Her work mystified and fascinated Claire and very often she found some particular Westhuizen profoundly satisfying, as if Katrina's pulsating splashes of colour on the waste of a broad canvas interpreted the empty deserts and living oases of the human spirit, its aloneness and its togetherness. Yet her portraits were almost conventional, for her subjects were recognizable. But she discovered and revealed some particular mood in them – some moment of truth. That insight, combined with her unusual use of vivid colour, marked her work as surely as her dashing signature. Claire owned a Westhuizen abstract, which had been given her by her aunt. It was her most cherished possession.

Katrina perched on the wide parapet of the roof-garden and put her palette and brush carefully beside her.

'You make me dizzy,' shivered Claire, looking at the casual figure outlined against the sunset, high above the busy artery of Beach Road. Katrina laughed.

'I have a good head for heights. Now what's with you?'

'Sarah thinks she can use me as one of her assistants. But I don't want to commute daily from Constantia.'

'Maybe not. And maybe you want the freedom of being on your own?'

Katrina flashed her wide friendly grin at Claire, who laughed a little self-consciously.

'I think it's time I spread my wings.'

'As a matter of fact,' Katrina said, 'I might know of something.' She turned to Sarah. 'The Dupont boy was married last week and Mrs Dupont told me only yesterday that she was thinking of taking a P.G. Actually, she wants a man, but she might be persuaded to consider a working girl who'd be out all day.'

'What's the exact accommodation?' asked Sarah. 'I don't remember.'

'A bed-sitter, bath and tiny kitchenette and – really important – a little stoep and a car-porch. Jannie Dupont was quite independent. He had electric plugs for everything, pot, kettle, the lot. And he had his own little fridge in the tiny kitchenette. The family are delightful, Ma and Pa Dupont and two kids – boy and girl, aged ten and eight – the afterthoughts.'

'Sounds too good to be true,' said Claire. 'Where is this paradise?'

'Clifton. High up, approached from the beach by steep

winding steps carved out of the granite cliff. Not everybody's cup of tea. You need to be young and nimble.' She hesitated, and Claire cut in quickly.

'You're thinking that I sometimes limp. That's nothing. It's a hang-over from polio. It doesn't worry me. I'm rather good at games really – what you'd call nimble.'

'I'm sure you are. Personally I think this place would be just right for you.'

'So do I,' said Sarah briskly. 'We must do what we can about it. After all, Claire's a properly brought up child and she won't put a red light over the door.' She turned to Claire. 'By the way, is there a boy-friend – a steady?'

Katrina rose from the parapet.

'Don't nag Claire about boy-friends, Sarah. At her age nothing and nobody is a settled proposition. Life is evanescent —'

'Spare us a lecture on life,' commanded her friend. 'It's more to the point to telephone the Duponts immediately.'

An hour later Claire was parking Vale's little car in the garage of Silverglade. She'd have to buy one of her own now. The trustees would surely be co-operative. Her father had made that clear. Her eyes shone with excitement. Everything had changed entirely in the course of the day. She must ring Aunt Helen and tell her the news. She hummed a snatch of the latest dance tune. Daddy would be pleased with her. Really, she ought to have launched out on her own months ago. Out of evil cometh good. Vale's letter had become shadowy and unimportant. Jef Broome, whose image had returned so vividly to haunt her, had receded once more into the past and all her own future sparkled across the mountains on the rocky cliffs above the Atlantic. What was more she must hurry and change. Guy was taking her dancing tonight. She'd wear her green. That leaf-green suited her. What a lot she'd have to tell him!

When she went into the house she heard voices on the stoep, Vale and her father were talking. They fell silent as she joined them, bursting with her news. The new job, the flatlet at the Duponts. But when her father looked up at her she saw that something had happened.

'Vale's mother has been taken ill,' he said gravely. 'John Rorke phoned from Johannesburg. Vale will be flying up tomorrow.'

Claire said: 'I'm sorry. I hope it isn't serious.'

'We don't know,' Vale said. 'Mother has always been a bit of a hypo. I can only hope it's a false alarm.'

Claire's eyes rested on Vale's inscrutable face.

'When was the last time – September, wasn't it?'

'Yes. She was confined to bed for three weeks.'

'I remember. You were away nearly a month.'

Vale's eyes met her stepdaughter's, dark and unfathomable.

'So I was.' She turned as a child trotted out on to the terrace. 'Micky!' Her arms were extended and the little boy ran into them.

'Here I are!'

'Oh,' she laughed as she hugged him. 'Here you are indeed. All warm from your bath in your snugly teddy-bear dressing-gown.'

She released him to let him go to his father who swung him into the air, tossed him still higher and caught him. Micky chortled with glee.

'More! More!'

'Careful,' warned Vale. 'He's just had his supper.'

Her eyes had lost their secret look. They brimmed with joy in her little son. Love made her beautiful and a cold little trickle of fear encircled Claire's heart as she watched her, chilling her spine. The child had his father's fair curly hair and his mother's soft dark eyes. He glowed from his recent bath, apple-cheeked and sturdy, and now he was running to Claire. She bent to meet him and clasp him in a quick embrace. They mustn't hurt him. Nobody must hurt Micky. But the goose-flesh rose on her arms and the taint of danger was all mixed up with the soft smell of talc and baby shampoo. She buried her face in his silky curls and felt his firm chubby cheek against her own as he squirmed suddenly, eel-like, from her grasp, and called, 'Catch me, catch me! See how fast I can run!'

As she chased and caught him he gurgled with laughter, safe, adored, utterly secure. Who would do anything to break the circle of safety in which he existed with such childish confidence?

'I'm going to miss you,' said Claire. 'Oh, Micky, I'm going to miss you.'

Vale froze. 'What's this? What do you mean? Why should you miss Micky?'

'I'm leaving home and taking a job. Not far. The Sea Point side. That's all. I've found somewhere to live at Clifton.'

'I don't know what you're talking about. What job?'

'Sarah Verity in the S.A.B.C. has taken me on as an assistant. So, by the time you come home, I'll be gone. Sarah's friends, Mr and Mrs Dupont, have a sort of flat to let – just what I need.'

Hammond smiled at his daughter. His quiet voice and warning glance gave his wife her cue.

'Well done, Claire. You're a fast worker. You must tell us all about it later. Now it's time Fedora fetched Micky. Bed-time, my lad.'

'*Not* bedtime!' contradicted Micky forcefully. But the dark form of the Xhosa nannie appeared as if by magic, her gay red *doek* tied round her head, her blue uniform straining at the seams, her face gentle as a black Madonna as she lifted the kicking protesting child into her strong arms and bore him away.

7

RORKE–MOTHER AND SON

JOHN RORKE WAITED FOR HIS SISTER ON JAN SMUTS Airport. The veld under the late afternoon sun was radiant green after the recent summer rains, but far away thunder grumbled as clouds massed heavily along the horizon.

The young man drinking a cup of black coffee by the plate-glass window looked more than his thirty years, for the way of his life was already beginning to slacken his sallow handsome face. The brown eyes were shrewd and shifty, the well-shaped mouth was weak, but he had his sister's wavy dark hair springing from a broad brow and her lithe frame and natural grace of movement. Behind him the usual crowd milled, people bringing the family to the Airport on a Sunday afternoon to watch the come and go of international air traffic. They pressed past each other and thronged the stairs leading to the observation terrace. There was a separate staircase for the non-Europeans, of course, and those who used that were more shabbily clothed, more serious and more purposeful. They had come to meet friends or to see them off, not to while away a lazy day. And seeing off friends or relatives frequently meant for them a final farewell, for the Bantu passengers leaving the country were not necessarily issued with permits of re-entry.

A woman's voice announced the incoming and outgoing flights in English and Afrikaans and suddenly John Rorke put down his coffee cup and sprang to his feet. The Cape Town plane was ten minutes early.

A few minutes later Vale was approaching across the apron, carrying her small hand-grip, her curls blowing about her head in the warm gusty wind. She gave him her baggage check.

'There's only one suitcase. Is it bad, John? Is it really Mummy at all?'

Porters were piling luggage on to the broad low counters and it didn't take Vale long to pick out her bag. As her brother carried it to his car he answered her question after his own oblique fashion.

'Mum's not too good, not too bad. She believes she's had an attack – God knows what she means by that – but it wasn't only that. I thought you'd like an excuse to pay us a visit. I have somebody staying with me. Here we are. In you get.'

He hoisted her case on to the back seat and opened the door for her. She took her place beside him.

'You've no accommodation for a guest,' she said suspiciously.

'There's a sofa in the living-room. For a few days it's good enough.'

'Jef Broome, I suppose.'

She was looking away from him across the open veld. Areas of cultivation turned it into a vast patchwork, the cloud shadows moving like armies across its face. Presently there were farms and shabby locations, and the miniature man-made mountains of white and sulphurous yellow among nature's green koppies. The towers of the Golden City rose dream-like in the evening sun.

'So it's that,' she said. 'You deliberately brought me here to see Jef.'

'Right.'

'I don't agree.'

From the corner of her eye she saw the smile of smug

satisfaction at the success of his ruse, and out of her mixed, tumultuous feelings the old familiar exasperation with her brother and his devious ways came to the surface. All the same she could not keep the excitement out of her voice when next she spoke.

'What's Jef doing staying with you? I'd no idea he was going to be in Johannesburg so soon.'

'Nor had he. It was a sudden decision. He's changed his job.'

'Why?'

'His firm asked him to represent them permanently in South Africa and he didn't want that.' For a moment John Rorke looked irritated. 'Jef makes such a thing about our . . . atmosphere . . . the tensions and the pressures. I don't notice them, why should he? They have plenty of tensions and pressures in America too – probably more than we have. Anyway, he's joined the staff of a paper – the *Illustrated Weekend News*. It's a fairly recent American publication sponsored by a powerful daily. His firm advertises in it, thanks to Jef, so he had a foot in the door from the word go.'

'What's he here for then?'

'To get material so that he can write a series of articles on South Africa.'

She groaned.

'Who doesn't? Why should Jef think he can write, anyway?'

'Because he can. He's done advertising copy and folders for years. He has plenty of punch.'

'When have you planned for me to see him? You seem to have everything taped.'

'I'm having supper with you and Mum this evening. Afterwards I'll take you back to my flat. I've told her I have some old friends coming in to see you. I'll leave you with

Jef. I have another engagement – a late one, all night probably. Jef will take you home.'

'How well arranged! You've missed your vocation,
Johnnie. Have you borrowed money off Jef in advance for
services rendered?'

His mouth turned sulkily down at the corners and she
knew that her random shot had gone home.

'I don't like your attitude, Mrs Hammond. How long are
you planning to stay?'

'Not long. I promised to telephone Charles tomorrow
morning. I'll go home as soon as I can reasonably leave
Mummy.'

The squalid areas of the city lay behind them, so did the
heart of the metropolis and the new suburban shopping
centres all steeped in their Sunday quiet. Church bells were
chiming.

John drew up at a block of modern flats set in pleasant
gardens, and a few minutes later Vale was in her mother's
arms.

'Darling child, so wonderful of you to come!'

Mrs Rorke was a small soft creature with haunted myopic
dark eyes magnified by strong-lensed glasses. She was one of
those fragile little women who are destined to watch their
friends fall out one by one as life plays its perpetual game of
musical chairs.

'How are you, Mummy? What happened?'

'Just one of my attacks, darling. I'm better today. Just
knowing I'd be seeing you helped. I've felt so poorly this
last week, so *collapsed*, that there were moments when I was
sure my last hour was at hand, and yesterday Johnnie said,
"I'm going to telephone Vale." So here you are.'

Vale smiled crookedly. 'Yes – as my little Micky would
say – here I are!'

She hugged her mother, torn as ever between affection,

pity and fury at the vapourings of this ineffectual self-centred parent who had seldom, to her daughter's knowledge, put herself out to do anything for anyone. Once, long ago, Agnes Rorke, or Agnes Vale as she was then, must have been the original 'sex kitten' of her generation – pretty, spoilt, arch, petted, and indifferent to anyone's comfort except her own. Now, at fifty, her main concern in life was cosseting her health and playing her bridge.

'The old ticker,' sighed Mrs Rorke, subsiding into an easy-chair in the luxurious sitting-room of the bijou flat as frivolous and superficial as she was herself. She touched her breast with a dainty hand. 'It's all over the place. Hammers when I lie on my left side at night, stops altogether on the slightest provocation. Darling, I *dare* not let myself get upset or over-stimulated. Anything could happen any time! But don't let's talk about me. How are dear Charles and little Micky?'

'They're well. I wish you could see Micky now. When last you stayed with us he was two and now he's four – and such fun, lively as a flea and mischievous as a wilderness of monkeys.'

'I'd love to see him again before . . . well, don't let's think sad thoughts. Perhaps I really will get down to the Cape one of these days. I would have tried long ago except that I hate being away from my doctor. You know how it is. One becomes so dependent. You must tell me all about Micky. Everything.'

So genuine and disarming was her mother's welcome that Vale was touched and her impatience evaporated. It was perfectly true that her mother's heart was shaky and her nervousness about herself was a symptom of her condition. It was not like Vale to be demonstrative but suddenly she came and sat at her mother's feet and laid her head against the older woman's knee. She wanted her reason for coming to Johannesburg to be real, she wanted to believe in her mother's recent 'attack'. But the region of her own troubled heart was filled with terrible confusion and wild palpitations that had nothing to do with any malady of the body. She felt the soft fingers touch her hair tenderly, and she heard her mother say,

'You're looking very pretty, darling. Beautiful, in fact. Are you happy?'

So unexpected was the question that Vale was taken unawares.

'Of course. Why shouldn't I be?'

'That gap in age between you and Charles. It's always worried me —'

'Don't let it!'

Vale jumped up and went to the window. The flat was on the tenth storey and the veld spread to the far rim of the world, its expanse broken here and there by the pale angular artificial hills and the blue distant ranges. Lightning stabbed the purple dusk and the evening was close. If only it would rain!

'I'll go and unpack,' she said. 'John says he's coming to supper.'

Mrs Rorke's small kitten face crumpled.

'Now, there's something else that worries me. John. He's gambling again, Vale. He can't let the horses be – or the cards. I know he's in debt, he tried to borrow off me —'

'Then he succeeded?'

'Not to any great extent. I'm not a rich woman and my doctors' bills are high. I don't honestly know what I'd do without the banker's order from your beloved Charles. Even with that I can barely manage. There are a thousand things that need doing to the flat. I ought to have new covers. These are terribly shabby, as you can see – positively threadbare – and the carpet! But John just laughs and says that's fashionable. Antique. He's so weak, Vale, and, though I hate to say it, rather sly. He has expensive tastes – there's a girl, some fly-by-night in a very fast set, and his mother's comfort doesn't concern him at all these days. In fact, ever since your dear Charles began to make me a regular allowance, John has stopped contributing to my support. I dare say he may try to touch you, dear. I'm only warning you.'

Vale's face hardened. 'John's not only weak, he's unscrupulous. I hate asking Charles for money to help him. Charles does enough for my family as it is.'

'Well, I may be doing your brother an injustice. But perhaps out of your personal income . . .'

'Don't let's anticipate the touch. It may not come.'

But Vale was sure it would. There was evidently to be a percentage both ways, the middleman getting a double cut off the cake – the kind brother selling his sister's honour down the river. No, that was absurd. His sister was responsible for her own honour and she'd better guard it well!

When her mother had retired to bed John drove Vale to his flat a few blocks away. It had begun to rain, heavy drops as big as coins pitting the dust. He pulled up at the entrance.

'I'll drop you here, you know your way. You won't need a key. There'll be someone to let you in.'

In the dark she was aware of the quality of his grin and she squirmed.

'I'll be out all night,' he added.

'Gambling or girls?'

'Both, dear.'

'I promised Mummy I wouldn't be late.'

'You needn't worry. She takes a whacking great tablet and sinks into oblivion. She won't be any the wiser if you're home at ten or at two.'

'Good hunting,' she said, trying to play it light. But her

voice was choked and she stood as if paralysed watching him drive away. The fat splash of rain on her face and hair brought her to her senses and she went slowly into the building. The entrance was quiet and discreet as befitted a block of flats tenanted mainly by business men who were seldom in. Outside the elevator she paused and scrabbled in her bag for a mirror. The face that looked back at her in the dim light was strained and almost ethereal, with the eyes over-bright. She put the mirror back and snapped her handbag to. Please, she whispered inwardly, please, please let me be strong! It was very strange – this sensation of fate, of knowing that the future of those she loved was in her hands, that tonight she might have to make some terrible decision. Queer the way this lift didn't seem to be moving at all, yet it was bearing her up to the top floor, to Jef Broome and an hour of destiny.

The number 13 showed in lights above the elevator door and it slid back. Vale stepped out and walked down the corridor to her brother's flat. Her steps were muffled by the heavy carpet. Her hands were cold as she pressed the bell.

8

THE LOVER

THE DOOR CLOSED BEHIND HER AND JEF LOCKED IT.
He stood with his back against it, his arms outspread. Vale
turned towards him. Without a word uttered between them
she felt those hungry arms enfold her.

For once in his life Jef Broome could not speak and it
seemed to him that he could scarcely breathe. They were
much of a height and standing face to face, their bodies
pressed together as if they could never bear to be separated,
they were thigh to thigh, breast to breast and mouth to
mouth. His heart pounded so violently that he felt as if it
would break through the thin strong wall of flesh and bone
to become one with hers. When at last he let her go his eyes
were misty.

He drew her into the living-room. There were drinks on a
side-table and he poured whisky and soda for her and one for
himself.

'Steady,' she protested. 'I don't, as a rule.'

'Tonight there are no rules.'

He drew her on to the sofa beside him. 'I love you, Vale.
Dear God, how I love you!'

'I love you too.'

The words were wrenched from her and he realized with
intoxicating triumph that this was the first time she had ever
used them to him. Those other times – their secret meetings
at the Cape, or here, and even during their stolen three days
in John's cabin in the lowveld – she had never said those three

precious words. Oh, there had been endearments in plenty. 'I'm yours' – how could she deny it? – 'I want you', and a thousand others, but not the three words that could elevate a transient *affaire* into the reality, or perhaps the illusion, of permanence. He had tried to force them from her, but it had seemed that they lay outside her scope. They were for another man – for the man she had married. In withholding them from her lover she had made clear the nature of her need for him – temporary, physical, something to be got out of her system. This half rejection in the very act of such abandoned giving had only served to increase his own possessive desire for her – for every part of her, body, heart and soul.

'Vale – honey love – you've never said that to me before. You've never said "I love you".'

'Perhaps I never knew it before, in spite of everything. I say it now, Jef, I love you – and I mean it – but it makes no difference. I can't leave Charles. You must understand and accept that.'

'I don't understand or accept it.'

He caught her cold hands and held them flat against his chest in the gesture she knew well, pleading, cajoling.

'This sort of thing – these furtive meetings – can't go on. I want you for my wife – for always. I wrote and told you that. You never even answered my letter.'

'My love,' she said, and that too was new. 'I can't go away with you. And I didn't answer your letter because it lay hidden in a hedge for over a fortnight. I only received it on Friday. Just before dinner, to be precise.'

'What on earth do you mean?'

'Claire found it there with the stamps slashed out of the envelope. She was rescuing a hurt bird or some silly thing. The postman, it seems, has been stealing foreign airmail stamps.'

'Claire . . . our little red herring.' His voice contained a note of anxiety. 'She wouldn't have read it, would she?'

Vale's smooth brow furrowed.

'I wonder. It was quite possible to draw the letter through the tear and put it back without anyone knowing. I tried it.'

'But Claire's not like that. Surely —'

'She's a woman. She's in love with you – at least she was—, A look of guilt shadowed his face at Vale's words – 'And she adores her father.'

'If she . . . then there's very little she won't know . . . about us, I mean. I asked you to go away with me, I mentioned that time we stayed in John's cabin in the wilds. Not this, I didn't ask you to come here, of course, because when I wrote I didn't know that I was going to be in Johannesburg so soon. So she can't have any valid reason for suspecting this visit of yours. But still . . . do you think she guesses?'

'Only that the gap in the envelope showed the words "Honey love, if you were free". As a matter of fact, Charles saw them too. Claire threw the letter at me in front of him. He asked to look at the envelope.'

Vale drew away from Jef's embrace and he watched her go and sit on the arm of a chair as if she needed to be apart from him. She was silent, her face averted. He made as if to follow her, but she said quickly,

'No! Stay where you are. That night, when he came to my room, I offered him your letter. I said, "Read it, if you want to." I'd meant to tell him then that it was finished between him and me, that I wanted to go to you, but that wasn't the way I behaved. I was crazy mad for you – so mad I needed Charles, needed him desperately, so I could make believe he was you loving me —'

'How dare you! How could you!'

He was on his feet, furious, but she held him off.

'Keep away from me, Jef! How can you understand

women – the things we do, the reasons? Substituting in the dark, giving our bodies to one man and our souls to another all in the same act of love and betrayal.'

He saw her heightened colour and glistening eyes, the pulse fluttering in her throat, the rise and fall of her thrusting breasts, yet he knew her to be suddenly and terribly unattainable. Presently they would make love, she would be his entirely for a while – the anticipation had been around them like an aura ever since they had stood inside the door so close, so deeply desiring, ever since she had said, 'I love you' – but now, for all he knew, she might call him Charles as she lay in his arms.

'The letter,' she said. 'He took it from me. He didn't read it. He tore it into little pieces and dropped them into the wastepaper basket. Then he came to me and we slept together.'

Jef gripped her shoulders; his eyes, staring down at hers, were hot with rage.

'He's clever! He's experienced. Can't you see through him? That show of trust and forgiveness was meant to appeal to everything loyal and good in you – and you're falling for it. You can't, Vale, you mustn't! In a few years it'll all be over between you and him. It'll be a travesty – an old man and his darling – whereas you and I have our lives before us. Too many years wasted already. We want children, a family, a home of our own. We'll live in America. It'll be a totally new life – and he can forget. For God's sake let him forget! Why can't you make a new start? Why?'

She put her hands up and removed his gently. Still holding them, she said:

'You're hurting me. Listen, Jef, there's something you seem to have forgotten. There's Micky. If I desert Charles he'll never give up Micky.'

'The child – if it's a young child – is almost always given

into the mother's custody. Who else could take care of Micky? You're making difficulties.'

'Claire could look after Micky – until she marries. She loves him. And after that, Helen Terblanche, Charles's widowed sister. She's forty, younger than Charles. It's not unreasonable.'

The emotion had gone out of her voice. It struck him that women were always the practical ones, the realists, the ones who saw exactly where the pound of flesh lay and sharpened the knives.

'Then prove your love for me and if Charles is intransigent – which I doubt – give up Micky.'

'You don't know what you're asking. I love you, but I love Micky too. And, in a different way, I still love Charles. You're asking the impossible.' Her face was pale and shocked.

'I come first,' he said arrogantly. 'I'm your future and you're my whole life. There's a price and I'm demanding it – the greatest sacrifice. Everything.'

She looked up at him, dark eyes abrim, resistance melting in tears, her lips still whispering the refusal he would not accept.

'I can't make that sacrifice, Jef. I can't.'

He knew that for the present he could no longer persuade her with argument. There could be no more discussion between them now.

'Honey love – come!'

They went into John's room as if it were their own. They had made it so on other occasions. Its bachelor austerity was tempered with comfort, for John Rorke was a sybarite.

Her dark head on the white pillow turned towards Jef, and her body moved into his embrace, inviting the touch of his hands, the enjoyment of his body, and the consummation that could reach the pinnacle of ecstasy that he alone could give her. For a while she forgot everything. There was nothing in the world but Jef and the pleasure that verged on pain.

It no longer mattered that the price of such loving might be her son – or even that it might beget some other child. She was lost in the fire of madness that only Jef could spark and only he could quell.

It was midnight when she made coffee and took the tray into the living-room. The action was prosaic and pleased her with its suggestion of domesticity. He watched her pour it, black and strong and only slightly sweetened, the way they liked it. He loved her hands, smooth and small. She was a woman of slender bones, but not angular. Even her elbows were rounded. Her thin sleeveless silk summer dress showed her voluptuous curves and the tantalizing slimness of her hips and her long bare legs.

'There's so much to talk about,' he said. 'Where do we start?'

'Your job. John says you've changed it.'

'I'm working on a paper now – the *Illustrated Weekend News*. I'm doing a series of articles on apartheid for them.'

'Oh, Jef, why? It's such old hat. Every foreign correspondent wears the subject to death.'

'Because this old hat – as you put it – comes up in a new form every day. Each time your Parliament meets it passes new apartheid laws – laws of fear – and more and more people are expelled or imprisoned for expressing their views.'

'They do much more than that before they're imprisoned,' she said with heat.

'They're fighting for their rights – the right of a majority for fair representation.'

'One man one vote, and chaos. Can't you see that African domination in this century would turn our prosperous country into bedlam. Children – even black political children – don't grow up overnight.'

'This century! You're hardly putting it as overnight development.'

'The British social revolution took over fifty years – and

those revolutionaries had a better start than these, who are still steeped in tribal superstition.'

'You don't want them to outgrow that tribal superstition either. You'd like to see them kept tribal.'

'Look what happens when they get control. Look to the north. Ghana, Nigeria, the Congo, Zambia, Tanzania. Confusion and anarchy everywhere. Only Southern Africa – and I include Rhodesia – has true stability. Face it!'

'You never did like my political ideas – my view on apartheid – did you, Vale? It was the little one, Claire – who cared.'

'Cared for what?'

'For the many. You, my love, care for the few. And let anyone question the magnanimity of your Government – your white Herrenvolk – and up you go in a sheet of flame.'

'I'm not going up in a sheet of flame now,' she said. 'I'm going to tidy these glasses and coffee things away and then I'm going home. If Mummy wakes she'll worry.'

He tried to hold her back as she rose, but she eluded him. As he helped her dry the cups in the tiny kitchenette, he said remorsefully:

'So silly to fight. So crazy when our time is so short. Politics – that's always the battleground here, public and private. But not for us, for heaven's sake! Surely, surely lovers don't talk politics. Honey love, when will I see you? Tomorrow?'

'I doubt if you will. You must be very busy collecting your precious material. And my mother expects me to be at her beck and call.'

'John said your mother played bridge on Mondays, come hell or high water. There's a place I want to take you. It's a corner on a private farm – an oasis. The owner's away. We can be alone.'

He had his way, and the next afternoon she made a flimsy

excuse to go shopping. They met in a quiet avenue not far from the shopping centre and within half an hour they were in open country. The air smelt of sun-warmed grass, of hay and ripe millet, dust and cattle, and a cool stream that widened and petered out in a pond where wild geese took to the air at their approach, the white arrowhead of a small flight of lesser birds.

They left the car in the shade of a thorn tree and he led her down to the willow-fringed water's edge. The grass here was green and soft and he spread a rug and threw two cushions on it and she found that he had brought a basket with a Thermos of tea, some cakes and a few apples.

'At sunset the springbok come here to drink with the cattle,' he said. 'Jerseys – so pretty and soft-eyed. Eyes like —'

'Don't say it!' she laughed. 'I'm not bovine, not a bit. Jef, I telephoned Charles this morning and I'm going home tomorrow by the midday plane.'

'What about your mother? Is she well enough for you to leave her?'

'She's playing bridge. Doesn't that speak for itself?'

'I suppose so. And me? I have three more days in Johannesburg.'

'They'll be very full.'

'But the nights! Why must you go?'

'I must go back because of Micky. Claire is taking a job and going to live on the other side of the Peninsula. How can I leave Micky alone with Fedora all day?'

'And Harmonia, to say nothing of Josiah, who'd lay down his life for Micky. And Charles coming back each evening. For heaven's sake, he'd be all right.'

'I'm sorry. It's not on. One doesn't leave a little child to the care of one's black servants all day. At least I don't. If Claire were at home it would be different. Or if my sister-in-law, Helen, were staying at Silverglade.'

'You'd stay here if you had to. You'd make a plan.'

'I don't have to.'

'Not for my sake?'

'Least of all for your sake.'

'What are you trying to tell me?'

'That you must forget me.'

'Try telling me to fly to Mars.'

'I'm tired of fighting you – of fighting myself. Let me be, Jef. Just let me be.'

But she pleaded on a note of defeat. He touched her hair gently as she lay on her back with her head pillowed on his chest. She could see the hot blue sky through the willow tresses, already sere with autumn gold. Little birds twittered in the branches and noisy yellow and black weavers hovered round their exquisite nests overhanging the water. A fish plopped and a haze of tiny insects wavered and moved on. Dragon-flies darted in the sun. A sense of peace pervaded her, a profound idleness. Such a day was not made for battles and decisions, it was made for love.

'When I was a child,' she said drowsily, 'there was a picture in my bedroom – a reproduction of a water-colour of a man and a girl in a meadow. They were kissing. They were very young and she was beautiful with long hair and a poppy behind her ear. He had some sort of hat on, I think. Funny, that. I imagine he was a shepherd. It was called "Pastoral Idyll". I've no idea who painted it, but it appealed to me enormously. I think I envied the girl. I haven't thought of it in years.'

'So now you do. Pastoral Idyll. This is it, honey love.'

Later they had tea and when they repacked the basket it was long after five o'clock.

She looked at him, the sun so bright on his bright hair, its alchemy bringing out the gold in his skin and at the roots of his thick brown lashes.

'This is our real good-bye,' she said.

He shook his head like a frisky pony maddened by a persistent fly.

'Get this straight,' he told her. 'I'm coming back at the beginning of August. It's then I'll want your final answer.'

'Take your answer now,' she said. 'Take it as *no*.'

'I can't,' he said. 'From the very first moment I saw you there was only one woman for me. You are the one.'

Once Charles had said much the same and he too had meant it. Charles and Micky. How could she abandon them? As she stood with Jef in the rich grass like the shepherd and his love in the Pastoral Idyll, as they kissed under the weeping willow, she could have wept, for, in her heart, she believed this was indeed a last farewell.

When he dropped her outside her mother's block of flats it was half-past six. The bridge game was over and the four ladies were sipping their respective drinks with satisfaction. This, after all, was the best part of the afternoon, the half-hour devoted to a nice little gossip.

The cards still lay on the open bridge table and Vale knew that after her guests had departed her mother would play one game of patience. If it came out she would regard it as a good omen, if not she would fear some nebulous disaster. After the greetings Mrs Rorke said:

'Dear girl, the shops closed ages ago. Where *have* you been? We were getting in a state.'

'I met an old school-friend and went home with her for a cup of tea. I didn't notice how late it was.'

She felt the three pairs of inquisitive eyes boring into her, salacious and disbelieving. Did she look like a woman warm from love-making? She put up a hand to touch her hair. Was her lipstick smeared?

'You missed a call from your husband,' said Mrs van

Tonder, her soft predatory hands busy with her cigarette case. 'He rang half an hour ago. Smoke, dear?'

'No thanks. What's this about a call from Charles?'

'Oh, yes, darling,' fluttered Mrs Rorke. 'Isn't it wonderful, he can spare you till Friday.'

'But he can't, Mummy. Claire —'

'That's the point, Claire will be home. She went for her interview today but she isn't taking up her new job till the end of the month. So there isn't a thing for you to worry about.' Mrs Rorke turned smiling to her guests. 'You've no idea how devoted Claire is to her little half-brother. She dotes on Micky.'

'How nice,' said Mrs Blair, her beady black eyes on Vale. 'Such difficult relationships —'

Mrs Rorke cut in. 'Anyway, Vale, I told Charles it was just too wonderful and generous of him to spare you, and of course I accepted the sacrifice with gratitude. So there it is. We must make the most of our few days together.'

'Yes, Mummy,' said Vale. 'We must.'

Her heart plunged and lifted. This was fate, this was something she couldn't fight any more.

'Does John know?' she asked suddenly.

'Yes, darling. John happened to be here when the call came through. He took it. Really, he was most persuasive. Dear John.'

'You have such kind successful children,' said Mrs Erasmus. 'You are a lucky woman, Agnes.'

Vale felt the colour rise in her cheeks.

Kind, successful children? John, the sly opportunist, gambler, womanizer, pimp for his sister. And she, the sister, under the influence of a man who urged her to cheat a good husband and abandon a beloved child. The surface and the depths, how different!

9

BACHELOR GIRL

THE SUN HAD ALREADY BEEN SWALLOWED BY THE sea when Claire and Guy arrived at her new flatlet.

Mr Dupont, a meagre but lively little man, and the two children, Kate and Eugene, helped them carry her cases from Guy's car.

Kate fell in love with Boo, the soft toy monkey Claire tossed on her bed and Gene immediately wanted to try her record player.

'Leave Miss Hammond in peace!' ordered Mr Dupont firmly. 'My wife'll soon be over to welcome you, Miss Hammond. She's out just now.'

By the time Mrs Dupont's broad smiling face and matronly figure appeared in the doorway, Guy had gone and Claire was in a turmoil of half unpacked garments and possessions, investing Jannie Dupont's vacated flatlet with an unfamiliar feminine atmosphere. A large framed photograph of a football team lay face up on the pillow next to Boo, and in its place against the wall was a Westhuizen aquatint so elusive that Mrs Dupont could make neither head nor tail of it.

'I hope you don't mind,' Claire said, following Mrs Dupont's baffled gaze. 'I didn't feel at home with the football team.'

Mrs Dupont laughed. 'Jannie meant to put that away. I'll take it with me. Have you everything you need? Shall I show you how the gadgets in the kitchenette work?'

Claire swept some clothes from a chair.

'Do sit down, Mrs Dupont, and don't worry about the

gadgets. Kate and Gene showed me the lot. They really are terrific – the children, I mean. They know all about everything. As for odds and ends, I can get them later – groceries, bread, tinned stuff and all that sort of thing – but maybe your milkman could let me have half a pint daily.'

'Of course. I'll see about it. In the meantime I can lend you half a pint for tomorrow.'

Claire was wearing a cocktail dress in a shade of hyacinth blue that was not unlike the dominant colour in the Westhuizen picture which might have signified anything from a bluebell wood in spring to a cow jumping over the moon at midnight.

'You're just going out, Miss Hammond?'

'Yes, Guy's coming for me later. Please call me Claire.'

Mrs Dupont smiled. 'Then I mustn't be a nuisance, Claire. I just wanted you to know that if there's anything you need you must say so. We want you to feel at home.'

'Oh, I will! You're so kind. Don't hurry away. I'm only putting out a few special things. I'll get settled in properly tomorrow.'

Mrs Dupont picked up a large double leather frame. 'Your parents?'

'Yes. It's a recent one of Daddy, but the one of my mother was taken eight years ago just before her last illness . . .'

'She was lovely – but you're more like your father.'

The face of the woman in the photograph was coldly beautiful. So it had been taken eight years ago? When had she died? Probably when this girl was still a child. As if in answer to the unspoken query, Claire said:

'My mother died when I was thirteen. Daddy married again. My stepmother is young – in her twenties.'

She showed Mrs Dupont a framed coloured snapshot of a picnic party on a river bank.

'See, here she is – the dark one in green shorts – and there's

Daddy and me, and the little boy in front is Micky, my half-brother.'

'A nice cheerful picture, and what a pleasant place!'

'It's a stretch of the Hex River near our farm, Leopard Bush. It's glorious there.'

Mrs Dupont cocked her head and listened. 'A car. Your boy-friend, I expect.'

Guy's footsteps crunched on the shingle path as he went round from the car-porch to the front stoep which looked down the dizzy descent to the sea. Claire went to the door.

'Come in and meet Mrs Dupont. Mrs Dupont, this is Guy Steele.'

'I'm glad to meet you.' The plump woman beamed as if she meant it. 'We hope Claire is going to be happy here. And now I must be off.'

She took her departure, carrying the football team with her and promising to remember the milk.

'Well,' said Guy, when she had gone. 'How does it feel to be an independent bachelor girl? Just a bit lonesome?'

Claire's eyes shone. 'It feels wonderful! And if I get lonesome I'll send for you.'

'Do that thing. Could be dangerous, though.'

Suddenly all the implications of independence flooded over her, intoxicating and just a tiny bit frightening.

'Anything in your fridge?' he asked. 'And I don't mean food.'

'Bitter lemon and beer.'

'And I've brought some gin. What shall it be?'

'Gin and bitter lemon for me.'

'And beer for me.'

He filled their glasses. 'Here's to it – the emancipation of Claire Hammond – and the new job.'

Claire hung up the last of her dresses hastily and flung the rest of her garments haphazard into drawers while Guy watched her with a new proprietary air.

'I can tidy this mess later. Just now I'm hungry as a wolf. Where are we going?'

'A little Italian place I know where we can eat well and dance to discs. They haven't a liquor licence but I've got a bottle of wine in the car. One takes one's own.'

'I feel high already.'

'Drunk with freedom.'

'I guess that's it.'

The Italian restaurant was crowded as usual on a Saturday night. Candle-lit, intimate, pervaded with tantalizing culinary aromas – garlic, minestroni, savoury fish, pasta, veal, grilled steak, crêpes Suzettes and the more exotic forms of ice-cream. Overall lay a film of cigarette smoke and on the limited floor space couples danced to the music of long-playing records. Rinaldo, the head waiter, was attentive to Guy with a flattering gleam in his black eyes as he presented the menu to the *signorina* and advised her what to order.

Over the *poussin en casserole* Claire said suddenly:

'Do you think Vale went to Johannesburg to see Jef?'

'Why?'

He took the bottle of Paarl Riesling from the ice bucket and filled her glass. She turned the stem delicately between her fingers and thumb and watched the candlelight reflected in the dry white wine.

'She came back yesterday in a queer mood. I met her with Micky off the afternoon plane and she was terribly thrilled to see him. She hugged him as if she was scared to death of losing him. She seemed genuinely glad to be home – yet, underneath, there was a sort of sadness.'

'Worried about her mother, perhaps.'

'Could be – but it didn't come out when she talked about her mother. It came out when she thought nobody was noticing – just a look in her eyes . . .'

'Did she mention Jef's name?'

'Not a word. And none of us asked. After all, why should he be in Johannesburg?'

'Did you suspect that the letter had something to do with her visit?'

'Why should I? John Rorke rang from Johannesburg to say Mrs Rorke was taken ill. And when Vale found her mother was crying "wolf", she didn't want to stay. She meant to come home on Tuesday. I was there when she phoned Daddy early Monday morning. We were at breakfast and she said she'd come back next day. She didn't like leaving Micky without me being at Silverglade and she thought I might have to start the new job straight away. Later, when we found I was only needed at the end of the month, Daddy rang to tell her not to hurry back. She was out, but John and Mrs Rorke answered and they were the ones who fixed up for her to stay on for the inside of the week. So you see, none of it really adds up to Jef or a plot – except just . . .'

'Just what?'

She shrugged her shoulders and pushed back her hair in a perplexed manner.

'Just that lost look when she was off guard – like the sadness of parting. Let's dance.'

He steered her between the tables and they danced close. There wasn't much room for manœuvre. Everybody was dancing the way they wanted – together, apart, conventional, eccentric, or with the rapt oblivion of lovers. Suddenly, in Guy's arms, she wondered where her new freedom might lead her. The other couples on the tiny floor were a haze in the dim light. They were nothing – but a fairly substantial nothing, as she had to admit when a pair in a trance collided with them.

Claire soon settled in to her new existence. Her work absorbed her. She found Sarah Verity an exacting but interesting boss. Sarah encouraged initiative but she was a martinet where matters such as punctuality were concerned. She expected a great deal of her assistants. If it was necessary to work late they must do so.

'Like newspaper reporters,' she explained. 'A great deal of our programme is concerned with news – happenings or personalities in the news – and our private engagements have to take second place.'

On Sundays Claire went home to Silverglade, and, as often as not, Guy took her. After all, she found it unnecessary to ask her father to help her buy a car. The bus stop on the High Level Road was practically next door to the Dupont home and the bus that conveyed her to Rocklands and her work also ran all the way through to Wynberg where Vale, her father, or Josiah could easily meet her on a Sunday and drive her up the hill through Wynberg Park to Silverglade. For the rest she was usually out with Guy, and it was his little car that was most often parked in the car-porch attached to her flatlet.

Guy lived in one of those fantastic blocks that cling to the perpendicular cliffs like vast concrete limpets between the road and the beach. The flat roof at road level was marked out with the numbers of tenants entitled to parking space. The block had its own access to and from the beach. His tiny apartment was like a ship's cabin. To Claire it was a never-ending shock of pleasure to enter that L-shaped room with its seascape window right across the outer wall. The narrow American kitchen-diner and the bathroom took a slice off the wide bed-sitter in which Guy slept. The beach, three floors below, was only visible from the narrow balcony outside, so that the effect from the window was of mighty rollers surging shorewards in uninterrupted majesty. Sea birds wheeled and cried, the roar of the ocean and its salty tang seemed part of the air of the room.

'I love it!' said Claire. 'I'm mad about it. To sleep and wake with this – how wonderful!'

Guy grinned. 'On moonlight nights it's rather disturbing. You must try it sometime.'

She laughed, wondering where her new freedom might lead her.

In the middle of June Judge Hammond took his winter vacation and went for a month to Durban, taking Vale and Micky, and, of course, Fedora, who was delighted as she had several friends in the beautiful semi-tropical seaport which was as bright and sunny in midwinter as the Cape was in spring.

Harmonia arranged to go to her daughter in the Transkei for a holiday and Josiah remained in charge of Silverglade with instructions to contact Mrs Terblanche in case of emergency.

During their absence Claire and Guy formed the week-end habit of walking up the Glen and over Kloof Nek to lunch or supper with Helen Terblanche. She always made them welcome and both young people felt at home with her. Sometimes Claire visited her aunt alone. Mrs Terblanche invited her niece's confidence.

'That nice horse-faced young man of yours has what it takes. Why aren't you head over heels in love with him? That deep voice —'

'Perhaps he isn't head over heels in love with me.'

'I'd say he was. For instance, do you ever talk about marriage? Or is it just an unspoken thought in the back of both your minds?'

'We never talk about it. It isn't on. He's still studying.'

'But he attracts you? Very much.'

Claire sat forward, looking solemnly at her aunt, chin on hands.

'I s'pose if one's the right age and normal one's bound to be attracted by somebody. If there was nobody else around a baboon might seem fascinating when the moon is at the full. It's nature, isn't it? Well, possibly not the baboon, but the rest. Chemistry. So, yes, at certain times, like an animal, I want Guy madly. But not hauntingly – like —'

'Go on. Like what? Like – who? Somebody you can't forget?'

For no reason that she could clearly define Claire suddenly found the tears welling into her eyes and Jef Broome's face swam before her. It was as if her aunt had put her finger upon some secret spring of half-forgotten pain.

'I don't know,' she said. 'I just don't know.'

Mrs Terblanche put her arm round the girl's shoulders.

'My child, don't worry. You'll find out. One day, in its own good time, the truth will be clear and bright and you'll know who is for you and who is not. Be patient. And, if your Guy is the man I think he is, he'll be patient too.'

'But it isn't fair,' choked Claire. 'It really isn't fair to Guy. He's a man with all a man's needs and I'm holding out on him.'

'Since when have women been fair to men?' said Mrs Terblanche. 'Be your age, Claire. Nineteen, isn't it? Let me hear no more nonsense about what's fair and what's not.'

A few days after the Hammonds had returned from Durban Claire invited herself to Sunday supper with her aunt. The winter evening was fading, and, although the sky to the west held an afterglow, the lights of Cape Town were already winking far below, wavering in the dark waters of Table Bay, and climbing the steep slopes of the mountain to the scenic drive that marked the limit of residential development. Mrs Terblanche drew the curtains together.

'Let's make ourselves snug. Lena is out so we'll get our

own supper when we want it – soup and eggs. Meanwhile you know where to find the drinks, whisky for me and gin and bitter lemon for you. Am I right?'

When they were settled Claire said:

'I've news for you.'

'Out with it.'

'Vale is going to have another baby.'

'When?'

'End of November.'

Mrs Terblanche made a quick calculation. 'And it's near the end of July now. She's kept it wonderfully quiet – even considering they've been away over a month.'

'It's the loose clothes we all wear – shift dresses, chunky jerseys —'

'Didn't you guess?'

'No. I never even thought of it.'

Mrs Terblanche sipped her whisky and digested Claire's information. Presently she said: 'Of course Vale has wanted another child for quite a while. Ever since that miscarriage when Micky was a year old. To tell you the truth, I was afraid, then, that something might have gone wrong – that there might never be another baby.'

'Well now we know differently.'

Mrs Terblanche looked sharply at her niece.

'How do you feel about it, Claire?'

Claire was curled up on the sofa, her legs tucked under her. Her hair was drawn back off her face by a blue bandeau and the pure grace of the line from chin to neck and throat was unbroken. Her blue sweater revealed the young curves of her slight form and her long delicate hands lay lightly in her lap. The expression on her face was enigmatic.

'It'll be a good thing for Micky.'

'Surely for all of you.'

'I hope it'll settle Vale.'

'Settle Vale? What makes you say that? Is Vale . . . un-settled?'

Mrs Terblanche saw some inner conflict reflected in her niece's shadowed eyes. There was something she wanted to say but loyalty of some sort was holding her back.

'I don't know,' said Claire at last. 'But she wants to go and see her mother in Johannesburg again. She wants to go away for a fortnight in August.'

'She was there at the end of February.'

'Yes, just before I took up my job.'

'It's natural, Claire. A girl wants to be with her mother at a time like this – just for a bit.'

'Vale and her mother aren't all that close.'

'Still – it's understandable.'

'Anyway, Aunt Helen, they're going to ask you to hold the fort at Silverglade while she's away.'

'I will, of course, but why doesn't she take Micky to see his grandmother?'

'There isn't room in Mrs Rorke's flat.'

'I dare say not. But if Micky were my grandchild I'd make room. There are ways and means – if the will is there.'

'You don't know Mrs Rorke. She's neurotic. She wouldn't like her routine upset.' Claire smiled at her aunt with affection. 'She couldn't be less like you. In fact, the will isn't there.'

'Do you know the dates I'll be wanted at Silverglade?'

'Not exactly – except that it'll be sometime early next month. Vale is ringing her brother, John, tonight to make a plan.'

'Why not her mother?'

'Mrs Rorke likes leaning on other people. She loves to feel dependent, and Vale says she gets agitated over long-distance telephone calls. Or thinks she does. It's the same thing.'

'You've met Mrs Rorke, of course?'

'Yes, when I spent a holiday in Pretoria I went to Johannesburg specially to see her. She's the clinging type – not a bit like Vale.'

'What's the brother like?'

'Not to be trusted. Dark and dirty, the type a lot of women fall for. I believe he's having an *affaire* with a wealthy Greek divorcee – so Mrs Rorke wrote Vale – and the old lady's delighted because if he marries this Maria Triandefiledes he'll have no more excuse for borrowing off his mother. Honestly, Aunt Helen, John Rorke's rather a heel and Mrs Rorke is fatuous.'

Helen Terblanche laughed outright.

'You aren't exactly enamoured of your step-relations, are you?'

Claire grinned. 'I don't think Vale is either. She does her best, but I think she's glad to be living a thousand miles away from them. I tried to be friends with John Rorke, but I couldn't. He made passes at me. Slimy. I was sorry, because I really wanted to like Vale's people. It was soon after she married Daddy and I knew he hoped Vale and I would be friends – like we had been before.'

'Why shouldn't you be? Friends, I mean?' Mrs Terblanche watched her niece's thoughtful face and the tell-tale wash of colour stain the high cheek-bones. 'Was it your fault?'

'I think it was,' said Claire slowly. 'You see, I was jealous of Vale. She was so self-confident – and those gorgeous eyes and legs – especially her lovely legs. I always felt clumsy and gauche beside her, and when I brought boy-friends home they found Vale more interesting than me.'

The words poured out in a breathless torrent, all the old resentments trembling in her voice.

'There was Jef Broome,' she added. 'You remember —'

'Very well. That extremely dynamic young American

wished on to you by John Rorke in the middle of the sabotage trial.'

'Yes, him. If it hadn't been for Vale I think he might have —'

She broke off and Mrs Terblanche knew that suddenly Claire had been carried into admissions beyond anything she had intended. She came to the rescue.

'It's very difficult for a teenage girl to compete with a more sophisticated woman. The sense of inferiority is built in before she even begins to fight.'

'That's it, Aunt Helen, and it is a fight – to hold one's own. Daddy, of course, would never understand.'

Mrs Terblanche backtracked the conversation. 'Jef Broome – was he attracted to Vale?'

But her niece was cautious now, and Helen Terblanche sensed the withdrawal.

'Like all the rest, yes.' Claire's face was deadpan, her tone impersonal. Her aunt smiled.

'Guy, at least, is yours.'

'So long as Vale doesn't want him.'

'Vale is going to be very busy in the near future. A well-advanced pregnancy is hardly the time for luring men away from their girl-friends.' Mrs Terblanche rose. 'It's time we foraged for food. Come and see what we can find in the kitchen.'

The telephone rang in the library where Vale and her husband were sitting by the wood fire. Fir cones sparked and crackled with a resinous scent and a blue glow among the logs.

'That'll be Johannesburg. John.'

She sprang up lightly. She carried her child well and easily as tall women often do. Hammond heard her end of the conversation.

'Yes, Mrs Hammond here. I'm ready . . . John, yes, I want to get the dates fixed. We have to arrange for Helen Ter-blanche to come in. I won't leave Micky otherwise. Claire lives miles away now and does a full-time job and Charles is out all day. But he says I can go any time I like so long as Helen can fit in with us . . . You suggest August 10. That should be all right . . . Mother has someone staying before that? I see. How is she? . . . Oh, dear, same old story. Is there anything to worry about? . . . No, not really. That's good . . . No, we're all fine here after our holiday. Charles is looking splendid, quite brown after all that glorious Durban sun . . . Well, I'll be seeing you soon. Give Mother my love and explain everything to her. Good-bye, John . . . Good-bye for now . . .'

She hung up the receiver and turned to her husband, her eyes shining.

'Now to fix up with Helen.'

'Yes,' he agreed. 'Ring her at once. You'll be away a fortnight, you said?'

She came to him and sat on the arm of his chair.

'You said that as if . . .'

'As if what?'

'As if it hurt – as if you hoped it wasn't true.'

'It does hurt. I don't like parting with you – not for one night or a fortnight. Not at all.'

Suddenly she knelt beside him and took the evening paper out of his hands so that she might clasp them and hold them against her cheek.

'Charles – dear Charles – I don't like parting with you either. It hurts me too.'

He raised her face and looked into her dark brimming eyes.

'You're strange these days – ever since this baby began. Sometimes gay, sometimes sad. There are times when I feel as if I hardly knew you, when you go right away from me. And your sad moods? You never had those with Micky. You were radiant then. You want this baby, Vale – we both do – so why the melancholy, my darling? There should be only happiness.'

'I know, I know. One gets fanciful, subject to silly fears. Any woman would understand. Any doctor. Don't pay attention to my moods. Don't let me distress you, Charles. Never let me hurt you. You're so strong . . .'

He bowed his head and covered her trembling mouth with his. He held her close to him and wished that he need never let her go. He dreaded losing her – even for two weeks.

LONG WEEK-END

MRS TERBLANCHE SAW VALE OFF ON A MONDAY BY
the early afternoon plane and Micky went to the airport
with them. There was a slight delay at the weighing-in
counter as Vale's two suitcases were overweight.

'Silly of me,' she said. 'I packed my heavy coat. It can be
so cold up country once the sun goes down. I should have
carried it.'

Helen Terblanche glanced at the tweed suit and fur-trim-
med matching coat Vale was wearing and the smart water-
proof over her arm but said nothing. Micky hopped on to
the weighing machine.

'Here I are! Weigh me too!'

The obliging official weighed him and swung him over the
counter and set him on the moving conveyor-belt with the
baggage, but he squealed and was quickly lifted back again
and into his mother's arms.

'Take me! Take me to 'hannesburg,' he begged.

Suddenly Vale squatted down on her heels and pulled him
to her and held him as if she could not bear to let him go.
When at last she released him her eyes were wet and her face
contorted as she struggled for composure.

'Your mummy will soon be back,' Mrs Terblanche con-
soled the child, as they stood outside in the cold sunshine to
watch the jet roar down the runway and take off steeply into
the clouds. 'Today fortnight we'll be here again watching
that jet come down.'

She ruffled the soft fair curls blowing in the chilly winter wind. The idea of returning to the airport pleased the child. He loved any excuse to see the planes land and take off and the prospect of another such jaunt soon chased his tears away.

As the Viscount rose into the air Vale looked down upon the Cape scene she had grown to love so dearly – the Flats swampy after the rains; the gaunt old mountain, a grey angry sea; intermittent sunshine on vine-growing valleys just beginning to bud among the blue haze of lupins and the green of young crops. They ascended into the clouds that hid the jagged peaks ahead. Beyond those hidden peaks lay the empty spaces of the Karoo, the wide open highveld, tawny as a lion after the dry winter months, and Jef Broome waiting for that terribly final – that fatal – answer. She felt sick with uncertainty. Even the quickening of the child she carried brought her little comfort. She was life and continuity, she was justifying the whole pattern of nature's purpose, yet her spirit walked in the cold mistland of near death. To part is to die a little. How true that was!

During her stepmother's absence Claire made a point of going home to Silverglade as often as possible, with or without Guy, who had now established his position as her boyfriend however much she might protest to the contrary. Somehow she felt that her father was going to need her, that it was important to make an effort to get back on to the old easy intimate footing that had been theirs before the disruptive intervention of Vale. Now there was Micky too, and Claire's affection for her little half-brother increased her pleasure in returning to her home. She often hurried straight from Broadcasting House to be with him in time to read to him after his bath.

One evening Hammond found her in the nursery, chuckling to herself, while Micky looked up at her from his bed with round expectant eyes. As she turned to her father Claire's own eyes were dancing.

'If you can stay and listen,' she said, 'you'll hear what Micky tells me is "one helluva good story".'

When she had read the satisfying episode from *Noddy and his Little Car* Hammond remarked:

'You really do read rather well. Even that half-witted Noddy. When I was Micky's age I was reading Chums.'

'To your mother, no doubt.' She laughed. 'You must have been a very precocious four-year-old!'

'Four and three quarters,' corrected Micky indignantly. 'Nearly five.'

When they had tucked the little boy up and kissed him good night they went down to the library where Mrs Terblanche sat by the fire.

'Your turn for good night kissing,' said Hammond. 'He's waiting.'

As his sister went up to the nursery he poured Claire a sherry.

'It's too cold for your abominable gin and tonic or bitter lemon. Be civilized and join me in this.' As he passed her the glass of South African sherry, he added: 'You know, I never was any good with tiny children – not even with you, Claire. It's when they've passed the age of nappies and begun to ask questions and think for themselves that I appreciate them. Micky now, he's more interesting and amusing with every day that passes. He asks quite intelligent questions and his mental development is striking. I believe this age is the one at which the biggest advances are made. Even after only two weeks Vale will find changes in him when she comes back – new expressions —'

'Like helluva good story. That, I may say, comes straight from Guy. Guy was reading to him last Sunday.'

Hammond grinned. 'I suppose Guy will be here to dinner later.'

'Yes. It's nice for me having a lift back. If it weren't for Guy I'd need to buy a car.'

'You'd certainly miss him. How's your job going?'

He sat in his accustomed wing-chair conveniently near his pipe-rack on the wall by the fireplace.

'Are you still enjoying it?'

'I love it. As a matter of fact, I've been recruited into Children's Hour for the Bedtime Story feature. It's a serial about a little Bantu boy lost in the bush. Rather exciting.'

'I'll tell you something, my girl. You interest me as much as my son and in something the same way. You too are learning something new every day – and you could afford to. You've developed poise since you left home and began to earn your own living. A new completeness.'

'Completeness?'

She stared at him, astonished. So it was perceptible, this feeling she had of being daily more entirely herself. It was as if – without the unconscious rivalry of Vale – she had found the secret of her own personality, of not playing second fiddle, of not trying to vie with Vale, but of simply being herself. Even her dress sense had become more definite and was no longer influenced by her stepmother's taste or example. And her father had noticed. He had observed her as he observed his son, and he was satisfied.

'Yes,' he said. 'Completeness was the word I used. Perhaps I should have used the contemporary jargon – well-adjusted.'

'Completeness is a better word,' she said. 'You're right. And you were so right when you told me I ought to get a real job and work with other people. It was lucky for me that Aunt Helen knew what sort of job it ought to be. I'm grateful to you both.'

But, as she spoke, she realized that there was someone else who had built her up and increased her dubious self-confidence. Guy. But between them – her and Guy – there was, as yet, no completeness.

Helen Terblanche came in, rubbing her hands.

'Really, it's bitterly cold. Even moving from one room to another.'

She stood by the fire, warming her back. Guy, who had just arrived, joined them and helped himself to a whisky at his host's request.

'There's snow on all the mountains,' he said. 'And the weather report predicts more. It's the last gasp of winter before the spring. Even Table Mountain has a sprinkling of snow on the summit, and that's rare enough.'

'We should use that snow,' said Hammond. 'It's a Public Holiday next Monday which gives us a long week-end. Why don't we go to Leopard Bush and get some ski-ing?'

'Wonderful idea,' said Claire. 'We could go on Friday – that's tomorrow – straight after work and come back Monday night. Can you manage it, Guy?'

'Can I! Nothing I'd rather do.'

'Then I can take Helen and Micky, Josiah, Fedora, the dog and the supplies, in the station-wagon,' said the Judge, 'and you can pick Claire up at Clifton and bring her in your car.'

Vale was not due back till the Tuesday following the long week-end, and after dinner the Judge telephoned her to tell her their plan.

Mrs Rorke answered the phone with the panicky witless flutter a long distance call invariably provoked in her.

'Oh, dear, yes, Vale's still here. She was just going out . . . Vale! It's Charles. Hurry, dear . . .'

Vale's voice came over the line, slightly sardonic.

'Is the house on fire? Mummy seems in a state.'

'She has no reason to be. I just wanted to tell you we're all going to Leopard Bush for the long week-end – leaving tomorrow evening – and back Monday night . . . The snow should be good if the cold snap holds . . . I wondered if you wouldn't like to cut your holiday short and join us. You love ski-ing . . . I see. No, well then, let the arrangement stand, darling ... How's your mother? ... Fine, I'm glad to hear it. She sounded agitated ... Then we'll expect you back on Tuesday ... Helen will meet the midday plane ... What? Oh, I see. Well, we'll expect you some time that evening. Good night, darling, take care of yourself.'

He put down the receiver and turned to his sister.

'There's no need to meet that plane. Vale's spending the long week-end with friends in the bushveld and they'll drive her back to Cape Town on Tuesday. We must expect her when we see her – probably late afternoon. They've no telephone, so she won't be able to ring us.'

'What friends?' asked Claire sharply.

'Van der Merwe, she said. Friends of John's. Does it matter?'

'I don't know,' said Claire. 'I s'pose not. It's just that I hate being out of touch ...'

'It's only for the week-end,' said Mrs Terblanche. 'Don't fuss, dear. Micky is well and contented. Nothing alarming will happen between now and Tuesday.'

Guy fetched Claire at her flatlet soon after six o'clock on Friday evening. The weather was perfect. Clear and very cold. He switched on the warm air in the Mini, and Claire, in woollen slacks, chunky jersey and loose, cherry-coloured anorak, snuggled close to him as they sped across the Flats on the National Road to the north. Soon they were ascending the mountains dividing the broad fertile Paarl Valley from the Worcester plateau and the Hex River range beyond.

High on Du Toit's Kloof they stopped at a lonely little fishing inn above the river. The frosty air bit them as they got out of the car, the stars pierced the sky with a myriad glittering stilettos, the Milky Way swept its silver dust across the night and the Southern Cross hung low and brilliant over the snow-crowned peaks. Here the proteas grew like trees, their twisted branches bearing the first stiff enduring flowers to welcome the mountain spring.

Guy and Claire entered the inn and warmed their hands at a cheerful blaze. They ordered a grill and half a bottle of red wine to be uncorked and mulled in front of the fire.

'Do you know,' said Guy, as they tucked in to a tender rumpsteak, 'It's a year since last we ski-ed up in these mountains. It was soon after I'd met you. You were just back from Italy and you'd been ski-ing in the Dolomites.'

'I remember very well. Daddy was teaching Vale to ski that year.'

'And was she quick at getting the hang of it! I'll never forget. She has natural balance, and being athletic helped.'

For Claire Vale's aptitude at ski-ing had been just another instance of the many ways in which her stepmother outshone her. Learning to ski had been a big struggle for Claire. Her father had begun to instruct her the winter after he considered her polio-weakened leg strong enough to risk the strain.

'It's good for you,' he had explained. 'New muscles come into play. You can enjoy the nursery slopes even if you never get beyond them.'

She had got beyond them, but only by the exercise of her considerable will-power. Now she could admit that the speed with which Vale mastered the new sport had been a stimulus. To be outstripped by Vale, the beginner, would have been too humiliating. During her year in Florence Claire had spent a winter holiday in the Dolomites under expert instruction. She had meant to keep ahead of Vale, and somehow she had done so.

'Your father and I both learned our ski-ing at Murren,' Guy was saying. 'It's extraordinary how my student days at Oxford followed much the same pattern as his, although so many years came between.'

Both Hammond and Guy had each in their time, been

Rhodes Scholars. Both had been at the same college and both considered Oxford the great experience of their lives. To Hammond, of course, it had fallen into perspective, taking its place with the many other highlights in a well-lived life. To Guy it was still the high point of much more than his education. Oxford had opened many doors of enlightenment and companionship, and the old city remained to him the most beautiful in the world – a place of dreams and ambitions which he had been privileged to share. He had taken a degree in science, intending a scientific career of some sort, but had then discovered that he was not, after all, a scientist at heart. He had written to his parents in Durban that science was too impersonal. 'I've made a mistake and I feel I must alter course while it is still possible. I want to study Law.' His father had been surprisingly understanding.

'All knowledge stands a man in good stead. You'll probably find your scientific studies very useful at some time or another in legal work. By all means make the switch. But it'll take you longer to get going and will cost you more. You'll have to help pay your way.'

Guy had remained at Oxford for an extra year and had then returned to South Africa to complete his studies in Roman Dutch law at the University of Cape Town while working as registrar to Judge Hammond. Although his home was Durban he had chosen to come to the Cape which he loved.

'You and Daddy have a lot in common,' said Claire. 'Even now.'

'We have indeed. We have your father's cases – and we have you.'

She smiled, warmed by his words and the look in his eyes and the red wine, most of which had found its way into her glass, as Guy made a rule of drinking very little when he was driving.

They went out into the night in holiday mood, well

content to be together. Soon they were driving through the high valley of De Doorns only a few miles from Leopard Bush.

'How lovely it is – with the snow on the ground, blue-white in the starlight!' he said.

Although the surrounding mountains were snow-topped every winter it was seldom that snow fell in the valleys.

'Look, the Katz family must be here for the long week-end.'

Guy indicated a little homestead on a vine-growing rise. All the windows shone with orange light in the lonely darkness, a charming and welcoming sight.

'You wouldn't think it would be worth-while for a popular surgeon to have a farm,' said Claire. 'Abel Katz is terribly busy. It isn't often he gets a chance to come up here.'

'He adores the place,' said Guy. 'And as for being worth-while, the busier he is the more it's to his advantage to own a farm. Why do you think half the Members of Parliament have farms?'

'They love the land. Afrikaners – in fact, most South Africans – do. But Abel Katz is a Jew.'

'Jews love the land too. Some of our most enterprising farmers are Jews. And you only have to look at Israel. The Jews have made the desert productive. I grant you Afrikaners have a particularly strong feeling for the land – *this South African land* – it's almost worship, part of their nationalism, but there's another reason. If you have a farm you can set it off against your income tax.'

'Even if it shows a profit?'

He laughed. 'Find me a farm that shows a profit! If there were such a thing it would plough back the profit and show a loss.'

He turned off the National Road on to a dirt track and soon they were within sight of Leopard Bush.

'The others have beaten us to it,' said Claire.

As in Abel Katz's farmhouse, lights were burning in most of the windows.

'There'll be hot coffee waiting for us. Oh, I'm going to sleep and sleep in this divine mountain air. So still and peaceful. Guy, Leopard Bush is my favourite place in the whole world.'

'I think it's mine too,' he said. 'And you are my favourite person.'

Helen Terblanche had never been a skier. She had made two feeble attempts to get the hang of it and had long since given up.

'I value my bones far too much,' she'd said when her brother had urged her to try again. 'I'll go for walks in the valley while you swoop about on the heights.'

So now, on this dazzling Saturday morning of sun and snow, she took Micky with her to play on the banks of the narrow fast-flowing river while Hammond, Guy and Claire set off in the station-wagon with their skis. The glistening slopes that beckoned them were some miles distant on the far wall of the valley.

'I'll take your binoculars,' she said to her brother. 'then we can watch you at play.'

'Keep an eye on us,' he laughed. 'We'll be back for a late lunch.'

'I want to ski too,' announced Micky, his underlip trembling.

'Next year when you're a big boy and your legs are stronger,' said his aunt. 'Now go and fetch your tin pail and we'll see if we can find some fish in one of the rock pools.'

Helen Terblanche loved Leopard Bush almost as much as Claire did. She and her brother had spent most of their school holidays here and they knew every inch of the golden river gurgling over its rocky bed, cascading over rapids and miniature waterfalls, and running merrily between steep green

banks where the weaver birds built their nests in the willows
and ferns and lilies grew in profusion. Like Claire, she too
loved the little graveyard where her forebears rested and at
times she almost regretted that she would never be buried
there herself, for she was no longer Hammond but Terblanche. One day this place would be Micky's. She hoped
the boy would grow up to care for it as much as Claire did. It
would be sad if it were to be sold out of the family. Five
generations of Hammonds had owned Leopard Bush, even
if they had not all lived there.

Micky trotted ahead of her, refusing to hold hands. As she
watched him she thought of his young mother and hoped
that all might continue to go well with her brother's marriage. She had feared for it and hoped to prevent it, but now,
with a second baby on the way, she felt that perhaps, after
all, it might succeed. If Charles had married a woman of 'a
suitable age' there would have been no young family. No
Micky. Her eyes lingered lovingly on her nephew as she reflected that in November, when the Cape summer was at its
loveliest, there would be another child to keep him company.

'Here, darling,' she said. 'Let's stop here. This is a good
place.'

They clambered down to a shady spit jutting out of shallow water with rocky pools that in summer were dry.

Away on the steep snow-covered incline they could see the
three skiers. Through the binoculars they looked to Mrs
Terblanche as swift and free as swallows in the spring and she
was tempted to wish that she had persevered in her own
efforts. She could pick out her brother's tall figure zigzagging
down the steep slope ahead of the other two. Really, few of
his colleagues on the Bench could match him at tennis or
golf, much less in winter sports. He was an exception to
many rules, a man who might indeed hold the love of a
young wife. Thus Helen Terblanche's thoughts returned to

Vale. They were gentle background music to her conversation with her nephew, who always had so much to ask and to tell.

'See,' she said, pointing to the distant white mountainside. 'Way over there, that's Daddy and Guy and Claire.'

He tried to use the heavy glasses but soon gave up. His own eyes were good enough.

'Daddy's in front,' he said with satisfaction. 'Look, Auntie! Daddy's turning somersaults!'

She saw the 'somersaults' with horror, and the two figures converging upon the fallen body on the snow. She waited for her brother to rise, her heart sick with anxiety. But Charles Hammond did not rise. There was evidently some consultation between Guy and Claire and then Guy was racing down the slope at breakneck speed and Claire was left alone kneeling, it seemed, by the still figure.

'Why doesn't Daddy get up?' asked Micky.

Mrs Terblanche made no bones about the answer.

'He can't. And I'm going to find out why not.'

Very firmly she led the little boy back to the house and turned him over to Fedora. She called Josiah and told him briefly what they had seen. Josiah's face was grey with trouble as she explained.

'Master has been hurt. Get hot-water bottles and blankets, and I will telephone Baas Steyn to come in his car now. Strip the folding stretcher-bed and we will take that too. And brandy and hot coffee.' Then she went to the telephone and called the manager's number. Klaas Steyn was out in the lands but his son, Jaapie, was there.

'I know where Pa is, Mrs Terblanche. I can get him for you in ten minutes. We'll be right over.'

'Good,' she said, grim-lipped. 'But make it five minutes, Jaapie. There is no time to lose.'

II

DISASTER

MR ABEL KATZ, THE FAMOUS ORTHOPAEDIC surgeon, was at peace with the world as he sauntered through his vineyards singing an unidentifiable song under his frosty breath. The sun was shining, the vines were healthy, the orange-flower scent of the lupins was sweet in his nostrils and the green grass seemed to him more radiant than ever before.

He was a short thick-set man with powerful shoulders and strong dexterous hands that might have belonged to a sculptor of marble. He was used to dealing with recalcitrant material, breaking, shaping and stripping the human scaff-olding, and he enjoyed his work. When he looked at the tortured boles and twin branches of his vines outspread in the classical traction devised for them by man, he would like to have straightened and planed the gnarled, twisted trunk and arms, but he knew that soon the dark limbs would be fleshed in lavish green, the little pale flowers of the grape would announce the spring, and bunches of fruit would proclaim summer. Then his coloured labourers would carry their great wicker baskets into the vineyards and fill them to over-flowing with the crop that would be sold to the Government Wineries to be pulped and crushed. In its turn the juice of the grape would ferment and grumble in the tanks, and sleep in the great teak vats till it reached maturity and was finally bottled and labelled as wine of the Cape of Good Hope. Be-hind the house was a smaller vineyard and in that he grew his trellissed table grapes. These he cherished most of all.

He wore faded corduroys, a thick fisherman's jersey knitted by his wife many years ago, an old tweed jacket whose pockets bulged with his pipe and tobacco pouch and a pair of gardening gloves in case he decided to do some pruning, for Abel Katz treated his hands with the utmost respect. They were his bread and butter and jam and he took no risks with them. On his grizzled head was a wide-brimmed straw hat. He looked up in some dismay as he heard a station-wagon turn into his rough dirt drive. It was eleven o'clock, a favourite hour for holiday visiting, but he wanted no visitors today. He just wanted to relax after the week's exertions and responsibilities. Ah, well, the visitor was probably somebody for his wife, Rachel, or – since the driver appeared to be a young man – for his daughter, Miriam. But his hopes were soon dashed as Miriam came rushing out of the house to call to him.

'Poppa, Poppa, there's been an accident! Judge Hammond – over on the ski-ing slope.'

Guy followed closely on her heels. Katz had met the young man several times at Leopard Bush.

'What's happened?' he asked, his dreams of peace vanishing.

'It's Judge Hammond, sir. He was ski-ing on the southern incline when he hit a tree stump. Quite a small one, only just covered by the snow – but enough to trip him and knock him out. He's unconscious and I think he may have injured his back and broken a leg. He's bleeding from a gash in the head too.'

Katz wasted no time. He led the way to the house, questioning Guy as they went.

'Where is he now?'

'We didn't try to move him. His daughter, Claire, is with him. We've covered him as much as possible.'

Katz observed that young Steele was in his shirt-sleeves and shivering slightly in the keen air.

'Give Guy a pullover,' he said to Miriam, and, turning to Guy, 'I'll come with you at once. I'll just get a few things together.'

His first-aid kit was always kept up to date, but he checked it quickly. Splints, morphia, a heart stimulant. Yes. They'd probably need a stretcher too. What could he improvise? A board? How about blankets? His mind raced along on the same lines that Helen Terblanche's had done. Guy was already on the telephone to Leopard Bush and Josiah was able to tell him that Mrs Terblanche had seen the accident through the binoculars and was on her way to the spot. He also recounted what she had taken with her. Guy relayed the information to Katz who expressed brisk approval.

'A folding stretcher-bed. That'll do if we need it. Well done. Mrs Terblanche has her head screwed on.'

Within minutes they were on their way.

'It's too bad,' Miriam Katz sighed to her mother. 'Poppa was so happy just loafing.'

'A doctor's leisure is never his own.' Mrs Katz spoke gloomily from long experience. 'We'd better have a cup of tea, Miriam. Looks like our week-end's gone for six.'

Tea was her cure for all ills and evils.

When the station-wagon reached the end of the rough track nearest the southern incline, Guy and Katz had to get out and plough their way upwards through the snow to reach the place where Hammond had fallen. Klaas Steyn's car was ahead of them and Helen Terblanche had covered her brother with blankets and wedged hot-water bottles against his icy body. The glistening snow was stained with blood and the recumbent figure was lying in an awkward distorted attitude. Claire had managed to remove the skis and she had folded her anorak and put it under her father's wounded head. But she had not dared try to dispose his limbs more comfortably.

Katz knelt down beside the Judge who was breathing stertorously. Every now and again he groaned and tried to rise, although he was obviously too concussed to know what he was doing. Claire, white-faced, crouched beside him in the snow. Steyn had insisted upon putting his jacket over her shoulders, nevertheless her teeth were chattering as she looked up into the wise wrinkled face of Abel Katz.

'Now, young lady, you get out of the way. All of you, except Guy, move to one side and let me see what's what.'

Helen Terblanche put her arms round Claire and they stood clinging anxiously together. A thousand fears and worries surged through their minds. It was Claire who voiced the immediate difficulty. Through lips shaking with cold and shock she said:

'How are we going to get hold of Vale?'

'We must telephone John Rorke. He must get a message to her immediately.'

'Yes, of course. As soon as we get back to the house I'll do it. My mind seems numb. I'm numb all over.'

'How did it happen?' Mrs Terblanche asked.

'That tree stump there.'

Claire indicated the blackened stump protruding through the snow. Steyn joined them and he looked at it in disgust.

'There's a plantation near here was burned out last summer. It's on Frikkie Maritz's land. He cut down his burnt pines afterwards to use for firewood and the bloody woodsmen must have left a few odd stumps about on the slopes. The silly beggars evidently didn't realize this area was used for ski-ing. The Judge must have thought he was on a firepath, and then he strikes a death-trap like that!'

Katz had risen. With Guy's assistance he had made a cursory examination and had roughly splinted the damaged leg.

'There's a nasty head wound – possibly a fracture – a

badly fractured leg, and there may be spinal damage. I've given him an injection. Now we must get him to Groote Schuur Hospital as quickly as possible. The X-rays I shall need can be done there better than anywhere else.'

'Do we call an ambulance, Dr Katz?' asked Steyn. As to most South Africans, all medical men, whether surgeons or not, were 'Doctor' to him.

For a moment Abel Katz hesitated while a pang of almost physical disappointment shot sharply through his whole being. He had looked forward greatly to this long week-end of complete relaxation. Now he had no choice other than to disappoint his wife and family and to deprive himself of a well-earned and much-needed holiday. Charles Hammond was not only a man of distinction, he was a friend and a neighbour. There was no choice. He must return to Cape Town with his patient and prepare to perform a complex and risky operation. At best, Hammond would be on the critical list for some time.

'We'll take him in the station-wagon. Thanks to your foresight, Mrs Terblanche, we can make him reasonably secure and comfortable on the folding stretcher-bed.'

'I'll come with you,' said Mrs Terblanche firmly. 'I can drive the station-wagon while you take care of Charles. The only bit of bumpy road will be the few miles between here and the National Road. From then on it'll be smooth going and we can make good time.'

Katz said: 'Claire, will you telephone my wife and explain that I won't be back this week-end. She must do as she likes. Come home or stay on here. Our cookie is at home and she can look after me if Rachel wants to stay.'

Guy and Steyn were standing by with the improvised stretcher and Katz bent down and eased the injured man gently on to it. 'Now to get him down as carefully as possible.'

The two younger men carried the stretcher with painstaking care while Mrs Terblanche, Katz and Claire walked beside it, Claire still on her skis.

'Where is Mrs Hammond?' asked Katz.

'She's in Johannesburg, visiting her mother,' said Mrs Terblanche. He frowned.

'She must come back at once, Mrs Terblanche. *At once.* This is a case of the very greatest urgency.'

'I understand.'

Helen Terblanche turned to her niece, her face pale and drawn.

'Claire, you must do as I say. I will go with your father and Mr Katz to Groote Schuur in the station-wagon. Mr Steyn can drive Josiah, Fedora and Micky to Silverglade as soon as possible. And I leave it to you and Guy to get in touch with Vale somehow. She *must* be found, you understand. Then let Guy bring you to Silverglade. You can telephone me there or at the hospital. Is that clear?'

'Yes, Aunt Helen. And I'll ring Mrs Katz the moment we get back.'

'Put through your call to Johannesburg first. Explain that it's a matter of life or death.'

Katz opened the back of the station-wagon and arranged the seats so that Guy and Steyn could slide the stretcher in along the side. The Judge's face was grey and lifeless. Katz wondered if he could survive the journey. Ninety miles. It would be touch and go.

'Your shoes and coat, Claire.'

Guy pulled them out of the station-wagon and gave them to her. She stood holding them, her eyes agonized, as her aunt took the wheel and started the engine. Abel Katz was sitting by the drugged man, his hand on his patient's pulse. The station-wagon moved slowly forward, avoiding the potholes wherever possible and taking the corrugations as gently as the springs permitted.

Suddenly Claire felt deathly sick and giddy. She swayed on her feet and the next moment Guy was letting her down softly on to the snowy track. He made her sit forward with her head on her knees while Steyn quietly unstrapped her skis. As the malaise passed she said faintly:

'Thank you, Klaasie. We must hurry home now. There's so much to do. We must hurry!'

Mrs Rorke was alone in her flat when the telephone rang. It was noon and she had sent her maid out to the corner Greek shop to buy some vegetables for the long week-end.

The operator said: 'Hex River wants you. Very urgent.'

Hex River? That would be Leopard Bush, the Hammond farm. Appalling fears instantly assailed her. Something had happened to Micky, and Vale had gone off only yesterday – heaven alone knew where.

'Yes, yes, yes . . . I'm waiting.'

Mrs Rorke's heart was thumping and the horrible familiar sensation of nausea and suffocation was in her chest and throat. Vale should never have left her all alone. Or, if she had to go anywhere, it ought to have been home to her family. There had been something wrong with Vale these last ten days. She hadn't been her usual cheerful self at all. She'd been irritable and distrait. What were those extraordinary noises at the other end of the line?

'Yes, I'm here,' she repeated. 'Who is it wants me? What's wrong? I can't hear a thing.'

She slumped down in the low chair by the telephone table. If only she could get herself a horse's neck. Why not? It wouldn't take a minute. No need to bother about ice. The brandy and ginger ale were right handy in the corner cupboard. She got up, leaving the receiver off the hook, and hastily poured herself a large tot. She emptied the ginger ale into the tumbler and took a good gulp. The unattended telephone was muttering to itself and she hurried back, feeling fortified, the nausea already slightly abated.

'Who is it? Who is it?' she asked loudly. Mrs Rorke believed that if her voice was to carry nine hundred miles it was obvious she must shout.

'It's Claire, Mrs Rorke. Is Vale there?'

'No. I thought she told Charles she'd be away for the long week-end.'

'She did. I just hoped . . . you see, there's been an accident. Daddy was hurt out ski-ing this morning. We don't know how bad it is —'

'Oh, dear, oh, dear – I'm terribly sorry – quite horrified. Your poor father. But what can one do?'

'I must get in touch with Vale. It's desperately important. I've tried John's number but there's no answer.'

'There wouldn't be. He flew to Athens on Thursday. There's this girl, my dear – this charming rich Greek girl, Maria Triandefiledes. I really do think something will come of it. It must! He's gone with her to meet her parents. He'll be in Athens for a week. That's surely a good sign – the best possible, wouldn't you agree?'

'Mrs Rorke – I can't just chat with you. I have to find Vale. Did she tell you where she was going?'

'Not a word. Really, Claire, Vale's been quite peculiar these last few days. I couldn't get a thing out of her. She just said she was going to the lowveld with friends – somewhere near the Kruger Park. But she left no address and no telephone number. But I've got two suitcases of hers here. She's picking them up on Tuesday on her way through to Cape Town. I won't see her till then.'

Mrs Rorke had taken another swig at her horse's neck and she felt much better. In fact, this was really rather an exciting conversation and she was settling down to enjoy it. After all, long distance wasn't so bad if the wretched operator would only shut up instead of interrupting constantly with rubbish about three minutes being up. That was what made her feel jumpy, in danger of being cut off. Most disturbing. Claire said:

'What's the name of the people who own this place? Perhaps we can trace it.'

'Van der Merwe, dear. But I've no idea which Van der Merwes – just friends of John's, I gather. Vale gave no details. She simply said "Take care of yourself, Mummy" – and she knows I need to, in my condition – then off she went with that American fellow. He was giving her a lift.'

There was a little gasp at the other end of the line.

'American – you mean Jefferson Broome?'

'Some such name. Fair-haired, with a fine pair of eyes, and a drawl. But, really, I don't know him from Adam. It seems he's a friend of John's – or of the Van der Merwes. They went off on Friday – yesterday morning.'

'Can you give me John's address in Athens?'

'No dear, I can't. I never even thought of asking for such a thing. Why should I? He'll be back in a few days, in any case. And Vale will be at home at Silverglade by Tuesday night. Won't that do, Claire? I really can't see how we can get hold of her before that. With John away, there isn't a thing we can do. Now is there?'

'We must do something – we must! This is a matter of life or death. My father has been badly injured – he may ... not ... live ...' The young voice so far away broke and recovered itself. 'Listen, please. What is the address of John's cabin near Nelspruit?'

'Good gracious, I'd have to look that up in my address book. What's the point, dear? What has John's cabin to do with it?'

'A good deal, perhaps. Please go and look in your address book.'

'Then you must just keep talking while I go, or the operator will think we've finished and cut us off. You know how they are —'

'Please, just find that address!'

'When I'm nervous I'm all fingers and thumbs. Hold on, dear, and whatever happens, keep talking.'

After what seemed an interminable delay she returned.

'It's very simple, dear. It's Avocado Kop, P.O. Nelspruit. But there's no telephone and you know how it is right out in the bundu on the week-end. Even if you send a wire now it probably wouldn't be delivered till Tuesday because of the Public Holiday on Monday. The country isn't the city, after all. And, in any case, there's no earthly reason to think the party is anywhere near John's cabin, much less at it. In fact, John would most certainly have mentioned it to me if people were going to be at his place in his absence. Or Vale would have told me.'

'I don't think she would, Mrs Rorke.'

'What do you mean, Claire?'

'I don't know what to think. But, please, when she gets back to you on Tuesday to fetch her suitcases, tell her to catch the very first plane home. She must telephone Silverglade at once.'

'Of course, of course. She'll be so shocked, poor child. Poor Charles, poor Vale! You must be sure to keep me informed about Charles. You haven't even said how it happened.'

'I can't stop now, Mrs Rorke. Aunt Helen or I will contact you later. And if you can think of anything – any way of getting a message to Vale – please, please do so! Good-bye for now.'

Mrs Rorke hung up in a state of horrified bewilderment. Poor dear Charles! Really, after all that talk, she was none the wiser about the accident. And now she came to think of it, it was disgraceful of Vale to rush off into hiding with these mysterious Van der Merwes without leaving proper instructions as to her whereabouts. If only John were here, he'd know what to do. Mrs Rorke finished her brandy and ginger ale and went to lie down. Shocks were the worst possible thing for a woman with her cardiac condition. People were really most inconsiderate.

Nine hundred miles away, at Leopard Bush, Claire turned to Guy, white as chalk, her hands moist and trembling.

'You heard most of that?'

'Yes, she was deafening. So what now?'

'Vale's gone away with Jef Broome and it's my bet they've gone to John's cabin, Avocado Kop. It's utterly out of touch with civilization. Nelspruit's the nearest post office, and that's thirty miles away. I've never been there but Vale has told me about it.'

The telephone was in the dining-room and she sat down at the stinkwood dining-table and put her head on her arms and burst into tears. Guy sat down beside her and stroked her hair gently.

'It's a long chance. The whole thing may be perfectly innocent. The fact is, we don't know where they went.'

She looked up at him, her tear-stained face taut.

'I swear I'm right – I swear it!'

'You could be. Whatever happens, we have to find her.'

'They've gone on a sort of honeymoon, Guy. That's what they've done. There aren't any Van der Merwes – except the ones they've invented to satisfy Mrs Rorke.'

The head of Josiah peeped sorrowfully round the door and he came in, followed by Dart, the Alsatian.

'Miss Claire, I must set this table for lunch. Then, after, we go back home in Baas Steyn's car. He come here to fetch us two o'clock.'

She stared at the old Xhosa. Of course they must be fed –

Micky and Fedora and Josiah. Dart too. Josiah's face was gloomy and his eyes and the dog's seemed to her to hold the same questioning apprehension. Josiah had heard the details of the disaster from the manager, Mr Steyn, and he feared greatly for his master's life.

Guy took over.

'Josiah, Miss Claire and I don't want lunch. Make us some sandwiches – plenty of sandwiches – quickly! And two Thermos flasks of black coffee. We are going to fetch Mrs Hammond.'

'But Madam is in Johannesburg.'

'Madam is in the lowveld with friends and there is no telephone where she is. We must go and bring her back. You get lunch for yourself and the others later, but make our sandwiches and coffee right now. Fast!'

'Yes, Master.'

As he went back to the kitchen, Claire said:

'What are we going to do?'

'The Mini-Cooper can cruise at ninety easily. It's about eleven hundred miles from here to Nelspruit if we go via Johannesburg. We can be there early tomorrow afternoon. *If we find Vale at Avocado Kop*, wherever that may be, we could come back the same night and we'd have her home before daybreak on Monday morning. We must follow your hunch and hope for the best.'

'You're right. It's the only thing we can do. We can take shifts driving. It's no good ringing Silverglade or Groote Schuur now. They wouldn't be there yet. I'll give Josiah a note for Aunt Helen and we'll get on our way.'

'Do that,' he said. 'And make it snappy.'

12

THE CHASE

THE AFTERNOON SUN, HIGH IN A CLEAR SKY, poured on to the low scrub of the Karoo spread like a knotty grey-green carpet as far as the eye could see. Flat-topped blue mountains, sugar-loaf koppies, the gleam of a dam, a tin roof or a tall iron windmill broke the monotony, and yellow, pink and purple everlastings blazed on the roadside among a froth of white and yellow daisies. At the fork marked by the blue breast-shaped hills of the Three Sisters they kept due north on the Kimberley–Johannesburg road.

Guy was at the wheel and the speedometer registered a steady hundred miles per hour. Towards sunset they changed places and Claire kept up the pace.

'You seem very sure of this hunch,' said Guy. 'Any good reason?'

Her profile was clear cut, secret and reserved. Suddenly he remembered the letter – the evening they had found the wounded bird. Had she read it and learned something from it that he didn't know? He refrained from asking her.

'Call it intuition,' she said.

'It better be good. We're travelling a long way on intuition.'

She half smiled and her hand left the wheel for an instant to touch his.

'You're a wonderful friend – to all of us.'

'I'm not doing this for friendship alone.'

She didn't encourage him to say any more.

'When we come to a place with trees I'm going to stop for a ten-minute break. A sandwich and some coffee, and I want to stretch my legs.'

She slowed down as they came to a clump of willows and gums beside a dried watercourse. Thorn trees grew in the empty river-bed. Here they were beyond the climate of the coast and the winter had been rainless. With sunset the night frost sharpened the air. As Claire drank the hot black coffee she found herself for a moment forgetting her father's plight. Shafts of glowing colour impregnated the cotton-wool clouds and above them the sky was pure aquamarine.

'Where in the world could one see such colours at sunset?' Her tone was touched with the impersonal melancholy peculiar to the hour and the vast lonely drama of approaching night.

'Every colour of the rainbow and molten gold into the bargain,' he said. 'On we go.'

The Karoo, with its sheep and citrus farms, fell behind them as they ascended the plateau on to the grasslands of the veld. East of them lay the Orange Free State and ahead was the Rand, both richly veined with gold. The Mini-Cooper devoured the superb National Road as if the night air added an extra stimulus. They took turn about – two hours for Claire and four for Guy – and each dozed while the other drove. At dawn they were in the Transvaal and it seemed that the flat tawny highveld spread away to the ends of the earth.

'I suppose a prairie is like this,' Claire said, and he knew that she was thinking of Jef Broome, the man she had once loved and who now threatened her father's home.

'We'll be in Johannesburg by half-past nine,' he said. 'I hope Mrs Rorke lays on some breakfast for us. I could do with it.'

'She will. She'll be expecting us. Aunt Helen will have telephoned her last night, so we should get the latest news about Daddy. Mrs Rorke may even have got in touch with Vale.'

They stopped for a few minutes to drink the last of their black coffee. The grass at the roadside was webbed with rime and glistening dew-drops, and pools of shallow water were coated with ice. When they left the warmth of the car, their breath steamed on the biting air of early morning.

Mrs Rorke greeted Claire with tearful agitation.

'You must be exhausted and hungry – both of you! There's breakfast ready. Mrs Terblanche phoned me at seven last night. Your father was about to undergo an operation and she said you were to ring her as soon as you arrived.'

'I'll put a call through at once,' said Claire. 'It takes a little time.'

When she had done so, Mrs Rorke joined them at breakfast and helped herself to a cup of tea.

'I have no news of Vale. I couldn't attempt to track down those Van der Merwes. After all, my dear, I didn't even know the initial and the telephone book is thick with Van der Merwes. It was very naughty of her not to leave me a telephone number. I suggested to your aunt that we ask the S.A.B.C. to broadcast an S.O.S. after the news, but she wasn't keen on the idea. She said it could be done as a last resort if you fail to find Vale.'

Claire sprang to her feet leaving her eggs and bacon untouched. 'The phone! That must be our call.'

When she returned to the table she looked dejected and the weariness of the night drive had sharpened her features.

'He's holding his own – but only just. His back was badly injured and his leg is broken in two places. The head wound was superficial and needed stitching, but, at best, Mr Katz reckons Daddy will be on the critical list for the next few days. Mrs Rorke, we must get on.'

'Eat your eggs, my dear. It's no good killing yourself.

And I'm sure you'll want a wash. You'll find cosmetics in the bathroom and there's powder in Vale's room. Besides,' she added sensibly, 'Guy hasn't finished his breakfast yet.'

Claire had no more appetite but she took some coffee with her to Vale's room. When she looked in the glass she was shocked by the apparition staring back at her. Suddenly it struck her that a few hours hence she expected to meet not only Vale but Jef Broome too. It was eighteen months since last she had seen him, and she looked terrible. As she faced her pinched reflection, she faced her inner self as well. Once she had believed herself in love with Jef, now she told herself she hated him, but it was untried hate that could only be proven when she saw him again. She feared their meeting for many reasons.

She went to the bathroom and washed her face and hands. She used Mrs Rorke's cold cream and skin freshener and remembered that she had seen a moisturizing lotion on Vale's dressing-table. Her skin still felt taut and parched as it usually did in the dry electric air of the Transvaal. She sat down at the mirror and patted the foundation into her skin. There, that was better. She felt refreshed and better able to meet the day ahead. Now rouge. Perhaps in the drawer? She opened the drawer, but it was empty except for a few tie-on luggage labels. As they caught her eye her heart stood still. She took them out and studied them carefully. Then she glanced at the two packed locked suitcases in the corner of the room, unlabelled as yet. So that was it! She shivered. She heard Mrs Rorke's step and the door opened.

'Is there anything you need, Claire?'

Claire pushed the labels hastily back into the drawer and shut it. She tried to smile.

'I wonder if you could lend me some rouge. I look so horribly pale.'

'Of course. I'll get it.'

She came back with a little pot of cream rouge and a box of powder.

'Here it is, and I brought my powder. Vale's is really too dark for your fair skin. I'm so glad you've done a new face, dear. You looked so tired when you arrived and I always say there's nothing like a new face when one feels down and out.'

'Thank you, Mrs Rorke. Did you say Vale was coming back here on Tuesday to fetch her cases?'

'That's right. She only took a little hand-grip with her for the week-end and she told me to expect her about ten o'clock, that she'd be going straight on from here to Cape Town by car with friends. The Van der Merwes, I suppose.'

'I see. Well, we hope to find her today. We'll try John's cabin. The . . . Van der Merwes probably have a place near there. Anyway, it's a chance.'

Mrs Rorke shrugged her shoulders.

'I wish you luck. If only John were here! You have to pass this way on your return journey, so you must come in and get the latest news of your father. I'll keep in touch with Mrs Terblanche. You'll need to pick up Vale's cases too.'

The window was open and a peal of church bells chimed with musical resonance, their echoes filling the room.

'That's St John's Church,' said Mrs Rorke. 'I love the sound of church bells, don't you? Really, hearing them now is like a good omen. I shall go and pray for your father at this morning's service.'

'Please do.' Claire rose, looking young and revived. 'Please do, Mrs Rorke.'

Suddenly she leaned down and kissed the little woman with something approaching affection. She heard Guy call her.

'Time we hit the road.'

They took their leave, assuring her that they would be back as soon as possible.

'This evening with luck,' said Guy. 'Though we can't say what time. It may be late.'

'I'll have food waiting for you,' she promised. 'At any hour.'

'Sandwiches, please,' said Claire. 'Then we can take them with us. We'll just be calling in for half an hour.'

When they had gone Mrs Rorke went into Vale's room to retrieve her rouge and powder. Or perhaps she ought to leave them there in case Claire needed them again. And face tissues? There should be some in the dressing-table drawer. Better make certain. She opened it. Empty. No, a few labels. She took one out and peered at it in her myopic way, holding it close to her eyes. How strange, how very strange! Suddenly she sat down on the stool in front of the dressing-table, her heart beginning to jump about like a fish out of water.

'Mrs Hammond', she read. 'Charlottesville, Virginia.' And the label was marked Pan-American Airways. No, it wasn't possible!

Mrs Rorke rose shakily and went to the sitting-room. She helped herself to a tot of neat brandy to subdue the noisy thumping of her heart. Then she sat down at the telephone and called the airport. There was always someone on duty, even on Sundays.

'Tuesday?' said an Afrikaans voice in answer to her inquiry. 'Ja, there's a Pan-Am flight on Tuesday at twelve noon. New York via Dakar . . . you want to check your booking? What name did you say? Hammond, Mrs Hammond . . . yus' a minute. . . .' After a long pause, in which Mrs Rorke prepared herself for the answer, the voice came back on the line. 'Ja, lady, here it is. Mrs Hammond. You've booked through from Johannesburg to New York . . . What did you say? . . . Oh, you want to check your nephew's booking too. Broome . . . Let's see, Bezuidenhout – Bisset –

ja, here we are. Broome, Jefferson. So that's okay. Nie te danke nie. What's that, lady? . . . You want to cancel your flight? And what about Mr Broome? . . . Mr Broome's is okay, but you want to cancel. I see. It's a bit awkward with today being Sunday and tomorrow a holiday . . . Ja, I *can* fix it here, but you got to get your deposit back from the office later . . . That's okay then. Good-bye, Mrs Hammond.'

Mrs Rorke sat very still, overcome by rising nausea. No, even the brandy couldn't help this. Nothing could. She went unsteadily to the bathroom. Afterwards, she knew, she would have to make some calculations. She hated calculations, and at this moment she hated her own daughter too. She felt soiled – a cat's-paw in a dirty game.

Vale sat under the big umbrella-shaped kaffirboom. In other lands it would be called a coral flame tree. Its flowers had already appeared on the leafless branches, blood-red against the hot blue of the sky. Here in the lowveld it was much warmer than in Johannesburg six thousand feet above sea level. Here, only two hundred and fifty miles from the city, it was almost tropical although the nights were still cold. Soon the real heat would begin and even the game in the near-by Kruger Park would become languid and out of condition, seeking new water-holes as the sanctuary waited for the summer rains that would flood the rivers and turn dirt-tracks into mud.

John Rorke's small log cabin was surrounded by brilliant shrubs and tropical fruits. There were paw-paw trees, tall mangoes with their dense dark foliage and little sweet-scented flowers, a grove of avocados with the young pears almost invisible among the stiff green leaves, poinsettias spreading their flat uneven flowers in various shades from pale pink to vermilion, and yellow cassias adding their abundance of blossom to the wild garden that had grown as nature intended. There were no formal flower-beds, unless you cared to call a border of aloes formal. Small gem-like birds, scarcely bigger than butterflies, hovered over the succulents, their wings quivering as their tiny scimitar beaks robbed the scarlet blooms of honey and moisture. Exotic starlings preened their metallic plumage and pecked at the crumbs Vale spread for them, and stumpy toucans called harshly to one another as they fought for their share of the manna from heaven.

Vale looked up as Jef joined her, cool in his khaki shorts and bush shirt.

'It could be paradise,' she said. 'I love the Cape when I'm there, but I was born and bred in the Transvaal and this cabin in the bundu is my idea of the Garden of Eden.'

'Mine too. What are we going to do today, honey? Shall we go into the Kruger Park – have lunch at Skukusa?'

'Why not? I'd love it. Spend all day there and come back after sunset when the Park closes. I love seeing the animals at the water-hole in the evening.'

'We'll do that. I'll tell Wilson.'

Wilson was John Rorke's Bantu caretaker, a man from the Shangaan country. His duties were flexible. He lived with his family in the little Bantu settlement a few miles from Avocado Kop and, so long as he kept an eye on the cabin and the garden and was available when John or his friends appeared, he could take any other jobs he liked to supplement his small income. When John was there for a week-end or longer Wilson was chief cook and bottle-washer and received extra pay for his trouble.

But in spite of his words, Jef didn't immediately seek out the Bantu. He squatted on the grass beside Vale's chair and breathed a deep sigh of contentment.

'I didn't ever guess that perfect happiness was within a man's reach,' he said. 'Yet here it is.'

'Almost perfect,' she corrected.

'Ah, love, don't qualify it.'

'I must. Happiness taken at somebody else's expense can't be perfect.'

'We must forget that flaw – the only flaw. Don't you know I feel badly about hurting a fine man like Charles? But it has to be. There isn't any choice any more.'

'But there's the guilt, darling. Underneath the happiness there's the guilt. Charles doesn't deserve what I'm doing to him.'

'The guilt will pass. Charles will marry again. You'll see – some woman of a sensible age, who will make him happy and look after him.'

'And what about Micky? When I desert Charles I lose Micky.' Pain was in her eyes now. In the end it always boiled down to this – her dread of losing Micky.

'Give him a chance and Micky will forget. The little fellow will adapt himself. Children do – the younger the more easily. He isn't even five. Leave it till he's six or seven and it's another matter.'

'I wonder if that's true. Would you forget at five? I hate to think of Micky being brought up by old people – by Charles and Helen. Even by some . . . sensible woman Charles may marry some day in the future.'

'He'll have Claire – young Claire – to love him and be fun.'

'Young Claire may marry and go far away like I'm doing.'

'Anything could happen. The sensible woman might have a daughter of your age who'll adore Micky. You can't look into the future. We've made up our minds. Let's just try not to spoil our happiness with futile regrets – and they are futile because nothing can stop what we mean to do.'

'I s'pose you're right. Let's go.'

She rose, tall and beautiful in her shorts and thin loose

overblouse. He had to touch her, to hold her in his arms. She was all his, but he needed the constant reassurance of her yielding physical body, for there were times when she seemed distant and remote from him, prey to the past from which he was trying to prise her. Part of her still belonged to her husband, and only time would sever the invisible natal cord that held her so tightly to her child. He hoped that when she was far away in another continent with another child to comfort her, her sense of guilt would relinquish its hold.

On the dusty road to the sanctuary they spoke of the future.

'Tuesday,' she said. 'It seems so near. The day after to-morrow. On that day my whole life will be cut in half. Not even John knows.'

'You'll send Charles a wire from Johannesburg and the letter will follow.'

'Yes. But there's Mother. The shock . . . you see, she thinks the world of Charles. And he makes her a generous allowance. She'll be afraid of losing that.'

'Will she lose it?'

'I don't know. Charles may continue it. He's so kind.'

'If not, we must find a way of helping her.'

But she knew that Jef was not a rich man. The sun was on his bare arms as he drove, glinting on the golden down that covered them. He looked young and worried.

'I must write a book,' he said. 'Not just articles but a best-seller about South Africa. A novel. Our story. Why not?'

'There's nothing new in our story. Wife of older man falls in love with young lover, deserts husband. What's new in that?'

'Yeah, I guess you're right.'

They had reached the gates of the sanctuary. A tall chocolate Bantu holding a long assegai stood to attention to let them through. They did not even glance at the skull and crossbone warning. They knew they must not leave the car except in camp, they knew the speed limits. They had no firearms to declare. They knew the many contour paths and game trails and where they wanted to go.

'Virginia could hardly be less like this,' he said with a sweeping glance at the tall pinkish grass, the frieze of thorn trees and acacias, the rocky ridges and hills and the broad opaque green river with its sandbanks and ledges where crocodiles sunned themselves and its pools where hippos wallowed and frolicked in their massive way.

'I suppose not,' she said vaguely.

Virginia, her future home, was still only a word to her although in a matter of days it would be a reality.

As they drove slowly along the dusty track a herd of grazing impala suddenly scattered and crossed the road with flying leaps, soaring over the car with incredible grace.

'A leopard, or possibly a lion,' said Vale. 'Let's stop and see what gives.'

He thought of the luscious fields of his home countryside, of pedigree horses and cattle, of parks with great trees and honeysuckle hedges. Always the smell of honeysuckle. So different from this dry scent of dusty earth and of the deep rooibos in which a lioness could stalk her prey unseen.

'There!' said Vale, suddenly. 'The ears and the tail.'

He peered at the spot to which she pointed and he saw it too, the movement in the long grass, the twitch of a dark ear and the tuft of a lashing tail. As they watched, the lioness emerged into a glade and was joined lazily by her heavily-maned mate and two cubs. They sprawled in the hot sun. The lion turned dog-like on his back with his feet in the air and the cubs played and tumbled each other with grunts and growls.

They drove on slowly and she exclaimed in delight at a

wart-hog family trotting in single file, tails erect, father in the lead, baby bringing up the rear. A herd of zebra and wildebeeste frisked under the thorn trees, giraffe cantered through an open space with their weird swaying movement and fantastic necks tree high, and a troop of baboons crossed the road, babies astride parental backs or clinging to maternal bellies.

Vale laughed so gaily that Jef felt his heart lift and his cares fall away.

It was high noon when they reached Skukusa, the shady camp dotted with rondavels and surrounded by a thorn fence. Here after dark, when the gates were closed, tourists could feel safe from the marauders of the night.

They drove down to the restaurant above the green Sabie River. After lunch they would go to the hippo pool. They sat by a window looking down upon the river bend. A roller bird performed its aerobatics above the water and the sun caught its indescribably beautiful colours.

'It's all too lovely to be true,' said Vale.

'Don't break the spell,' he said. 'Enjoy it.'

They were half-way through their lunch when Jef saw Vale's eyes on the door, wide and disbelieving. Her face flushed and paled.

'What's wrong?'

He turned to follow the direction of her gaze.

Guy Steele's tall figure was advancing across the room towards them and with him was the slim fair girl Jef remembered so well – Claire, the girl he had kissed long ago, made love to just a little, the red herring. What were they doing here? Of all people, why should they be here?

'So we've tracked you down at last,' said Guy, standing over them.

Jef had risen, but Vale still sat as if she had been turned to stone.

'What is it?' she asked at last. 'What's happened?'

'We've come to take you home,' said Claire. She had scarcely glanced at Jef Broome.

'You can't,' said Vale. 'I'm not going home, Claire. Never any more.'

'Yes, you are, Vale. You're going home with us because my father has been terribly injured in a ski-ing accident. It happened yesterday morning and he was operated on last night . . .' Her voice broke. 'He may not live. That's why we must get back at once.'

Vale clung to the table as she rose. She stood, swaying on her feet, and Jef Broome grasped her arm to steady her.

'I'm sorry,' she said. 'I'm terribly sorry, Claire.'

'So you'll come? At once.'

'Yes,' said Vale. 'I have no choice. I'll come.'

13

THE WAY HOME

GUY TOOK CHARGE.

'If you've finished eating we should be on our way.'

'What about you?' asked Jef Broome.

'We've had sandwiches. Now, if you'll go with Claire, I'll drive Vale as far as Avocado Kop. I want to put her in the picture. There's a great deal she ought to know.'

'As you wish.'

'At Avocado Kop we can change over and Vale can go with you as far as Johannesburg. After that she'll be with us.'

His tone implied that what became of Broome when they reached Johannesburg was of no interest to any of them. He and Claire would be responsible for getting Vale back to where she belonged and was so desperately needed, and that would be the end of an unfortunate incident.

They headed towards the south-western gate of the sanctuary. Jef was driving a hired Chevrolet, and, as they travelled slowly along the dirt-track he said:

'This is terrible, Claire. Tell me what happened to your father.'

She described the accident. 'It's a case of life and death,' she concluded. 'The surgeon said Vale must come at once.'

'It was clever of you to find her,' he said, frowning. 'And remarkably lucky.'

'Yes. John's boy at Avocado Kop told us you had gone to Skukusa.'

'How did you find John's cabin? You've never been there before have you?'

'I asked Mrs Rorke for the address. It was P.O. Nelspruit, so we inquired the way at the hotel in Nelspruit. The manager was very helpful. He apparently knows John Rorke well.'

'But what made you think of John's cabin? What led you to believe you'd find Vale there? Or me either, come to that?'

'I had my reasons.'

Cars ahead of them had drawn up at the side of the road, and Claire changed the conversation.

'Elephant,' she said. 'We'll have to wait till they've crossed the road.'

The great beasts had left their trail of trampled shrubs and uprooted trees and now they emerged on to the road, apparently oblivious of the cars. There were several adult beasts and two babies. Even at this time, with so much on her mind, Claire couldn't help feeling a thrill of pleasure at the sight of the small herd and the baby elephants, obviously in charge of a pair of monster aunts or nannies.

'Baby animals! How enchanting they are!'

'Yeah,' he said. 'It's a wonderful sight. We saw a pride of lions this morning.'

The great grey shapes moved into the grass on their way towards the lower river and Claire thought of Kipling's classic, *The Elephant's Child*. Would one of the babies get his trunk pulled by a crocodile while drinking? It was only too possible! When they moved on, Jef said:

'There was a letter I wrote to Vale some time ago – one you found hidden in a hedge with the stamps torn off it. If you had read that letter – I don't suggest you did, but if you had done so – you would have had good reason to think we might be here.'

'I did read that letter.'

He bit back his surprise at her honesty and came up with a question.

'Did you tell anyone that you had done so? Your father? Guy?'

'No one at all.'

'Why not?'

She smiled bitterly. 'I wasn't very proud of reading somebody else's letter. It's not my custom.'

'Then why did you do it?'

'Because there were words showing through the gap —'

'I know those words. So what?'

'So I knew you might be trying to take Vale away from my father. I had to get the whole truth – how far things had gone between you and Vale and how far they were likely to go. A number of lives depended on that – and still do. My father, Micky, Vale, and now this new baby —'

'Leave the new baby out of it! And don't forget that I have a point of view too. I love Vale and she loves me. If you've read my letter you know that. What else do you know?'

'I know that you and Vale are lovers, that you plan to elope with her. What else? Oh, yes, your idea of paradise is Avocado Kop, and its owner, John Rorke, was your go-between. And, just incidentally, I also know —' She broke off.

'What do you also know?'

'That in the beginning I was the dupe.'

He turned his head to look at her and she saw that his eyes were troubled.

'Claire,' he said. 'I've wanted to say this for a long time. I'm sorry about that.'

'Why should you care? You take what you want, regardless. As for me, it was just another part of growing up. An essential experience, perhaps.'

'It hurt you,' he said.

'Since when have you minded hurting people? I was a good decoy.'

'You sound so bitter.'

'That's natural enough.'

'I couldn't know you'd take a kiss or two so seriously.'

'I was very inexperienced. I've grown up since then.'

'So I see. You've made a nice job of it. And Guy? I guess Guy's the lucky man.'

'We aren't here to discuss me. Or Guy.'

'Maybe not. You're here – self-appointed conscience – to show your stepmother the path of duty. Vale doesn't need you to arrange her life for her.'

'Just now she does.'

'What can you possibly know about the way Vale and I feel about each other? It's not a light passing intrigue. It's the real thing.'

She was acutely aware of him beside her. The desire she had once felt for him had turned to a hatred so vindictive that she wanted to hurt him physically. Suddenly she understood the passion that could drive human beings to kill in hot blood. This was a man who roused powerful instincts. There was something elemental about him, a single-minded ruthlessness. She looked at the blunt attractive profile, the strong compelling chin and powerful throat, the good forehead and thick bright hair, and as she did so, he turned his head for an instant and met her eyes. His quick smile broke.

'Perhaps, after all, you can – perhaps now you've grown up you can understand that certain people are made for each other – that no force on earth can keep them apart.'

'I understand total selfishness,' she said icily. 'My father and Micky must be swept aside like so many dead leaves because you want my father's wife.'

'I met Vale too late,' he said. 'It can happen. Two people meet and they belong. We did and we still do. It's hard on your father – and, believe me, I respect and admire him – but Vale is my woman and we are going away together —'

'You *were*,' she corrected. 'You intended to go away together on Tuesday – fly to America. Well, now all that must wait. Daddy needs her – if he's still alive —'

Her voice broke. He put out his hand as if to touch her in sympathy, but withdrew it quickly.

'I'm sorry,' he said. 'It's all very heart-breaking for you.'

'Yes,' she said in a stifled tone. 'It is heart-breaking, but you don't really care. Right now this minute you're planning to come back – wondering how soon you can have Vale for yourself, whichever way fate plays it – whether Daddy lives or dies.'

His face set. 'There's nothing more that we can say to one another. I'm sorry, Claire.'

He drove the Chev through the sanctuary gates and speeded up as they turned on to the rough track leading to Avocado Kop. From now on they were unlikely to see much game. It lay behind them – that kingdom of the predator and the victim, of tooth and claw, where man was of no account and nature had her way.

He must believe Vale is carrying his child, she thought. That time she went to Johannesburg at the end of last summer they must have met. It must have happened then. He reckons it gives him the right to take her at any price. Claire felt utterly defeated. If that were true, Jef would never give Vale up.

They were nearly there. At Avocado Kop Jef would leave Claire and travel to Johannesburg with Vale. The Mini-Cooper had gone ahead and Guy was waiting outside the cabin. He came to meet them.

Vale came out of the cabin with Wilson behind her, carrying her grip.

'Put that bag in my car,' snapped Guy. 'It'll save time later.'

Vale leaned against Jef's car, her curls blowing about her head, her loose tunic fluttering over the opulent curves of approaching motherhood. In the past few weeks those curves had become more pronounced, and, as Claire watched the thin silk caress the soft full body with its promise of fertility, she knew that this warm sun-laden wind was whispering the secret of Jef Broome's claim to the wife of Charles Hammond.

The stars had faded and the lights of Cape Town were beginning to go out as they reached the fringe of the city.

Vale, on the back seat, woke from a fitful doze haunted by the constraint of her parting with Jef. He had waited for her outside her mother's flat in Johannesburg to hear the latest news of Charles, and, while Guy and Claire stowed her suitcases in the Mini-Cooper, she had talked to him for a few hurried moments.

'Charles hasn't regained consciousness. There's no change.'

'I'm sorry. How will we keep in touch? Shall I ring you early Tuesday morning before I fly to America?'

'Do that. But where can I find you in the meantime, if necessary?'

'At the Langham. I booked in there from a call-box ten minutes ago.'

'Good-bye, then, Jef.'

'Good-bye, Vale.'

He had not kissed her. They had been awkwardly aware of the other two, hostile and impatient. She had felt hopelessly detached from Jef. Even the pressure of his hands grasping hers had not restored the sense of intimacy. It had been as if they had parted already, irrevocably.

She woke now with a little moan and Claire turned round from her place next to Guy.

'We're nearly there. What do you want to do?'

'Home, first. I must see Helen and change and tidy up before . . . before . . .'

'Before we go to the hospital. Yes, I agree.'

The sun was rising behind the Hottentots-Hollands as they drove into Silverglade drive. Dart rushed at the car, barking madly, and Josiah came out to meet them.

'What news of Master?' asked Vale.

The old Xhosa's face looked swollen and bruised as if he had not slept for nights.

'Master is still asleep. He does not talk.'

'Asleep?' asked Guy.

'Unconscious,' said Claire quickly. She knew that in his own language Josiah would have used the word 'dead' instead of 'asleep'. Unconsciousness was, to him, a state of death.

As they went into the hall they heard a step on the stair and Mrs Terblanche hurried down, drawing her quilted dressing-gown round her. She too looked inexpressibly strained.

'I heard that broken silencer.' She tried to smile. 'There's nothing new to report. At all events, he's no worse.' She turned to Josiah. 'Tell Harmonia to make breakfast for four.'

'I won't want any, thank you,' said Guy. 'I'll be getting right on.'

They did not press him to stay and a few moments later the little car was on its noisy way, and Micky was throwing himself into his mother's arms.

'Here I are! What have you brought me, Mummy?'

'A cuddly cub,' she said. 'Come and get him. He's curled up in my hand-grip.'

She had bought the lion at Skukusa – a most endearing toy. She heard Micky's cry of delight as he rummaged in the zip-bag and found it.

'His name is Cubby,' he announced. 'Cubby is my very favourite toy!'

She hugged them both, remembering, with a stab of remorse, how she had made the hasty purchase before leaving the camp when she had known that she must return to her home.

'Micky – darling, darling Micky! Are you glad I'm back?'

'Yes, I are – and Dart is glad, Cubby is glad, Josiah is glad —'

'That'll do,' she laughed, putting an end to what might develop into an endless liturgy like Micky's prayers were apt to do when they included blessings for a long list of likely and unlikely human beings and improbable birds and beasts. She must hurry and get cleaned up. A shiver of dread went down her spine. What would she find at the hospital?

Claire went with her as soon as they were ready. Helen Terblanche said: 'I'll come later.' But as soon as they had gone she telephoned Abel Katz.

'I hate calling you so early – eight o'clock on a Public Holiday – but you did ask me to let you know when Vale arrived. She's on her way to the hospital now with Claire.'

'Good,' he said. 'I'll meet her there as soon as possible.'

Poor man, she thought, as she put down the receiver. All his precious long week-end ruined. Instead he would spend most of the holiday at the hospital. But he had assured her that she must not worry. In fact, Mrs Terblanche had other worries on her mind .Claire's tense face and the coldness in her eyes when she'd looked at her stepmother had indicated greater antagonism than she realized. But why? Much as Claire loved her aunt, she had never told Helen Terblanche about the tell-tale letter. Loyalty to her father held her back. The very suggestion that his wife had a lover diminished his stature and that was something Claire was not prepared to do. Whatever her suspicions might have been, she had kept them to herself. Only Guy knew – but that had been inevitable from the start. But that something was seriously amiss was clear to Mrs Terblanche, and she could not help speculating about Vale's interrupted week-end. What had Claire discovered to upset her so much?

The Judge came muzzily out of the confused darkness of unconsciousness with a thumping headache. He opened his aching eyes cautiously and closed them again. Where could he be?

'Vale,' he muttered. 'Vale —'

He felt his hand lifted to soft lips and he turned his head and flinched as a wave of pain shot through it.

She bent and kissed him and he saw her wavering beloved face as if it were under water, a drowned face moved by slow currents, glistening with drops of water. Water running down her cheeks.

'Water . . .' he tried to say, and someone in a starched uniform held a glass against his mouth so that he might moisten his parched lips and flannel tongue. The hand that raised his head was Vale's. He was aware of her with a profound sense of comfort and tried to smile at her. If she was here it must be all right. But where? A square of light hurt his eyes when he tried to look at her. As if she guessed his pain, she said:

'Please, Sister, draw the curtains.'

The starched figure made a movement to shut out the light and he felt better.

'Charles – darling. It's Vale – and Claire is here. Everything is all right.'

'Where?'

'At Groote Schuur Hospital. You're in a private ward at Groote Schuur. You had an accident, ski-ing.'

'What hap . . .'

His weak attempt to make words failed, and Vale said:

'You struck a tree stump and took a most almighty toss.'

'When?'

'On Saturday morning. Today is Monday morning. You broke your leg in two places and cut your head. Abel Katz operated on Saturday night.'

He saw the mound made by the cage over his leg and fear rushed into the jumble of muddled impressions, terrifyingly sharp and clear.

'Not . . . cut off?'

'No, darling. Not cut off. Just set. Everything will be all right.'

The cool hand held his and he clung to it feebly. Now another figure was beside his bed, broad, stocky, familiar.

'So you're awake at last, Judge.'

Vaguely Hammond knew the voice. Of course. Abel Katz.

'My leg?' he said with a great effort. 'What —'

'We patched it up. It's in plaster. There's a bandage on your head too, my friend, and you have a pair of fine black eyes.'

Hammond closed his 'fine black eyes' and sank down once more into the nightmare darkness from which he had emerged.

'Stay with him, Claire,' said Abel Katz. 'I want to speak to Mrs Hammond.'

He led her on to the sun-warmed balcony outside the room.

'Mr Katz,' she said. 'I don't know how to thank you. Claire has told me all about the accident. We're all so grateful. How is he?'

'It's been a hard fight. You know about his injuries?'

'The broken leg, a gash in the head, and his back was hurt. Helen said you'd tell me the details.'

'Mrs Hammond,' said Abel Katz. 'There's a chair here. Why don't you sit down while we discuss this?'

She stared at him, cold in the sunshine. She did as he suggested, and he stood over her – a stalwart figure, grave-faced and compassionate. She clasped her hands as she asked her questions. He thought that she was wringing them in her great anxiety and he could hardly bear what he had to do.

'Mr Katz,' she pleaded. 'Charles will live, won't he? I mean, now that he's regained consciousness, we have nothing further to fear, have we?'

'Your husband will live, Mrs Hammond. But the spinal cord was snapped when he fell. It was a terrible fall – a shocking jar —'

'What does that mean – the spinal cord snapped – what will it mean to Charles?'

He drew a deep sighing breath. 'My dear, I hate to tell you this. It means that Charles will never walk again.'

'No!' she cried in a low voice. 'Not that! Surely there's something – some operation, some hope?'

'There is no operation that can help him. There is no hope that your husband will be able to walk. He will have the full use of his upper body – but from the waist down – no.'

She said nothing. Just sat in the bright warm sun and wept. Abel Katz left her there. His task was only half done. Later he would have to tell his patient what he had told the young wife. Pity was his weakness. In all his years as a surgeon – the young struggling years and the many successful years – he had never learned to rid himself of his burden. Pity.

14

'A HEAVY THING'

WHEN GUY CAME TO SILVERGLADE FOR NEWS SOON
after six that evening he found Claire alone in the library.
Vale was upstairs with Micky, and Helen Terblanche was
resting.

Claire was sitting in her father's high-backed chair by
the fire, her legs curled under her, her hands limp in her
lap, her eyes fixed on the flickering flames. Dart, sprawling
in front of the blaze, paid no attention as Guy entered, and
Claire looked up at him, her face pinched and despairing. He
strode across the room and took her hands.

'What's the verdict?'

'He'll live. But he'll never walk again.'

She saw horror flare in his eyes and felt his grip tighten.
The next minute she was up and in his arms, weeping against
his chest. He stroked her hair gently.

'Darling,' he said. 'I'm so terribly sorry. Cry, my darling . . .'

Sobs racked her. He felt that without his arms to enfold it,
her slight frame would burst apart, but the storm was as
brief as it was fierce, and soon she was mopping at her tears
with his clean handkerchief, struggling to control herself.

'Saying it . . .' she whispered, 'Just saying it . . . made it so
terribly . . . true.'

'So she's told you, Guy.'

They turned to see Vale standing in the doorway. She was
very pale and her eyes had sunk back into deep bruised

hollows. She wore a plain cherry-coloured woollen dress which accentuated her pallor and did nothing to detract from the thickening of her figure.

'Micky wants you to read to him, Claire. Why not take a drink up with you?'

Claire shook her head. 'I don't want a drink but I'll go up to Micky. What have you told him?'

'Only what Helen has already told him – that his daddy will be in hospital for some time because his leg is broken.' She added gently: 'Do something about your face before you go to him. He's sensitive to atmosphere – frightened, poor little boy.'

Claire raised a faint smile. 'I'll do my best.'

When she had gone Vale poured herself a whisky and soda and one for Guy. She stood with her back to the fire, and Guy, watching her profile, thought that the softness of her features had firmed and sharpened, graven by the sorrow and determination that haunted her eyes as she turned to him. She came straight to the point.

'You understand that this – what has happened to Charles – alters everything?'

'I haven't had time to take in all the implications. Are you sure you have?'

He lit a cigarette for her and one for himself.

'Yes. Abel Katz told me this morning. I've had all day to think about it. But really I knew at once.'

'What did you know, Vale?'

'That I couldn't desert Charles now. Not in these circumstances.'

Her chin trembled but she drew hard on her cigarette, fighting to maintain control of herself. He thought of Jef Broome, that stubborn young man who would not easily give her up, and he was silent.

'Nobody knows about Jef and me,' she went on. 'Except

you and Claire and my brother, John. Even my mother has no idea. Nobody must ever know. Claire swears she has never mentioned it to Helen – or to anybody else – and I believe her. It has to be kept a secret. Forgotten.'

'You have Jef to reckon with.'

'When I write and explain he'll understand.'

'I don't think he will.'

She stared at him in astonishment.

'Wouldn't you – in similar circumstances?'

'I don't know. How can one know such things till one's confronted with them? Your present unselfish attitude is fine in theory but can you sustain it? There's a long haul ahead – a lifetime of sacrifice.'

She shivered as if an icy draught had suddenly blown through the room. But her chin set.

'It isn't as if I didn't love Charles. I do. You may find that difficult to understand. But a woman can love two men at the same time. There are many ways of loving. It isn't just affection and gratitude because Charles has been wonderful to me and very generous to my mother, it's much more than that.'

'I don't find it difficult to understand that you love and respect him. His character exacts love – and loyalty.'

'Loyalty! I've let him down on that. To the limit. But the thing with Jef was a flood tide. From the moment I met him he was in my blood and my bones. Believe me, I tried to fight it. But I was fighting two of us all the time – him and myself. At the beginning I thought I could get it out of my system by giving in – by keeping it on the basis of a physical infidelity. I told myself he'd have to go back to America and that would be the end of that. But it wasn't. You know how it is in the sea around this coast. If you get caught in a strong current and you give in, you've had it. You're carried out of your depth towards the rocks. When you try to swim for shore again it's too late. You've lost your footing. The beach is far away and the reef is near.'

The colour had risen in her cheeks and her eyes were brilliant as she talked. It was as if a fever shook her. She'd been emotionally pent up for many months, fighting her lone losing battle, confiding in no one, resenting her brother's connivance, carrying a child in her body that she believed was her lover's and finding herself at last helpless in the deep waters of a love affair that was bearing her into irresistible currents far from home.

She flicked her cigarette stub into the fire with trembling fingers and sat down suddenly in the wing chair with her face in her hands. Guy said gently:

'I suppose that when you went to Johannesburg this last time you'd made up your mind? You thought you'd said a final good-bye to your life with Charles.'

'Yes.'

'But you weren't sure – a hundred per cent sure of yourself?'

'I was sure then. The only thing that tortured me was leaving Micky and the fear that Charles would insist on retaining the custody of his son. Jef thought he'd be bound to let me have the child, but Jef doesn't know Charles as I do and what Micky means to him. Anyway, none of that is relevant any more.'

'Does Claire know your decision?'

'Yes. Charles must never find out about Jef. I have to trust you and Claire to keep that to yourselves – for his sake. For mine.'

'Of course.'

They heard voices coming down the stairs. Mrs Terblanche and Claire.

'Don't forget,' whispered Vale. 'Helen knows nothing.'

Mrs Terblanche put out her hands to Guy as she came in. He pressed them and touched her cheek with his lips.

'It's so tragic. I don't know what to say.'

Her vivid blue eyes stared at him from her gaunt birdlike face.

'Somehow we must all help him to bear it. We'll find ways.'

'Does he know?'

'Not yet,' said Vale. 'He hasn't started asking questions yet. Abel Katz says he'll only be fully conscious tomorrow.'

'We must all get a good night's sleep,' said Mrs Terblanche. 'I'm going to spend the next few days here with Vale. Once the Press gets the news of the accident the phone will never stop.' She glanced at her niece's drawn face. 'And the best thing you can do, my girl, is get back to your job as usual tomorrow. You can see your father in the evening.'

Claire nodded and turned to Guy. 'You can take me back to my flat right after dinner, Guy. There's nothing more any of us can do tonight.'

Josiah appeared and announced dinner in a tone so sepulchral that Mrs Terblanche rebuked him gently.

'This is only the beginning, Josiah. When Master comes back we will all help him to live again.'

'Yes, Madam. God will help Master too and Master will help himself.'

She smiled at the old Bantu gratefully. Vale rose.

'We'll come in to dinner right away, Josiah. Open a bottle of the red Cabernet wine and warm it a little.'

She held out her hands to the fire for a minute or two before leaving it. She was cold and deathly tired. Helen had been right. This was only the beginning of what Guy had called a long haul . . . a lifetime of sacrifice. No, it wouldn't be like that. It would simply be a different sort of life with different sets of values.

.   .   .   .   .

Claire sat close to Guy in the little car.

They avoided the coast road and went instead along the Foreshore between the bay and Table Mountain. A floodlit American round-the-world cruise ship added her touch of glamorous prosperity to the lights reflected in the quiet harbour.

She was light-headed with exhaustion, yet even the food and the red wine had not made her sleepy. Her mind was spinning round in circles, coming back again and again to one point.

'It would have been better if he'd died.'

She felt the shock pass through Guy, from her cold hand on his knee right through his body.

'No, Claire! People like your father are not expendable just because they have to face a great personal incapacity.'

'Don't you see that it's worse now where Vale and Jef are concerned?'

'Vale will stand by your father. She'll break with Jef Broome. She's made up her mind.'

She asked his own question. 'Will Jef let her?'

'He'd be a heel if he didn't. He's on his way back to America. Surely that's the end of that if Vale decides so.'

'All last night I kept thinking what would happen if Daddy died. Last night – in this car with Vale in the back – seems a thousand years ago. I kept thinking how easy everything would be for her if Daddy died. No problem over Micky, none over money. When they were married Daddy took out a big life insurance policy in her favour. He told us about it. He was so proud after he'd sailed through the medical. They couldn't fault him. And now this. How can he stand it? He's always prided himself on his physical fitness. How can he live totally crippled —'

'He has so much else. Brain, a great spirit. People of your father's calibre can rise above their afflictions. Look a

Roosevelt. He was a paraplegic, but it didn't prevent him from being America's President and the leader of a great nation in time of war.'

'Roosevelt didn't have a young beautiful wife,' she said sharply.

Again she felt the effect of her words tingle in the palm of her hand lying along his thigh. They turned towards Lion's Head, leaving the city behind them.

'I've struggled against a small affliction since I was a child,' she went on, 'a weak leg – a polio hangover. It made me mean – jealous of girls who excelled at the sports I found difficult. Things that were easy for them were a monumental effort for me. Ski-ing, that was the biggest battle. I was terrified Vale would beat me at it. I know how it is to have a disability.'

'You surmounted it.'

'Not entirely. It left ugly flaws in my character, uglier than a physical limp. I know them. Vale's gracefulness – the lovely way she moves – has been a whip to me. If I can be hurt with so little cause, how will it be for Daddy when he has to face up to the future?'

'It's no good torturing yourself like this, Claire. Letting your imagination run amuck. It's not going to help anybody.'

'I'm a realist.'

'What do you think Vale is?'

'A romantic. She sees herself in the role of the noble martyr.'

'Let's be thankful for that. If she acts the part well enough she may come to believe in it – to live it. And don't forget, Claire, she had a very real dread of losing Micky. She was convinced your father would never give him up.'

'Nor would he. I saw Daddy just after Micky was born. He was so thrilled to have a son. Just at the beginning I was jealous of that too, but it didn't last. Micky was such a darling baby and Daddy never let him come between us.'

'I don't believe your father would have been persuaded to relinquish the custody —'

'And hand Micky over to Jef Broome? Never! Even now he wouldn't do that.'

'So you see Vale's choice, either way, is between Micky and Jef. It could even be that it's a sort of relief for her to have the issue taken out of her hands. That was what I sensed. And it's not as if Jef lived here – as if he could go on putting pressure on her. It's when he's with her that he breaks down her resistance.'

'I pray you're right.'

Suddenly she let her head fall against his shoulder.

'It's awful,' she said presently, 'to love somebody so much you wish them dead. It's like having a sin inside you.'

The lights of Sea Point winked along the palm-fringed beach and they heard the surf pounding on the white sands as they ascended the Clifton road. Guy ran the Mini into the car-porch and got out to take Claire's suitcase from the boot. He carried it on to the stoep and waited while she unlocked the door. The tang of the sea drifted up the cliff and mingled with the aromatic scent of the herbs in Mrs Dupont's rockery.

He picked up the milk-bottle on the doorstep and followed Claire into the flat.

'Why don't you go to bed right now?' he said. 'I'll heat some milk for you.'

She hesitated. It would be lovely to be put to bed like a child – to be tucked up and kissed good night like Micky. Suddenly she was drowned and overwhelmed by weariness of body and mind. But before she could answer him she heard footsteps coming heavily along the stoep from the house and a knock at the door. Guy opened it and Mrs

Dupont lumbered in. She greeted him warmly while her kind anxious gaze sought Claire.

'My dear, I don't want to intrude, but it was on the wireless this evening about your father's accident – that he was at Groote Schuur Hospital. I just came to ask how he was getting on.'

Claire turned a stricken face to the older woman. 'Daddy was badly hurt in a ski-ing accident. His leg and back broken – but he'll get better. He isn't going to die.'

'I'm so relieved, my child. So very relieved. God bless you, and sleep well.'

She turned to go, but Guy stopped her.

'Claire is very tired, Mrs Dupont. I was just going to heat some milk for her.'

'Shall I do that?' she offered at once. 'I'll stay and see her safely into bed.'

'That would be very kind of you,' he said. 'I'll leave you then. I'll ring you tomorrow, Claire. Good-bye, Mrs Dupont.'

'Totsiens, Guy. And don't worry about Claire. I'll tuck her up with a glass of milk and a hottie.' Her broad gentle features relaxed into a smile of affectionate approval. The young man was right to leave the girl in her care.

Claire went with Guy to the door while Mrs Dupont pottered into the kitchen.

'Perhaps it's better this way,' he said, as he took her in his arms and kissed her tenderly. 'She's dying to mother you.'

'Yes, it's better this way. And Guy, maybe you'd better forget the things I said tonight. I wouldn't have said them to anyone but you.'

He stroked her hair back from her brow and held her small pinched face between his hands, looking down into her eyes with infinite understanding.

'You can say what you like to me. Always. I love you.'

'You've been wonderful – all through.'

'There's a long way to go. Good night, my darling.'

She watched his tall figure follow the path round the side of the flat and the words 'I love you' were a beam of glowing light in the chill darkness of her grief. She wished that he could have stayed. She longed to call him back. She needed him desperately, but Mrs Dupont would be shocked. She must let him go. She went back into the flat, her leg dragging, and found that Mrs Dupont had turned down her bed, filled her hot-bottle and prepared a mug of hot milk. Together they unpacked her week-end case and when she was ready for bed Mrs Dupont tucked her in, put Boo, the rag monkey, beside her and the milk on her bedside-table.

'There, now! Sleep well, little one. Alles sal reg kom. God bless you and your dear father.'

The plump woman bent and kissed her and Claire felt the tears well into her eyes. No one had treated her as a child since her mother's death. Not even Aunt Helen. She had long since forgotten how it felt to be tucked into a warm bed with a toy thrust into her arms. She had become totally and prematurely adult at thirteen.

'I'll leave your bedside lamp on,' said Mrs Dupont. 'And I'll drop the latch as I go out, but before you go to sleep put your door on the chain. Drink your milk first, though.'

'Thank you,' said Claire. 'You're very kind. Good night, Mrs Dupont.'

When she had finished her milk and locked the door and hooked up the safety chain she crept back into her warm bed and turned off the light. Tiredness flowed over her in waves, and with it a desolation she had never experienced before, an aching weight in her chest. She thought of the Bantu expression 'this is a heavy thing'. Her sorrow weighed physically in the region of her heart as if her father's plight had materialized and entered her breast, unendurably heavy. If

Mrs Dupont had not come to ask after her father she knew now that she would not have let Guy leave her. She would have been in his arms now, her body close against his, his lips on her hair. She would have found comfort in his warmth and strength, in his tenderness. She would have fallen asleep with her head in the crook of his shoulder. She would have passed some of her burden to him. The infinite weariness of her limbs would have relaxed against his, and his hand would have stroked her skin very softly. Passionless, but with the knowledge that it would not always be so. Her face was motionless in the dark, but hot searing tears poured down her cheeks on to the rag monkey's head. To cry with one's eyes closed – strange. To cry and cry. So, at last, she fell asleep.

15

HOME-COMING

CHARLES HAMMOND THANKED THE PRETTY DARK young night-nurse who brought him a cup of tea at 5.45 a.m. She looked as fresh as she had done ten hours earlier when she'd come on duty. Her dark hair was brushed into a bun that made her seem taller and older than she was. Perhaps the bun was false, he thought. When she had put down the tea-tray and opened his curtains she closed the door of his private ward softly and firmly behind her and he lay alone and looked out at the sky beginning to pale with the first light of dawn.

Over a month had passed since he had been brought here and today he would go home. He supposed he ought to feel pleased. Instead he felt nothing. It was as if the paralysis that immobilized his lower limbs extended cold tendrils into every part of his being, numbing his ability to accept his fate, sapping his fortitude and leaving him a prey to self-pity and despair. This, since the accident, was invariably his mood on waking from sleep – even from an afternoon nap – a stagnant black hopelessness that had to be fought back from the very threshold of his soul. He turned from the waist and poured his tea, added milk and sugar and sipped it, savouring its taste and warmth deliberately, as if thereby he could begin to employ some small part of a spiritual arm-oury. Every little action he could perform for himself was one more weapon against the great disability with which he must learn to live.

This daybreak hour between sleeping and waking, between tea and breakfast, was a good time for reflection, but his thoughts were not inspiring. He tried to visualize Silverglade as he would find it on his return, a home of shining beauty in the spring sunshine. There would be a new face, Angela. Vale had told him about Angela a week ago. She'd been sitting beside his invalid-chair on the balcony trying to prepare him for changes ahead, sensitive and apprehensive while he had been irascible.

'I've engaged a partly-trained coloured hospital nurse, Charles. She was with Jim Haggarty till he died —'

'Jim Haggarty! For God's sake, Vale, you don't imagine I'm going to be like that – a helpless vegetable!'

'Of course not, darling. Don't be silly. But there are several reasons why I must reorganize our household.'

'Such as?'

'You know quite well it isn't going to be possible to keep our Bantu staff. Fedora and Harmonia will be sent back to the Bantustans. We'll be lucky if we can keep Josiah. Fortunately he gets on well with the coloureds.'

Hammond knew she was right. The Bantu labour flocking to the Cape over the past half century had squeezed the Cape coloureds out of their traditional employment. Now the field was being cleared for them once more by a massive Bantu repatriation, inflicting severe hardship on many of those being arbitrarily returned to 'homelands' they scarcely knew. And most of the coloured population, who had long since moved a step up the economic ladder into more educated employment, felt little gratitude for the openings offered them by the receding tide of black unskilled labour. Government policies, however, must be carried out and adjustments made by those concerned, and this applied sharply to domestic service.

'If I have to lose Fedora later on,' continued Vale, 'it seems a good thing to have Angela on tap. She can help you so long as you need her and then she can take over the children. Her hospital training will be a blessing.'

'An expensive blessing – with me retired.'

'Some expenses are worth while,' she said, crisply. 'You must leave the management of the house to me, Charles.'

'Very well. Of the house, yes. Of me, no. I must find my own way through the wood. But let Angela stay for a while and then we'll see.'

He had been aware of his irritability, his unreasonableness, and of her reaction. She had been hurt. He must learn not to spurn all her efforts to help him. He must be fair to her. He must never hurt Vale.

He sighed and switched on his transistor radio and listened as usual to the Bantu early morning programme. There were records interspersed with commercials. Some of the records were 'top of the pops', some were operatic and a good many were Bantu choirs. These he enjoyed most. The range and purity of the voices was astonishing, flexible and true, intensely expressive. The Xhosa announcers put over the commercials with persuasive enthusiasm. They're irresistible, thought Hammond. If they can sell a product with such exuberance what can they do when they're selling something that really moves their hearts? Freedom, for instance, the paradise of Black Africa. You can judge the maturity of a man by his voice, you can sense a mood over the telephone or the radio, sickness or health. Listen to the laughter and the talk of our Bantu, to the quality of their voices, and know them for what they are – born orators, born actors, and, yes, born warriors, a vital dominant race.

The first fingers of spring sunlight were reaching on to the balcony outside his room; the Bantu music faded and the sound of birdsong announced 6.30 as the English programme came on the air. The doves outside cooed noisily. It amused him to distinguish the real birds from the recorded ones. The sun entered his room, dispelling shreds of the cloud upon his spirit. The clock on the Union Buildings in far away Pretoria was striking the hour, and the newscaster in the Johannesburg studio was launching into the seven o'clock news. The pretty dark-haired night-nurse popped her head through the door to wish him good-bye and a happy home-coming. He smiled stiffly and made some suitable rejoinder.

A happy home-coming? Oh, my God! But somehow he must make it so. For Vale's sake and Micky's. For Claire and Helen and the friends who were so eager to help him to live again, even for that nice blonde physiotherapist who had been teaching him how to get the best value out of his invalid-chair and how to help himself in and out of bed with the help of the 'monkey swing' hanging from an overhead rod. 'This accident doesn't make an end of your independence,' she'd said. Whatever happened he must refuse to allow his personal 'cloud' to engulf his family. He must put up an act, and go on putting it up till he learnt to believe in it. '. . . the Cape Peninsula, sunny and mild, wind southwesterly, showers later; Namaqualand, Bushmanland and the Karoo area, partly cloudy, wind south-westerly . . .' He switched off the weather report and reached out his arm for his electric razor.

At 11.30 punctually Vale had arrived with Helen, anxiety ill concealed under their bright masks. There had been hospital good-byes and the difficulty of transferring his helpless limbs and plaster cast from a wheel-chair into Vale's car, and then again of showing Josiah how to help him from car to chair at the other end. They had all been waiting for him on the doorstep, Harmonia and Fedora beaming and bobbing their welcome, and a new pleasant face in the background. Angela, of course. Dart had gone crazy with joy, jumping all over his chair, his big paws against his master's chest as he uttered cries and whimpers of greeting. Micky had raced to fling his arms round his father's neck, hair glinting gold in the sun.

'Can I push your chair, Daddy?' His lovely excited laughter rang true as a bell in his genuine happiness. With his throat constricted Charles Hammond thought that only the laughter of children was genuine. Of all the smiles that surrounded him now only Micky's did not cover pain or embarrassment. He wanted to answer his son, but he could not speak and he heard with relief the deep voice of Josiah.

'You help Josiah, Micky. We push this chair together, you and Josiah. Careful, not too fast.'

Hammond pulled himself together. 'Nobody pushes this chair. I drive myself. Micky, go and get your tricycle and ride beside me while we take a look at the garden. It's only when I have to go up or down steps that Josiah and Angela must give me a hand.'

'Claire's at work,' said Vale. 'But she's coming to dinner tonight with Guy.' She had already told him that at the hospital, and her unwonted nervousness saddened him.

The silver trees glistened in the October noonday sun, every narrow velvet leaf scintillating, the banks were ablaze with many-coloured daisies, the lawns dazzling green. The valley of the vines spread in young emerald leaf towards the sparkle of the sea, the violet mountains above were clear and soft, their flanks embroidered with the spring tapestry of forest and glade. He had forgotten that the mountain oaks climbed so high! The half-forgotten beauty of his surroundings enveloped him with a sense of gratitude and the aching pressure in his throat began to relax. This lovely place – this Silverglade – was his home. His.

When he turned his chair towards the house Vale said:

'Darling, shall we go and see how the library has been fixed up as a suite for you? I hope you'll approve.'

'Vale's taken immense trouble,' said Mrs Terblanche. She's done wonders.'

Hammond smiled at his sister. 'I'm sure she has.'

But the need to assert himself as master of this house was upon him. He wasn't going to be pushed around by his womenfolk – neither physically, nor in any other way. He allowed Josiah and Angela to manœuvre his chair up the shallow steps to the front door and into the hall.

'No,' he said. 'We won't go to the library just yet. We'll have a drink first – out on the stoep. Josiah, fetch the tray.'

He propelled himself through the long sitting-room and out of the open french doors.

'It's good to be home,' he said.

Vale touched his hand lightly. 'It's wonderful to have you back, Charles. There's Veuve Cliquot on the ice, or would you rather have something else?'

'Let it be champagne.'

'Me too!' begged Micky. 'Just a sip.'

'Just a sip,' agreed his father.

'See, the little back wheels of your chair go sideways,' observed Micky, as Hammond turned into the position that commanded the view he loved.

'That's to make it easy to turn in the smallest space,' explained Hammond.

Josiah appeared with the champagne in an ice-bucket and a tray with glasses. The wine, primrose as the spring sunshine, winked and fizzed and the Judge's wife and sister drank his health with Micky taking an outsize sip from his father's glass. When the bottle was empty Hammond glanced at his watch.

'A quarter to one. Well, Vale, let's go and see that transformed library.'

The beautiful room with its big windows and bookshelves and its teak panelling and open fireplace had been cleverly converted into the heart of a suite. A dressing-room and bathroom had been added, and a carved teak screen shut off the sleeping alcove during the day. Vale folded the screen back to let her husband see his bed with the new straight wicker and wood headboard. Next to it a section of the bookshelves had been left empty so that he could use them for whatever possessions he wished to place there. A miniature of Vale, a leather-framed photograph of Claire, a bowl of roses, and his leather travelling clock were already in position. Other things too. A house telephone, and a 'monkey swing' on a chain. Seeing his eye on them Vale smiled.

'There's a slotted rod that hinges forward from the bed-head when you want to use it and the monkey chain can hook on to it. The phone is an intercom. You can get any of us. It also connects with Angela's room and Josiah's.'

'You've thought of everything,' he said. 'Everything. I'll be very comfortable here.'

Mrs Terblanche had taken Micky to wash his hands and brush his hair before lunch. Vale and Hammond were alone. In spite of his show of cheerful appreciation there was a look of bleak desolation on his face that caused her to turn away from him to the window while she fought to control the ache that held her throat. Unbearable tension gripped them both as all the unspoken tragedy of the future was manifest in this room where he would sleep alone from now on.

'Vale?'

She started, unaccustomed to the silent passage of his chair. He was next to her and a world of questions were in the short word that was her name. She answered one of them at once.

'Darling, I have to sleep upstairs to be near Micky and the

baby that's coming. I can't be here with you. You do understand?'

There was urgency in her voice. He must surely realize
that little children could not be left unprotected and alone
upstairs.

'Fedora sleeps across the yard, as you know. I have no
choice.'

'None,' he agreed, reaching for her hand. 'There is nothing
else you could possibly do. You must be near the nursery.'

She felt the fine delicacy and extraordinary strength of his
fingers as they clasped hers. She sat on the broad teak window-sill and let him draw both her hands up to his lips.
Words forced themselves through those shaking lips.

'My God, my God! What can we do, my love?'

She leaned her face against his and the scent of her skin
was sweet and fragrant, her hair was soft against his cheek.
The feel of her, the young healthy glory of her entered his
being with poignant intensity. Every undamaged nerve cried
out for her and defied the deathly peace that held his man-
hood prisoner. In this hour of his home-coming his spirit
scaled the Golgotha of suffering that he knew would crucify
him again and again.

'It'll be all right,' she was saying. 'We aren't the only ones
like this. We have so much. We have Micky, the baby on
the way, Silverglade, friends – above all, each other. We'll
be all right.'

But she knew that her words were a cry in the dark, a
false whisper in the void of their broken marriage. It had
been broken anyway, and now there was only this strange
sad patchwork where once she had known the completeness
of a husband – and later the ecstasy of a lover.

Guy fetched Claire after work and when they arrived at
Silverglade Vale was upstairs changing for dinner and Ham-

mond was entertaining a visitor in the library. The decorative screen hid the bed, and the room, though slightly altered, retained most of its familiar charm. The Judge-President of the Cape, Mr Justice Anton Erasmus, rose to greet Claire. He was a big broad-shouldered man with a shock of grey hair, a lined weather-beaten face and a reputation for toughness tempered with humanity in his dealings with delinquents. There were no frills about Erasmus, and, in or out of the courtroom, he was famed for calling a spade a bloody shovel with outrageous disregard for the conventions.

'Good to see you, my girl!'

He flung a brawny arm about Claire's shoulders and landed a smacking kiss full on her mouth with a mischievous sidelong glance at Guy. But Guy knew Judge Erasmus and was unconcerned.

'Glad you're here, Guy.' The big man reluctantly released his grip on Claire. 'I need a couple of allies. I'm telling my friend here that we can't afford to lose him from the Bench. I speak for all his colleagues.'

'We're with you, sir,' said Guy. 'The law needs Judge Hammond.'

Hammond shook his head. 'I'm retiring to write my memoirs – all those dramatic criminal cases I've saved up for years to delight a public hungry for stories of rape and murder and all the uglier vices of mankind.'

'You could do that, Daddy,' cried Claire. 'It's a wonderful idea! And the witchcraft murders would really make your readers sit up and beg for more.'

'Not so fast, my girl,' protested Judge Erasmus. 'Charles can sit back in the fullness of time and scribble to his heart's content, but we aren't prepared to let him go yet.'

'If you think I'm going to dispense justice from an invalid-chair you've got another think coming,' said Hammond.

'Why the hell not? I've talked to Abel Katz and he says there's no earthly reason against it.'

Guy saw determination freeze Hammond's features, honed down to a brittle sharpness by mental rather than physical suffering. The blue eyes were stony and the jaw thrust forward. Guy knew the signs.

'I've made up my mind. I'm not going to be the one and only – the unique – wheel-chair judge. Not to please you, Anton, or anyone else. I'm through with the active dispensation of the law.'

'And why?' thundered Erasmus, who never hesitated to hurl himself in where angels feared to rustle so much as a feather. 'Because, man, you're proud as Lucifer. It has to be the throne or bloody nothing for you. So your profession must be deprived.'

'That's right.'

Hammond was apparently unruffled, but Claire knew the whiteness round his nostrils proclaimed his inward fury. He was indeed as proud as Lucifer, she thought. How would he ever learn to take pity in his stride? She changed the subject quickly.

'Are you dining with us tonight, Judge Erasmus?'

'No, I can't do that. What's the time? Past seven o'clock! I must be on my way. Now listen, child. I leave it to you and your boy-friend to talk sense into your father's arrogant head. Vale's on my side too.'

He took his leave and Guy went with him to the car.

'It's no good,' the young man said. 'Even you won't be able to shift his stand. And certainly none of us will.'

'I'm afraid you're right. Let me tell you something. When Charles Hammond gives sentence he sees himself as God. And, to him, God doesn't talk from an invalid-chair – only from On High or from the Cross. Man, how senseless can a wise man be?'

'Perhaps – as things are – he'll be happier writing. Perhaps he'll find the outlet he needs that way. He may even find it profitable.'

Erasmus got stiffly into his car and rolled down the window to shoot another broadside at Guy.

'That's right, young fellow. Study your future pa-in-law. He's a man of quality.'

'I agree, sir. But as to being my future pa-in-law, you're jumping the gun, aren't you?'

Erasmus chuckled. 'I always do. Our first-born arrived eight months after our wedding on the dot. A premature infant with every toenail and fingernail as perfect as you could wish to behold. Totsiens, Guy, my lad.'

A hairy hand waved and rolled up the window, a heavy foot revved up the engine, and the car shot forward. Guy watched the bluster, the kindness and the uncouth wisdom vanish round the curve of the drive between the silver trees.

Guy took Claire home soon after dinner and they went in to her flat and made themselves some coffee.

'Judge Erasmus knows what he's talking about,' he said. 'Your father could carry on if he wanted to.'

'Possibly,' she said. 'But he knows what he's talking about too when he says Daddy's as proud as Lucifer. I see breakers ahead.'

'So do I. How can we help?'

'I don't know exactly, but I've got an idea – several ideas, in fact.'

'Tell.'

'Not yet. They're formless. I must knock them into shape.'

'How will you begin?'

'I'm going to talk to Sarah Verity tomorrow. And Katrina. Don't ask me now, Guy. As soon as I've something tangible worked out I promise I'll tell you.'

She sipped the hot coffee with a little frown. 'Vale looked terrible tonight – tired, half dead.'

'And your father was very tense. It isn't going to be easy for either of them at first. But it'll settle itself.'

'Life's frightening,' she said. 'From day to day one doesn't know what next.'

'Like a good yarn – like you and me.'

She caught her breath as his arms encircled her. It couldn't go on like this much longer. There'd come a breaking point. He was part of her now, part of her life, part of her family. She could no longer envisage any existence without Guy. He had said 'I love you', but that was not all. There was an institution called marriage. Did Guy's 'I love you' include that? How much could she take for granted? How much could she give without losing the slender advantage of a woman desired and not yet possessed? How much could she give without losing Guy?

16

TIME OF TRANSITION

'SO YOU'VE AN IDEA FOR OUR INTERVIEW PROGRAMME,'
Sarah Verity said to Claire. 'Let's have it.'

She sat at her big desk on the third floor of the S.A.B.C.
building on the sea-front, the light falling over her left
shoulder and the wide view of the Atlantic visible through
the open window. It was Thursday and the mailship was
steaming majestically out to sea, her lavender hull and scarlet
funnel picked out by the afternoon sun. Gulls circled in her
wake, white and erratic, as if windblown. Claire watched
them for a moment or two before turning to Sarah.

'There's a swell out there,' she said. 'There'll be a few
empty places at dinner tonight.'

Sarah smiled. 'I'd give a good deal to be on board and
outward bound all the same. Now – your suggestion?'

'Well, Sarah, I'd like to interview Miss Thorpe, the Head
Physiotherapist at the Paraplegic Centre.'

Sarah ran her fingers through her short black hair.

'From what angle?'

'She's a remarkable person. Daddy's physio-girl told me
all about her. She organizes our paraplegic teams and takes
them to international paraplegic sports rallies all over the
world, and she gives up most of her Saturday afternoons to
teaching them archery, swimming, bowls, table-tennis, and
various other games.'

A sudden brilliant smile illumined Sarah's strong features
and lent them great transient charm.

'Presumably you'd like to do the feature yourself, on the spot, one Saturday afternoon. Get a variety of views – from the paraplegics as well as from Miss Thorpe?'

'I'd love to.'

'It's a splendid idea. Go ahead and fix it. Get Jim and a couple of the technicians to go with you. You can record it and we'll fit it into Woman's Hour. You might try using a bow and arrow yourself.'

Claire's eyes lit up. 'I'll make the appointment right away.'

'Oh, by the way, when can you have a bite with Katrina and me? What about tonight?'

'I'd love it.'

'Come about seven-thirty. I'll ring Katrina and she'll fix us one of her *specialités de la maison*.'

They ate in the pent-house studio by lamplight. Katrina Westhuizen had prepared avocado pears and soles poached in white wine with fresh crayfish claws, followed by strawberries. A milky moon glimmered through the skylight, and a half-finished portrait on the easel watched them from the gloom. Claire recognized the leonine head and fanatic gaze of the conductor of the Cape Town Symphony Orchestra.

'That's going to be superb.' She indicated the picture.

'Katrina is at her best with male portraits,' said Sarah. 'Women bore her.'

'Women always want to appear pretty and prettiness is so dull.' Katrina went to the side-table to fetch the bowl of strawberries and cream, her tall figure throwing its angular shadow on the wall, her braided coronet of pale hair shining as she leaned into the glow of the lamp to serve Claire. 'Just a few more strawberries. They really are rather good.'

Claire helped herself. 'I can't resist them.'

'There's something I want to ask you,' said Katrina, as she resumed her place at the table. 'Do you think your father would let me come to Silverglade to paint his portrait? I'd like to do him in all his judicial majesty – the scarlet and slate blue. I've always wanted to. He has such a magnificent head.'

Claire considered. She knew her father liked and admired Katrina Westhuizen both as a person and as an artist. Time might well hang heavy on his hands now that he was no longer actively employed, and Katrina's company might be just the stimulant he needed. She said slowly:

'It might be a wonderful idea, but he needs to get more resigned . . . more settled first. Then maybe the strained look will go. You've seen him. You know how he looks now.'

'Yes,' said Katrina. 'He looks haunted. Somehow that evil spirit must be exorcized.'

Sarah said slowly, 'We've thought about it a lot. Perhaps it would help for him just to wear his robes – to be, so to speak, on the Bench again. We've discussed it with Helen. It was she who suggested the portrait.'

'It might give him confidence. I don't know,' said Claire. 'Judge Erasmus wants Daddy to continue to serve on the Bench. But he won't. He's determined to write his memoirs instead.,

'Why not?' Sarah leaned forward, her gipsy face intent. 'I've always felt that an intelligent writer can't fail if he has a knowledge of medicine or the law – preferably both – and the ability to state his case lucidly. I don't mean that he could become a novelist. That requires certain creative potentialities. But he can certainly become a writer. Your father's whole training has taught him to sift essential from inessential evidence, to pinpoint human motives, and to see where the drama lies and exploit it. His own case-book would make fascinating reading. Certain cases could blow up into a book on their own, and then there are other little known cases asking to be dramatized. Charles could launch out into a new career based on his legal experience, and make a first-rate thing of it. Goodness knows we'd be glad to serialize it for the S.A.B.C. if he really got down to it.'

'And while he sits for his portrait he could mull over his ideas with me,' added Katrina, refusing to relinquish her project. 'He'll be in the right rig, at all events. Very much the Judge. Persuade him, Claire!'

'I will,' Claire promised.

She left her friends that evening with a new lightness of heart. Between them all, they would give her father no time to brood and grow melancholy. Sarah could involve his mind, and she, Claire, would enlist Miss Thorpe to teach him physical recreation. Katrina would be a tonic.

So, when Hammond's leg was out of plaster and he was better able to face the future with resignation, three new interests entered his life.

To please Claire he allowed himself to be persuaded to meet Miss Thorpe and join her Saturday afternoon sports gatherings. His natural aptitude for athletics made it simple for him to shine as a swimmer, to master the art of archery and to learn to play a very reasonable game of table-tennis or bowls from his wheel-chair. He saw too how others afflicted as he was surmounted their disabilities with courage and cheerfulness and managed to lead normal lives in almost every sense of the word. He was enthusiastic when the paraplegic swimmers pitted a team against the best amateur swimmers the Cape could muster. The amateurs had their feet tied to equalize the handicap and the competition was fierce and close. Hammond himself made a good showing.

Vale, near her time, did not accompany him on these outings. It was Claire who was his companion and driver. The old closeness between father and daughter was renewed and strengthened. It flowered again as it had not done since his marriage to Vale, and he found a sweet and satisfying pleasure in the company of his daughter. With her encouragement he had made the first tentative notes for his memoirs, and with

Guy's help he had begun to assemble a considerable amount of material from which to pick and choose the stories for a book.

Then lastly he had consented to sit for Katrina. He soon found that he looked forward to her morning visits to Silverglade with eager anticipation. She was good company with a lively wit and a keen interest in world affairs. Moreover she made a point of egging him on to discuss the many and various cases that might be suitable for publication.

'You've any amount of material,' she said. 'I've discussed it with Sarah. She says you mustn't be tempted to use it all in one volume. Spin it out.'

She had set up her easel in the library and he sat for her in his high-backed chair. She wandered about, drawing a curtain here or there to alter the light, shifting the folds of his gown this way or that.

'You're most impressive in your canonicals – a splendid subject.'

The long fine hands emerging from the wide judicial sleeves delighted her as did the set of the grey proud head. The look of suffering had relaxed, and the new thinness accentuated the elegant bone-structure. She could hold his interest with her conversation and his alert attentiveness was reflected in his responsive expression.

'We're so fortunate in this country,' she said. 'Yesterday I was painting our native charwoman. She has a gorgeous coy chocolate head. And today it's you.'

'Apartheid is a myth,' he said. 'It can't be maintained. Our black brethren are with us wherever we may be, and thank God for it. However we happen to work we inevitably broaden our experience of humanity with our multi-racial contacts. We have the whole vast system of Bantu society and custom to enrich our outlook. In medicine and the law it's particularly so. You see the tragedies and comedies of a race emerging from the superstitions and animalism of primitive tribalism into the sophistication of the twentieth century as exemplified by our own white culture and industrial advancement. It's an absorbing anthropological study and we can't escape it.'

'I've done a good deal of work in the tribal territories,' she said. 'It's fascinating. The unspoilt primitive background, the complex but sensible morality – often much better than our own – the affinity with nature, the prestige symbols, a fat belly, plenty of beer, several wives, herds of cattle —'

'Not really so very different from our own,' he grinned. 'Whisky galore, exotic mistresses and fast cars or yachts for the international set —'

'Or in the top ranks of emergent Africa, come to that,' she put in. 'The whole of our continent is in varying stages of evolution. That's what's so interesting. In the emergent states the clever black politician knows just how to impress his fellow countrymen. He's a keen psychologist and he plays on the superstitions of the people.'

'He shares them. So do we all. We are riddled with superstition, whether we admit it or not. Take my old Josiah for instance, he's quite a wizard in his own right. Why, some time ago the police received an anonymous letter to say that Josiah kept a brothel and a shebeen in my servants' quarters and a tokoloshe – a hairy dwarf – in his cupboard. The police informed me and searched the premises but luckily they found nothing to justify any action. All the same, I swear Josiah dabbles in a little witchcraft, even if he doesn't sell women, brew illicit liquor or materialize evil familiars.'

'His father was a Chief, wasn't he?' she asked. 'Every Chief knows magic and passes it on to his children.'

'Yes,' said Hammond. 'And his elder brother is a Chief in the Transkei now. God knows they need magic in the territories – but it's the white man's magic. There's so much still to be done to fight the diseases of malnutrition and the erosion of the soil, to say nothing of the cruelty of ignorance.'

She put out her hand quickly. 'Hold it! Don't say anything for a moment!'

He watched her work fast, her face absorbed, making sketch after sketch. He was in no hurry to have her begin the portrait in earnest. With her he forgot his own preoccupations.

'What do you consider the most interesting case you know?' she asked presently.

He reflected, and she smiled to herself, catching a new expression in the blue eyes.

'It wasn't one of mine,' he said, at length. 'But I should definitely say the tokoloshe murders. The murderer worked here at Langa and for some reason he made an enemy of the witch-doctor who saddled him with the tokoloshe. At least that was his story. The criminal, Msomi, trekked hundreds of miles leaving a trail of corpses in his wake. He axed at least sixteen people and he attributed all the crimes to the tokoloshe who travelled with him. He couldn't rid himself of this bloodthirsty influence wished on him by his enemy. Well, perhaps that's one way of describing an obsession.'

She shuddered. 'I remember the case. He described the tokoloshe – his abominable familiar – as a hairy dwarf, sex-ridden and murderous, raping and killing. Even reading about it in the papers one seemed to feel the actual presence of this supernatural creature in the courtroom.'

'Every black witness believed in the tokoloshe,' said Hammond. 'So much so that before the case was over he near as dammit materialized in court! The day the murderer was executed three Zulu Chiefs were present to witness the execution because the people believed that the tokoloshe would spirit the criminal's body away.'

'And did he?' she asked.

'Not quite. But at the moment of his death his kraal in Zululand was struck by lightning and his eldest son was killed.'

'Uncanny,' she shivered. 'On the other hand when it comes to being possessed of the devil – as Msomi certainly was – take the weird delusion of the assassin of Dr Verwoerd. It wasn't the tokoloshe there, it was a tapeworm that was blamed for the murder!'

'The trick cyclists certainly played a big part in that,' he agreed. Like most of his colleagues Hammond regarded the evidence of psychiatrists with a certain scepticism, but he had valued it in his time.

'I've kept the newspaper records of the case,' he said. 'You'll find them in that bottom left-hand drawer of my cabinet, Katrina. If you'll bring them here you'll see the extraordinary similarity with the Msomi murders.'

She found the folder with no difficulty and put it into his hands. It was time for a break in any case and she poured him and herself a gin and tonic.

'Tell me,' she said. 'I'd like to hear about it.'

He put on his glasses and thumbed through the cuttings. In the *Cape Argus* of October 18, 1966, he found what he wanted. The assassin's defence had rested upon proving that he was a schizophrenic not responsible for his actions at the time of the crime.

'Now listen to this, Katrina. Here is the evidence of Dr Sakinofsky, one of the leading psychiatrists who examined Dr Verwoerd's murderer, Tsafendas, who was haunted, not by a tokoloshe, but by a tapeworm.'

He began to read and she thought how beautiful his voice was. She saw it in colour. She could paint his voice – soft and smoky, shot with tongues of flame or milky ash – and then the macabre matter of his subject gripped her with its sickening lunacy.

'"Dr Sakinofsky said his third interview with Tsafendas was at Caledon Square on October 14. 'I wanted to lead him on to the tapeworm and what it meant to him. We started talking about this tapeworm and he said it might have been a serpent. He described it as a viper, a demon, a dragon. He said, "There is a lot in the scriptures about tapeworms. I got to the point in my church where I could not take bread and wine at Communion. I was trying to make a demon holy by doing so."' Tsafendas said he was possessed by the tapeworm which had the effect of making him a robot. He quoted a passage from the Bible which said: 'Lord, I am a worm, I am a worm' . . .

'"Tsafendas said he fed the tapeworm. It was like a boa-constrictor. When he fed it, then it left off worrying him. It purred like a cat. He gave his concept life in a bizarre and grotesque way . . . *Tsafendas also said he had been hypnotized by the tapeworm when he killed Dr Verwoerd* . . . He said the tapeworm had corrupted him . . . Dr Sakinofsky said reports on Tsafendas's behaviour which included mention of the tapeworm delusion showed that Tsafendas could never have dreamt it up as a defence."'

'I remember that fantastic evidence,' said Katrina. 'It was – as Dr Sakinofsky describes it – bizarre. The demon tapeworm must have held the court in its coils much as the tokoloshe practically materialized in the Msomi case! But there was one striking difference.'

'Well?'

'Msomi was also the victim of a delusion but he had no battery of psychiatric evidence to prove him schizophrenic and get him off.'

He gave her one of his speculative looks.

'Consider the essence of the case, my dear, and you will see why not. The demon tapeworm was a pathological de-lusion while the tokoloshe was a deadly tool in the paraphernalia of witchcraft. We don't encourage witchcraft. We try to eradicate it.'

'Surely, then, it was the witch-doctor who should have stood trial?'

'As an accessory? Perhaps. But he had vanished, and, in any case, he would simply have denied everything.'

'Once, in medieval times, he would have been burned at the stake – condemned by the Church.'

'The Church has changed its methods since then. But it is still the duty of the Church and the State to stamp out witch-craft in its sinister forms. Sorcery is the scourge of Black Africa.'

'And liquor is the scourge of White Africa,' said Katrina, downing her gin and tonic. 'I needed that after such a grisly conversation. Now, my friend, back to work! Another half-hour before lunch.'

'You're a slave-driver.'

'Could be. A love of my work is my personal scourge and just at the moment you are my victim.'

He laughed and allowed her to settle him back into the pose. He liked to watch her at work. He regretted that he too was not a painter, for at times he saw rare beauty in her absorbed aesthetic face. She had a medieval cast of counten-ance herself, he thought. He could picture her in one of those tall pointed dunce-cap headgears with a flowing veil and gown. Guinevere? Or Ysolde? Yes. Ysolde.

'What are you thinking about?' she asked, smiling.

'You,' he said.

The Judge's portrait, when at last it was finished, was breathtaking. The wise arrogant head looked out of the canvas and gave compassionate judgement on the sins of all mankind.

'I must have it,' said Vale. 'This is something Micky must inherit. Will you sell it, Katrina?'

'I will give it to you,' said Katrina, 'on one condition.'

'What condition?'

'That Charles sits for me in my studio for a bust. I want to do a bronze – just the head.'

'I'll sit for it when I have my own car,' said Hammond. 'When will that be?'

'Soon,' he grinned. 'I've ordered it already. A car with manual controls. Then I can come to your studio whenever it suits us and I'll be completely independent.'

'Done,' she said. 'The portrait is Vale's.'

When Claire and Guy saw it they knew that her father had begun to live again. Katrina had caught the turn of the tide and immortalized it.

November, the blue month of jacarandas, agapanthus, lilies, hydrangeas and periwinkle banks was near its end. A summer heatwave crowded the beaches and parks and Guy called for Claire at Silverglade one Saturday evening to take her out to dine and dance. It had been too hot for the Judge to go out and he had been swimming in the pool with Micky clinging to his shoulders like a limpet. Vale looked pale and tired.

'Should I stay at Silverglade for a few nights – in case you have to go to the nursing-home suddenly?' Claire asked.

'Gracious, no. I have Angela in an emergency. And Josiah can drive me to the nursing-home. It's too simple. I think Charles is really relieved we have Angela now. He lets her do a lot for him, but he feels she'll be mostly for me and the new baby quite soon.'

'Getting Angela was a brilliant move.'

'Yes,' said Vale. 'It's worked out well.'

Guy ran Claire back to her flat and waited for her on the stoep while she changed. Kate and Gene Dupont found him there.

Gene said: 'It was my birthday last week and Daddy gave

me two rand. I bought four beautiful little cars.' He took the miniature toys from his pocket. 'This is the James Bond Aston Martin.'

'All gold with guns and an ejector seat,' explained Kate. 'I wish I knew a man with a car like that.'

Gene was making the appropriate noises as he raced the Aston Martin round the stoep and shot his passenger into the air and on to the track where Kate ran him over with a Ferrari.

'You going dancing tonight?' Kate asked Guy.

'Probably.'

'It's too hot for dancing,' she said. 'You should surf in the moonlight.'

'That's quite an idea. Pop in and tell Claire to bring her swimsuit.'

'Leave the Ferrari here,' commanded Gene, as Kate vanished into the flat. He turned to Guy.

'You know what girls are when they get together. They'll start gossiping and forget all about the cars.'

Guy laughed. 'You're learning young.'

'I have a mother and a sister,' sighed Gene. 'Ma says Claire's father'll never be able to drive again because his legs are paralysed.'

'Your ma's wrong. His legs are paralysed but he's ordered a special car with hand controls. He'll be able to drive it perfectly.'

'Gee, I'd like to see that hand-driven car. Maybe he'll let me have a look when he gets it, or even drive it. My legs are still too short for our pedals.'

'I'm sure he'll take you out in it.'

Claire, followed by Kate, came on to the stoep and Guy saw that she was carrying her towel and bikini. She looked cool and charming in her thin leaf-green summer dress with her fair hair just above her shoulders, springing up and away from her long slim neck. She locked the door and they called goodnight to the children as they went round to the car-porch.

Guy had booked a table at the latest sea-front restaurant and they ate out of doors round a small courtyard cleared for dancing. A crooner at the piano played soft music while they dined. He was relieved later by a three-piece dance band. But Kate was right. It was too hot for dancing and after a while they decided to swim.

'We'll go and change in my flat,' Guy said.

The tide was coming in when they ran down the bathers' stairway and on to the sandy beach.

'The spring tide,' said Claire. 'You can hear it.'

Under the roar of the waves there was a stronger palpitation as if the deep heart of the sea were beating to a fiercer rhythm, answering the distant call of the last full moon of the spring season. The beat of the rollers on the shore carried an echo of the mighty power of the whole wide Atlantic. They plunged into the surf, gasping at the icy impact, torn apart and washed together again in showers of moon-silvered spray. They could feel the force of the rising tide, the tug and suck of the sea, and, as the great rollers swelled and cast their white plumes into the night, they dived through them and surfaced in time to watch them tower and crash in a thunderous tumult of surf.

'That was wonderful!'

Claire dried her legs and arms as she stood on the cool shining sand, her body warm and tingling with the exhilaration of the bathe. They were alone in the moonlight and Guy longed to hold her in his arms but too many windows looked upon this beach, his own included, so he contented himself with taking her hand as they walked back across the sands to the stairs and up to his flat, refreshed and stimulated, no longer languid in the hot night.

Through the open seascape window they could hear the thump-thump of the waves and the monstrous murmur of the swell. The surface of the sea was fragmented by restless incandescent silver, matching Claire's mood of radiant excitement.

She went into Guy's bathroom and peeled off her bikini under the shower.

'It seems awful to get dressed again,' she called presently. 'But you'd better pass my clothes in through the door.'

She was standing with the towel round her when he came in, wearing a pair of very brief shorts.

'My clothes?' she inquired.

'I haven't brought them.'

He lifted her bodily in his arms and carried her into his L-shaped room and plumped her down on the divan in the full light of the westering moon.

'That towel is damp,' he said.

'Yes,' she whispered. 'Yes, darling, it is.'

Her arms were raised to encircle his neck and she felt his hands on her cool skin and her body drawn close against his. The light of the moon bathed them in white fire and his lips moved against hers.

'I love you, little one.'

'And I love you,' she said.

It was two in the morning when the telephone rang next to Guy's bed. He stretched out an arm to take the receiver.

'Who is it? . . . Judge Hammond!'

Claire stirred beside him, her eyes wide and startled. She could hear her father's voice clearly over the line.

'I tried to get Claire at her flat, but there's no reply. I thought she might be with you.'

'Yes, sir, she is. Just a moment . . . Claire!' he called unnecessarily, handing her the receiver, his eyebrows raised, his face concerned but half amused.

She let a few moments elapse.

'Daddy! We've been out dancing. We just came in for a nightcap. What is it?'

'It's Vale,' said the Judge. 'I thought you'd like to know. Vale had a daughter half an hour ago.'

'How wonderful! Where? At the nursing-home?'

'Yes, Josiah got her there just in time. She's doing well and the baby is magnificent.'

'We'll come to you at once.'

'It's very late – or should I say early?' But in spite of his words his voice told them how much he wished he could see them.

'That doesn't matter,' said Claire. 'Have the champagne ready on the ice.'

'I will.'

Within quarter of an hour they were on their way to Silverglade. The lights blazed in the hall and they found the Judge in the library with his favourite Veuve Cliquot cooling in the ice-bucket on a tray on his desk. He was wearing pyjamas and a tailored maroon dressing-gown. He looked happy and uncritical as he greeted them warmly. He poured the champagne himself and raised his glass.

'To Vale and baby Freya!'

'Freya?'

'She's a spring baby – little goddess of the spring.'

'Born on the night of the spring tide – a lucky night,' said Claire. 'To Vale and Freya.'

When they had drunk the toast Guy said:

'Judge Hammond, sir, I have something very special to ask you.'

'What is that, my boy?'

'I want to marry Claire.'

Hammond's eyes sought his daughter's and she ran to him and grasped his hands.

'Daddy, we love each other.'

'That's all I need to know,' he said. 'God bless you both.'

17

END OF THE YEAR

MRS DUPONT OPENED THE *CAPE TIMES* ON SATURDAY morning with pleasurable anticipation.

'There it is in black and white!'

She passed the paper to her husband, folded back at the appropriate page.

'Miss Claire Hammond, whose engagement to Mr Guy Steele was announced today,' he read aloud. 'But the photograph is too formal,' he added. 'Rather serious.'

'Let's see!' The children scrambled off their chairs and pressed against their father's side. 'Gee, she looks pretty.'

'Don't breathe egg and bacon all over me,' he protested. 'And don't put your buttery fingers on my sleeve, Gene! Well, Ma, I s'pose your mind is at rest now.'

Mrs Dupont exhaled a deep sigh of satisfaction.

'I admit it's a relief. There were times when I couldn't help worrying. After all, Robert, we've been young ourselves. One doesn't forget how it was.'

He took off his spectacles and wiped them. His plump girl hadn't always been on the verge of the roaring forties, and he too remembered the turbulent twenties with more than a touch of nostalgia.

'She's got a good man in young Steele,' he said. 'If Kate picks as well one of these days I shan't complain.'

'Pooh,' said Kate. 'I'm not going to get married and have babies being sick all over me. I'm going to be an air hostess—'

'And have grown-ups being sick all over you instead,' said her mother.

'And *I'm* going to be an astronaut,' announced Gene, and produced a strange supersonic sound from the corners of his mouth with the aid of two marmalade-smeared fingers.

'We're going to miss Claire very much,' said Mrs Dupont.

'And you were the one who thought a girl was too much responsibility,' her husband reminded her.

'I'm going to be her bridesmaid,' said Kate. 'She promised.'

Mrs Dupont looked at her daughter with swift indignant suspicion. 'Did you dare to ask her?'

Kate had the grace to blush. 'No,' she muttered.

Gene chirped up. 'She didn't exactly ask. She said, "Ooh, it must be fab to be a flower-girl at a wedding," and Claire said, "Have you ever been one?" and Kate said, "Not yet." Then Claire said, "You can be mine."'

'You women know what you want,' said Mr Dupont. 'You have no conscience and no decent feelings. You just oozle your way in anywhere. When is this wedding to be?'

'They haven't decided yet,' said his wife. 'But it won't be long. Guy's trying to get a bigger flat and when that's fixed up they'll go ahead.'

Mr Dupont grinned. 'I'd be surprised if they wait that long to go ahead.'

'You're incorrigible,' said Mrs Dupont severely.

'What's incorrigible?' asked Kate.

'The whole lot of you,' said her mother. 'Now, be off! All of you. I want to get the breakfast table cleared. I haven't all Saturday to play in, even if you have.'

The only person who was not entirely satisfied about the engagement was Sarah Verity.

'So now I lose my most promising assistant,' she complained.

Claire sat on the edge of Sarah's big desk.

'Not yet. Not for a year or so. I'd like to keep on with my job.'

'What about babies?'

'We want a family, of course. A boy and a girl, but not at once. We aren't solvent enough for that. I'm going to see Vale's doctor about the pill. Vale has Dr Mary Stern. I'd rather go into all that business with a woman doctor.'

'That sounds sensible. In that case you have my unreserved blessing.'

'Anyway, I don't see why I shouldn't work for you even if I start a baby. I could always free-lance after that.'

Sarah laughed and relented. 'You're quite right. Marriage isn't the end of a career. In fact it might even give you new slants on life, and, if the infants come, you'll be none the worse and a lot the wiser.'

Katrina did one of her lightning pastels of Claire standing against the sunny parapet of the penthouse roof with the south-easter blowing her long hair about her face and whipping her short silk dress against her body. It had a youthful magic about it that entranced Guy.

'You shall have it for a wedding present,' she said. 'And sometime I'll do the twin to it – you in shorts and a T-shirt.'

'It's extraordinary,' he said, 'how you capture a mood of transition. You did it with the Judge too. You caught a feeling – the shift-over from shock to living again – to being himself, but tempered. Fined down.'

'And this?' she asked with a smile. 'What do you see in this?'

'The future,' he said. 'It's looking forward.'

Helen Terblanche was frankly delighted to know of the engagement.

'It was inevitable,' she said. 'I can't think why you didn't get around to it sooner.'

Vale smiled approvingly with the new maturity that had changed her in the past month, setting her in a stronger mould.

'She's glad about us,' Claire said, as she sprawled with Guy beside the pool at Silverglade, the grass rough and cool against her bare limbs.

'As much as she can be actively glad about anything,' he said.
Claire glanced at him quickly.

'What do you mean? She seems so content at last.'

'If detachment is content – then, yes, she is content.'

Claire felt a sudden chill. The goose-pimples rose on her flesh.

'What a curious thing to say.'

'I have the feeling sometimes that she's been . . . de-sensitized, cauterized against emotion . . . against passion, if you like.'

She shivered in the sun.

'You frighten me. You're so terribly aware of Vale. You always have been. I could be jealous of Vale.'

He sat up and his face was full of laughter. 'Not again! I'm getting into bad habits. I say anything that comes into my mind when I'm with you. I must be more careful if you're going to be jealous.'

'Ah, no,' she begged. 'Let's have no secrets. It's worth a stab of jealousy.'

'Is it? I wonder. No doubt we'll find out. We've an awful lot to find out about each other. A lifetime of studying and learning.'

'You do study people,' she said thoughtfully. 'I've seen you study Vale. And Daddy. Even Micky.'

'And you. Most of all, you.'

'Sometimes I think you know me better than I know myself.'

It was good to be loved, to be studied and considered, to rest passive under the tender microscope and know oneself understood. Her own love was of another order. Intuitive, spontaneous, possessive, nothing analytical in its essence, but equally confident. With Guy she felt happy and safe. That other love – that early desire for Jef Broome – had been a flame in the wind, undirected and dangerous. Destructively painful.

She put out her hand and touched Guy as he lay on his face beside her, exploring the sun-warmed skin of his muscular back, stroking his shoulders and the cleft between them, her fingers running softly down his spine and over his flanks. In a flash he turned and she was in his arms, and then he had tossed her into the pool and followed her as she spluttered and laughed with her wet hair streaming across her eyes and cheeks.

'You wait!' he threatened, his arm about her. 'Just you wait, my little beauty! Touch by touch you sow the wind and what a whirlwind you're going to reap!'

'Don't boast,' she giggled.

They heard quick footfalls and the high voice of a child.

'Here I are! Catch me, Guy!' Micky ran to the edge of the pool and along the diving-board. He jumped into the water and Guy caught him and threw him up and caught him again, and then the wheels of an invalid-chair grated on the gravel path.

'Daddy's coming,' gasped Micky. 'I raced him and I won. Here he comes.'

Claire laughed with eager pleasure.

'That's good. The water's glorious.'

She was filled with love and happiness and gratitude that her father no longer hesitated to swim with them. Beloved Lucifer, she thought, you may well be proud of your victories. This is one of them.

The weeks that followed fled too fast for Claire. She was furiously busy. The wedding had been arranged for the end of January and she had decided to forego her Christmas holiday and take her fortnight for her honeymoon instead. Guy had managed to arrange the exchange of his one-roomed bachelor flat for a slightly larger one with the same wonderful sea view. There were curtains, crockery and linen to be bought, and Claire's trousseau to be chosen. Vale threw herself whole-heartedly into helping her stepdaughter.

'Your father's setting you up with almost everything you'll need. I can comb the shops and select samples, and you can make the final choice.'

Vale's taste was excellent and Claire was genuinely grateful for her stepmother's interest and assistance. But she said to Guy:

'I expect she'll be glad to see me settled – off her shoulders. I think she used to feel that she ought to entertain more for me, if you know what I mean.'

'But in the circumstances it hasn't been easy, what with Freya on the way and your father knocked out for such a long time – to say nothing of you being in a full-time job. You're rather hypercritical where Vale is concerned.'

'I know,' Claire conceded, with a touch of remorse.

The wedding was to be very simple.

'You can take your pick,' the Judge had said. 'A fashionable wedding with all the frills, or a quiet one and you can put the cash I would have had to spend on a big do in your pockets.'

There wasn't any choice as far as Claire was concerned.

'It's my day and I want no fuss. Just ourselves and Aunt Helen, and Guy's father and mother and sister must come down from Natal. I'd like Judge Erasmus, Abel Katz and their families, the Duponts and Sarah and Katrina. Kate Dupont can be my flower-girl and Micky can be my train-bearer. I don't want any other attendants.'

They were having tea by the stoep at Silverglade at the time. It was a Sunday afternoon but suddenly, as she spoke, Claire saw her father glance at Vale with a questioning look. In an instant a flash of mental telepathy told her what was in his mind. She turned quickly to Vale.

'Oh, and Vale, of course if you think your mother and John would come down from Johannesburg to our wedding it would be wonderful.'

'We can put up your mother and John easily,' said the Judge with evident relief. 'It would be nice to have them.'

Vale nodded without much enthusiasm. She preferred her family at a distance. They won't come, thought Claire hopefully.

But Claire turned out to be wrong. John Rorke wrote that he would take his leave at the end of January specially to be at the wedding, and Vale's mother, lured by the chance of driving down to the Cape with her son and of seeing her new granddaughter, Freya, decided to break out of her psychosis and visit her daughter. Maria, the Greek girl, found, oddly enough, that she could stay with friends at Hout Bay at the same time. In fact, it would all fit in very well, they said. Claire was so happy that it didn't seem to matter. Mrs Rorke and John were Vale's responsibility.

But Vale was obscurely troubled. John was a stormy petrel. She was even a little afraid of him. She had the curious notion sometimes that her brother possessed a vicious streak, that he played on the side of evil. But surely now she was beyond harm? She was in a strange passive state of mental, physical and emotional quiescence. Her home and her children absorbed her, the improvement in her husband's health gratified her, and he seemed to have become more resigned to his fate. She wanted nothing to disturb this atmosphere of calm. Yet, when she visualized her brother, she was reminded of tempests better forgotten, and the smooth surface of her unnatural placidity was ruffled as if by the first breath of a storm-wind feathering the glassy waters of a quiet cove.

On Christmas Eve Fedora was to sing in the choir of the Nativity Play in the Anglican Church at Guguletu. She had asked permission for the evening off and Angela had volunteered to take her place. But Micky begged to be allowed to go to the sacred play.

'Fedora says there'll be angels singing, and the Three Kings, and the shepherds watching their flocks by night, and Joseph and Mary and Jesus and the Star. I want to go. Please, please Mummy, take me!'

So Vale and Claire and Guy agreed to take him. To Vale that evening had an unforgettable enchantment, a naïve innocence that could never be recaptured.

The Xhosa vicar had obtained a permit for them and Guy drove them to the Bantu township in the Mini. The night was quiet as Christmas Eve should be, and the white dunes of the Cape Flats were silvered by starlight. But for the midsummer heat of the evening, they might have been drifts of snow on the desert of the Holy Land. Among them the scattered lights of the small boxlike houses of Guguletu winked yellow eyes at the dazzling Milky Way, and the Southern Cross hung low, the Cross of Jesus with one arm awry, throbbing in the blue-black velvet of the African sky.

The austere Anglican Church in its sandy setting was already packed but seats in the front pew had been kept for the Hammond party.

The vicar and his wife and Fedora greeted them as Guy parked his car outside the simple vicarage with a patch of garden where shrubs and flowers bloomed in the surrounding wilderness. Guguletu, which housed over 45,000 Bantu, lacked the established air of the older and larger townships of Langa and Nyanga, and the settlement round the church still had the feel of an oasis in the sandy waste.

'My wife leads the choir,' said the vicar, when he had made them welcome with the natural good manners and dignity of his people.

'And my brother is the curate. It is he who is responsible for the Nativity Play.'

His voice had depth and warmth and Vale could imagine him preaching a stirring sermon. She recalled Charles telling her of the voices that had impressed him so deeply in hospital when he had listened to the early morning programmes on the Bantu Radio.

The vicar led them to their places. The choir was grouped to the side nearest them. The crib was on the left of the altar steps with Joseph, Mary and the Holy Child already in position, and the shepherds watched their flocks on the right. Just above the steps were two rickety tables with boxes on them and the stage-managing curate helped two juvenile angels to ascend these perilous contrivances until they stood on the shaky summit visible to the entire congregation, which stirred and murmured in delighted approval. There the angels remained throughout the performance, their white wings illumined by electric bulbs that Vale feared would either cook their shoulder-blades or scorch their butter-muslin tunics. But they were stoical angels prepared to endure their martyrdom, not in silence, but in most glorious song. There was no organ and none was needed. The two young soloists filled the church with carolling so pure that Vale felt the tears sting her eyes. The adult choir also sang their carols and hymns unaccompanied, and the solemn beauty and vibrant flexibility of their voices poured forth in a range of notes of incomparable truth and quality. Guy murmured to Vale:

'I've heard the Vienna Boys Choir and the International Eisteddfod choirs competing at Llangollen in Wales but never have I heard anything better than this!'

There was a stir when the Star of Bethlehem, bobbing on a wire suspended between the back of the church and the altar, moved gradually – if a trifle jerkily – down the aisle ahead of the Three Wise Men and the shepherds who had abandoned their flocks to slip round and join the little procession.

Vale noticed a number of children clustered at the side unable to see the followers of the Star and she beckoned them to come up in front. They responded eagerly, smiling at Micky with great white grins in their lively black faces. At this point the actors all converged at the top of the steps between the two angels on their dizzy heights and the play was performed with the peculiar charm of children who were born singers and actors. Claire whispered to Guy:

'Look, the Blessed Babe is a white baby doll. Why white?'

'Borrowed, I expect,' he whispered back.

It was strangely out of place – the white waxen pallor of the Infant Jesu among the dark intent faces of Joseph and Mary, the Kings of the East and the little shepherds. The children at the feet of the Hammond party milled and exclaimed and enjoyed themselves hugely, and when the congregation joined in the Christmas carols they opened their mouths wide and sang with lusty glee.

Vale thought how alive they were – how different from a white congregation, not meek and dutiful but entering into the occasion with heart and soul and might and main. The spirit of peace and goodwill that prevailed seemed more positive and powerful here among the poor and underprivileged, who gave so much of themselves to this worship that expressed itself largely in song. Song was their medium. They are a gay and singing people, she thought, capable of fantastic merriment and joy and of melancholy and resignation far beyond our comprehension. Suddenly she found herself wishing that Jef could be here – Jef, who felt so strongly about the frustrations of the South African Bantu. If only he could see them now, happy and at peace. Yet he might well remind her that many in church that evening had relations who were political prisoners.

The thought of Jef was with her when the little procession had filed back along the aisle and out of the church, when the Angels had been helped down from their precarious perches and their lights switched out, when the congregation had gone into the night, laughing and talking, well satisfied with their sacred entertainment, with the carols and hymns of praise that had shaken the rafters of this church that was also their club and their meeting-place. If only Jef could have been here tonight.

They thanked the vicar and congratulated his wife and Fedora and the young curate on their part in the performance, and then they drove home under the summer stars from the black township on the Cape Flats to Silverglade on the high slopes with the world at its feet. As they parked the car Guy said:

'There it is, Guguletu – away down there among the sand-dunes under the same crooked Southern Cross that shines over us.'

'Tonight there is peace and goodwill – here and there,' said Vale. 'Come, Micky, my boy, it's long past your bedtime.'

But Micky rubbed sleepy eyes, determined to stay awake. Christmas Eve was a special night, a night of wonder, too thrilling for bed. There was a big tree in the hall – a young pine the gardener had brought in only this morning. It glittered with shining decorations, with snow and frosty tinsel, with gaudy geegaws, and Claire had poised a fairy with a magic wand on the very top. During the night Father Christmas would come and hang presents in the branches and stack them all round it.

Micky trotted into the hall eager to turn on the fairy lights, but his father was there already in his wheel-chair to welcome them and the circuit of many coloured lights was glowing among the branches, gleaming on baubles of gold and silver, ruby, emerald, sapphire and amethyst.

When at last the little boy had been swept upstairs by Angela, the others began to hang up the presents in their gay wrappings. There was something for everybody, including the absent families of Josiah and Harmonia. Helen Terblanche, Sarah and Katrina were coming to spend Christmas Day at

Silverglade. After the midday feast everybody would rest and relax and amuse themselves as they pleased. Later on friends of Micky's would come to play with him, and the Judge, who had recently had a miniature bowling green laid, looked forward to a contest with Helen, Sarah and Katrina in the cool of the evening. There was tennis or swimming for anyone who felt inclined.

Vale reached up to hang Micky's present from his father on the tree. A little bow and a quiver full of arrows.

'He'll be in raptures,' she said. 'His own bow! He's mad on archery.'

'And a Robin Hood costume from me,' said Claire.

Hammond watched his wife and daughter, amused and charmed. They were like children themselves.

'Pity you can't hang my car on the tree,' he said. 'But it won't be delivered till the end of January. Infuriating.'

'Never mind,' said Claire. 'You can take your pick of drivers in the meantime. We fight for the honour.'

'Fair enough. But, oh, for the joy of a modicum of independence! Is there anything more precious in the whole wide world?'

Claire ran to him and laid her cheek against his.

'You're wonderful, Daddy. There's nothing you can manage for yourself that you allow any of us to do for you. You work yourself too hard.'

Vale stood with a golden parcel in her hand and her soft dark gaze on her husband. She said:

'I can't think of any father who does more with his son than you do. Micky's only a little boy – just turned five – and already you've taught him to swim, to play table-tennis and quoits, and now you'll teach him archery. Next it'll be bowls. He counts on you and he adores you.'

'That's quite a speech, my love,' said Hammond. 'Bless your heart. But I did better for his sister. I taught Claire to play a useful game of tennis and to ride and to ski. Micky'll have to find some other teacher for those things.'

Vale turned away abruptly, her eyes bright with unshed tears.

'I must go up to Micky and kiss him good night. I'll give him a big bear-hug from you.'

'I'll come with you,' said Claire.

On the landing she touched Vale's arm.

'Poor Daddy. It's hard for both of you,' she said. 'No one could do more than you, Vale.'

Vale looked down at her stepdaughter from her greater height. She was smiling.

'We were great friends once, Claire – before I married your father. Let's be friends again. Real friends.'

'Let's,' said Claire.

It seemed to her that loving Guy brought everyone into the orbit of her goodwill. She was glad she and Guy were spending tonight at Silverglade. She followed Vale into Micky's room and felt the child's arms about her neck and his warm silky hair against her cheek.

'Angels watch you,' she said.

'Black angels with lights in their wings,' he murmured sleepily.

'Sure. Black angels, darling, and the Three Kings and the Shepherds and Mary and Joseph and Gentle Jesus.'

'And Father Christmas too?'

'And Father Christmas too.'

Vale opened the curtains and the scented summer night flowed into the room.

'I must peep at Freya,' she said, hugging Micky and tucking him in. 'I must kiss your little sister too.'

Contentment held her in its spell – a strange false sense of security that had been with her ever since she had made her decision to give up Jef and remain with Charles in his time of need.

18

ONE ROAD ENDS

CLAIRE AND GUY WERE MARRIED IN ST SAVIOUR'S Church, Claremont, at eleven o'clock on a Saturday morning. The flowers, provided and arranged by Sarah and Katrina, were beautiful and the guests were few, only those they really wanted. Claire was sorry that Josiah and Harmonia could not be at the service. She had known them all her life and they were part of her family, but they were needed at Silverglade to prepare the wedding buffet luncheon which was served under the trees in the garden.

The day was hot and languid and the champagne cold and sparkling. Judge Anton Erasmus made an amusing speech, proposing the health of the bride and bridegroom, and he had the grace to water down his robust humour, much to Guy's relief. Claire, in a fever of nervousness for Guy, relaxed when she realized that her barrister husband was quite capable of replying to the Judge-President's quips, and his thanks to her father and stepmother had a simple and touching sincerity that came straight from the heart. Abel Katz rose to the occasion and his sturdy feet to toast the parents of the young couple and Hammond replied with his usual easy charm. Guy thought that he had never seen a more lovely and appealing bride than the fair girl who stood beside him in her ivory angel-skin gown with a froth of tulle cascading over her shoulders. Micky took his page-boy duties with astonishing solemnity and refused any assistance from Kate Dupont. Once she tried to adjust Claire's train, but he threw her a sizzling glance, hissed like an angry goose and immediately rearranged it. After that she minded her own business and contented herself with nursing the bride's bouquet and her own, to the manner born. Her mother was proud of her.

Mrs Rorke was in a beaming mood, her blood-pressure forgotten. She approved of her son's Greek girl friend, Maria; her daughter had a beautiful house, her son-in-law was the most considerate of hosts, and her grandchildren were angelic. She must certainly repeat a holiday at the Cape.

At last, in the heat of the afternoon, the young couple were on their way to the Wilderness with an old satin slipper tied on to the Mini's rear bumper. They reckoned to reach their destination in time for dinner in their suite.

'Well, that's that,' said Guy when he had removed the give-away slipper. 'Now we're really on our way.'

'I'm sorry your sister couldn't come down for the wedding,' said Claire.

'Too bad. The infant's imminent. You charmed Dad and Mum. I could tell at once. I knew Dad would fall for you, but my old lady is inclined to be critical.'

'She didn't seem so. She was absolutely sweet.'

'Everything went like a dream, didn't it? Even the speeches.'

'Yours was marvellous.'

He laughed. 'I could feel you beside me, all of a twitch.'

'Not for long – not once you got going.'

The mountain passes lay behind them and the great wheat-growing uplands spread eastwards. By the time they reached the Indian Ocean coast at Mossel Bay the sun was low. The seals had slithered off their sun-baked rocks and the long white beaches and jungly sub-tropical cliffs were tinged with rose. The Outeniqua mountains raised their wooded heads steeply against the sky and the leafy town of George with its gardens and broad oak-lined avenues came and went in the sunset.

It was dusk when they entered the river gorge down to the coast. The golden river surged over its rocky bed between high precipitous banks clothed in dense vegetation and at last they emerged from the green canyon to a viewpoint of incomparable majesty. The Indian Ocean and its white beaches spread at their feet in the dusk, vast and lonely beneath the jungle forests and bush of the Wilderness. Their sitting-room in the hotel was gay with roses and a table had been set for two. They had their own cocktail cabinet, adequately equipped, and the gilded neck of a bottle of French champagne protruded from an ice-bucket.

'Shall we say dinner in half an hour?' said Guy. 'I'm famished.'

'So am I.'

Their suitcases had been put in the bedroom. Soon her things would be hanging in the built-in cupboard beside his. Suddenly she was nervous, even a little afraid. There was no going back any more. Here and now she had come to the end of her girlhood. As she stood uncertainly looking round the pretty room, wondering where to begin unpacking, she heard Guy's voice behind her.

'Do you realize we're alone at last – my wife and I?'

She swung round and into his arms and as he held her to him it no longer mattered that childhood and girlhood had receded into the past. She was a woman now, she was Guy's wife, and the road ahead was the only one she cared to travel.

The scents of the garden and mown grass came in through the open window and mingled with that of the roses. Crickets shrilled in the summer night and the sea purred under the stars. The lips of her lover were the lips of her husband.

'This is my happy day,' she said. 'The happiest day of my whole life.'

At Silverglade Vale was putting the last touches to her face and hair. She wondered what the party would be like. John had, as usual, been very casual in flinging out the invitation. It was after lunch just before Claire and Guy went upstairs to change.

'This is a great day. You can't just go to bed early. Maria's friends, Jason and Penelope Euclides' – he pronounced it in the Greek way, Efkleethees – 'want you to dine with us over at Hout Bay. There's that sea-front place where you get the most delicious sea-food and you can dance there on Saturday nights. They have a friend staying at the Vineyard – don't ask me who he is, he's just turned up from somewhere or another – and it's slap on his way to call in for you. Will Charles spare you?'

'I wouldn't dream of asking him.'

'Why not?'

'How could I leave him – and mother – on Claire's wedding night?'

'Mother'll have supper in bed, if I know her,' John had said. 'She'll be exhausted by this evening.'

Charles had heard him, and cut in.

'That goes for me too. If you want to go out tonight, Vale, you have my blessing.'

She had turned to him with a warm tender smile.

'You're too unselfish, darling.'

'On the contrary. I still tire easily and don't mind admitting it.'

She had met her brother's provocative, almost pleading gaze and suddenly her own eyes were young and eager as a schoolgirl's.

'Square it with Mother, John, and I'll come to your friend's party.' She laughed. 'Perhaps I should learn to know Maria better too.'

'You certainly should! I'll have a word with Mum and then I'll phone Jason Euclides.'

'Do, and tell him to arrange for Mr X to call for me.'

'That's fine. Say eight o'clock. We'll be a six to dine and dance. A good number.'

To dance again! After the long tragedy of Charles and the birth of Freya it was a ridiculously exciting prospect. Suddenly she'd felt young again – in the mood for a party. All that champagne, no doubt. It was ages since she'd been out anywhere.

Now she stood in front of the mirror in a long white evening dress, and what she saw gave her confidence. Her olive skin glowed with its summer tan in apricot contrast to her low-cut gown. Her hair had its own dark springing life and her eyes were limpid.

She went in to her mother's room. Mrs Rorke had retired to bed with relief after the delicious rigours of the day. Her eyes widened as her daughter appeared.

'You look like one of those Greek figures on my Wedgwood urn.'

'My host and hostess tonight are Greek, so is John's girlfriend. I thought I'd pay them the compliment of wearing this dress.'

'It's lovely. Simple and classical. Who is to be your partner?'

Vale smiled. 'I've no idea. As usual John wasn't specific. He just mentioned that this man was a friend of his girlfriend's friends. A blind date.'

'Well, don't get into mischief.'

'What dull advice!'

'It wouldn't be the first time,' said Mrs Rorke, shrewdly. She had a sudden and distinct recollection of Vale's suitcases, of labels for America, of the horrible realization that her daughter had intended to take an irrevocable step -- to abandon Charles, and, in so doing, to abandon her as well.

'Darling,' said Vale, smoothly. 'I don't know what you're talking about. Sleep well. I must leave you now and finish my rounds – Freya and Micky and Charles. Good night and happy dreams.'

'If my heartburn gives me a chance. Really, dear, champagne doesn't agree with me. Pass me my bicarb tablets before you go, will you? And enjoy yourself. Oh, and give me my patience cards, will you?'

Vale left her mother and peeped in at the sleeping Freya, and went on to Micky's room. He was still awake but only just. Light streamed into the room from the landing.

'That makes four,' he said, as she came to his bedside. 'One, two, three, four.' He counted drowsily on his chubby fingers.

'Four what, honey?'

'Four angels. Two black ones with wings and two white ones – Claire and Mummy.'

She hugged him gently. He had never forgotten the black angels at Guguletu. They watched over him every night.

'Happy dreams,' she said, as she had said to her mother. 'God bless you, my little Micky.'

She went slowly downstairs. The scent of flowers was overpowering. She had arranged bowls everywhere for the wedding and more had been sent. Only the library was austere, except for one small vase of roses. More than that Charles would not tolerate in his room.

He was sitting in his wing-chair when she went in, reading a book.

'Have you had your supper?' she asked.

He pushed his spectacles up on to his forehead and looked at her.

'Not yet. I told Josiah to bring my tray when you'd gone.'

He removed the spectacles and slipped them into their case and into his pocket. His eyes took in every detail of her appearance, from the soft short dark hair to the open gold sandals. She wore gold jewellery that might have come from the Mycenae tomb of Clytemnaestra, and the bands of gold braid that crossed her high bodice separated and accentuated her full breasts. Her eyes glistened and her lips were moist and enticing.

'You're very beautiful tonight – very, very feminine. A drink?'

'No, Charles. I've had plenty already and there'll be more to follow. Do you want to meet this blind date of mine? He should be here any time now.'

'No. I told Josiah to show him into the sitting-room. I've had enough people for one day.'

As he spoke he wondered if he were being a fool and a dupe. She was enough to tempt any man tonight. What man? Whoever he might be, Hammond didn't want Vale's 'blind date' to see her husband – a cripple exhausted by a long day. Vale accepted his excuse. She knew that too many people at one time tired him more than physical exertion.

'Can I pour something for you?' she asked. 'Whisky or brandy? Or why not have some more champagne?'

'Not now.'

Suddenly he did what she had dreaded. He leaned forward and drew her towards him. Don't, she thought, please, Charles, don't. But he raised his hands and straightened his upper body so that he could cup her breasts in his palms. He trembled violently as his hands stroked her body and followed the tapering curves very gently down over her flanks. She saw – as she knew she would – his face contorted with rapture and anguish, and she said:

'Why do you torment yourself – and me?'

But she stood passive and immobile, feeling his touch like a painful electric current, fearsome, exciting and yet repellent. He said huskily:

'I need this. When you've gone I shall remember . . . there'll be comfort in remembering.' She had turned very pale but he did not notice. His eyes were closed.

The doorbell rang and she moved away in relief, released from a tension she had come to hate.

'That's Mr X,' she said lightly. 'I must leave you, Charles. Dear Charles. It's been a good day. Your Claire made a very lovely bride.'

'It's you who look like a bride tonight – you in your white Grecian dress. Artemis – Goddess of the Moon, Artemis the huntress.' He smiled wrily. 'Would you like to borrow my bow and arrows? They're lethal weapons.'

She laughed and bent to kiss him.

'Not tonight. I have no quarry in view. Good night, my darling. Don't be late.'

'And you? You'll come in with the milk?'

'Who knows? Whatever happens, I'll try not to disturb you.'

They could hear Angela show the visitor into the sitting-room. Josiah was evidently preparing his master's tray. Angela came to the library door.

'The gentleman is waiting, Madam.'

'I'm just coming. Tell Josiah Master is ready for his supper.' She brushed the grey head with her lips.

''Bye for now, darling.'

'Be good!' he called after her.

That's the second time, she thought, and smiled. I must look better than I think.

There was no one in the sitting-room when she went into it. Only that overpowering scent of flowers like a presence. Almost funereal. Her blind date must have wandered on to the stoep to get away from it. But when she went out she found that he had gone farther. He had gone right down into the garden and was standing at a point on the lawn overlooking the Constantia Valley. She could see the gleam of his white tropical dinner jacket and his rather slight back. Suddenly she wondered what he'd be like when he turned round – this friend of John's girl-friend's friends. Absurd remote acquaintanceship.

'It's lovely, isn't it? Our valley,' she called softly, and with a certain pride. She saw him start.

The man in the white dinner jacket swung round as if her voice had stung him. He stood quite still and watched her come across the grass towards him, moving with fluid grace, a white wraith in a diaphanous dress. He saw the dark head on the slender neck, the full bosom and the rhythm of the long graceful legs, so well remembered. As she drew near, she repeated: 'It's lovely, isn't it?'

'Unbearably lovely,' he said, and put out his hands to take hers.

She drew in her breath with a deep broken sigh. 'Oh, no . . . not you, not you! What can I do?'

But her slender hands were in his, her high narrow heels were cushioned in the grass. She leaned away from him. Their eyes were almost on a level. He gazed at her as if he could never look his fill.

'Honey love . . . Vale, my love.'

She did not answer. She swayed a little and closed her eyes, and he knew that behind those closed lids she was weeping bitterly. Her face was as still as death, but her breasts, that had nourished his child, were swollen and shaking with emotion, her body was melting with the warmth of her inward crying, and she would have fallen if he had not drawn her to him and held her tight.

'No,' she said at last. 'Not you, Jef, please God, don't let it be you.'

But his hands, his mouth and his hard male body against hers left her in no doubt of his hunger for her – the hunger that never failed to rouse her own – and she knew that there was no escape. No escape ever.

The Saturday evening paper was always delivered late, nearer 9 p.m. than the weekday six o'clock, and Hammond was already in bed when Josiah took it to him with a broad grin. He had been unable to resist combing through it for a photograph of the wedding and he had not been disappointed. There it was on page two, a charming picture of the bride and bridegroom leaving the church attended by Kate, the flower-girl, and Micky, the page. The photographer had caught the very human moment in which Micky, the sun in his bright curls, had scowled thunderously at Kate for interfering with the bride's train. 'Hands off!'' read the caption.

'Miss Claire is in the paper,' said Josiah, with pride. 'And Master Micky too.'

The Judge turned to the page in question and shared a hearty laugh with Josiah at Micky's expression. Claire looked smiling and happy and her husband pleased with his bride and himself.

'Miss Claire was very sorry you couldn't be at the church today,' said the Judge.

'So was I,' said Josiah. 'But there were many things to do here.'

'You all helped to make a great success of the wedding,' said the Judge. 'Everything went just right. There's no need for anyone to wait up for Madam tonight. She has her key and she may be late. By the way, did the paper-boy bring the extra copies we ordered?'

'Yes, Master. Angela has taken one to Madam's mammy, upstairs.'

'Good. And leave one on Madam's bed.'

When Josiah had left the room Hammond settled down to enjoy the rest of his Saturday evening *Argus*. First he would read the news, then he'd concentrate on the Sporting Section and lastly the Magazine Supplement. As he refolded the paper the interview jumped at him from the front page.

U.S. JOURNALIST RETURNS

'I am going to write a South African novel,' said Jefferson Broome when I interviewed him at a Claremont hotel this morning. 'It will have a colour bar theme and the setting will be the Cape.'

Jefferson Broome's controversial articles on South Africa have been appearing in American magazines during the past few months. One in *Life* described South Africa as a 'police state' and one in *Time* highlighted the personalities of a number of Europeans and non-Europeans banned for political reasons.

'I don't intend to pull my punches,' declared Mr Broome, who is noted as a writer who packs a hefty punch. He will spend some months at the Cape before moving on to South West Africa. His unfavourable comments on the Republic after his last visit less than a year ago have received wide publicity in the world press.

'I reflect the truth as I see it,' said Mr Broome. We hope that he will discard his blinkers on this visit and take a look at some of the good that is being done for our non-Europeans, so that the truth he reflects will be more evenly balanced and fairly presented.

Jefferson Broome? Yes, Hammond remembered the young journalist only too well – the writer of controversial material, the writer of a love-letter to Vale which he, her husband, had never seen.

He closed his eyes and the night of the letter came into sharp clear focus – Claire's defiant flinging down of the gauntlet in the form of the long foreign envelope, his realization that Silverglade could no longer hold his wife and daughter. It had been a hot night on the stoep, with a fire on the mountainside, and afterwards he had gone upstairs and given his wife the chance to show him the letter. She had offered it to him with large frightened eyes and he had torn it unread rather than learn something that might sadden and anger him. Then he had made love to her and she had given herself – all of herself – as never before. Had she been giving herself to him or to Jef Broome that night in the summer darkness?

Fear and suspicion laid hands on his paralysed body and it seemed to him that his deadened entrails twisted in agony and rose up into his diaphragm, squeezing his heart with a sickening pressure that filled his entire chest, tightened his throat and made his head whirl. He broke into an icy sweat and felt that he might faint. He rang the bell communicating with Josiah's room, and within minutes his Bantu friend and servant was at his side, still buttoning his tunic, his reddened eyes wide with concern. He had been drinking young Missie's health with Harmonia.

'Master is ill?'

The Judge forced a grimace intended to be a reassuring smile as the sweat poured down his ashen face.

'Brandy,' he muttered.

Josiah fetched the liqueur brandy and poured a generous tot. He held it to his Master's lips and saw with relief the stimulant take effect.

The colour came back into the Judge's face as Josiah soaked a handkerchief in cologne and dabbed his Master's forehead as gently as any woman might have done.

'That's better,' sighed the Judge.

'Master has done too much today. Too many people, too much talk. Tonight I bring my blanket and sleep outside Master's room.'

'Nonsense. You'll do no such thing. Go back to your room – and Harmonia. But leave the brandy here.'

Josiah turned a darker shade of chocolate. His Master had the seeing eye. But he said quietly:

'If Master want anything I hear the bell and come.'

'I know,' said Hammond. 'Now go about your business. I am well again.' Yes, he thought, as the door closed softly behind Josiah. I am well but my spirit is very sick.

The moment he had read the interview he had guessed the identity of Vale's 'blind date – Mr X'. Had she known? Or had Jef exploded like a time bomb into her life – her vulnerable, empty, emotional life? So, after all, she was not Artemis, the Huntress, tonight. She was the doe, the soft-eyed victim, and Jef was the hunter. Hammond never doubted that it was Jef. He found himself shaken by a burning primitive instinct to order Josiah to fetch his bow and arrows, and then to await his wife's return. He could sit in his chair and be ready for them. As Jef crossed the threshold of Silverglade he would fall with an arrow quivering in his heart. Everything in the room was red and swimming. He felt as if vessels were bursting in his eyes. His head and heart pounded. He reached for the brandy and poured a strong tot. He tossed it back, searing his throat. He covered his eyes with his hands. This way madness lay. If he allowed jealousy to be his master he would torment himself and her to the death.

'Let her go on being my blind spot!' he prayed aloud. 'Only that way can I live.'

19

ANOTHER BEGINS

JEF HAD HIRED A SELF-DRIVE CAR.

'It's only till Monday,' he said. 'Then I'm going to buy a car. I've taken a flat in Protea Road from next week. It's quite near the Vineyard – no great distance from you. I'll be at the Cape several months.'

'Why didn't you let me know you were coming?' Vale asked.

'You'd have tried to stop me. Your letter was final. No compromise. When I wrote to you, you never even answered.'

'Then why, why, *why* did you come?'

'I had to see you . . . and Freya.'

'Freya?'

'Is she mine, Vale?'

'How can I swear to that, one way or the other? She's a baby – a blob. Little chubby features, indigo eyes, fair curls.'

'I'll know,' he said obstinately, his jaw out-thrust. 'I'll know the moment I set eyes on her.'

She made an irritable gesture. 'How absurd. Babies have no features. Likenesses are imagined at a few months old. Freya could be me at the same age – or Charles. Or, for that matter, I suppose she could be considered like you. She's still just herself, a cuddly little baby.'

A gold tissue stole covered her shoulders and she sat as far from him as possible, achingly aware of him, and of the beginning of a thaw within herself, the first excruciating twinges of a return to feeling and sensitivity after a long frozen period of almost total numbness. She remembered that it had never been easy to get her own way with Jef. He was headstrong and immovable, always sure what he meant to do and determined to do it. What did he intend now? As if in answer to her unspoken question he said:

'Everything depends on Freya. If I am satisfied that she is mine I shall take you and her away.'

'We've had that out already,' she said wearily. 'Forget it.'

They were coming down into Hout Bay. He turned the car towards the mountainside and took the steep rough track in bottom gear.

'We've plenty of time for argument,' he said. 'Here we are. Do you know the Euclides?'

'No. They're John's friends, or rather Maria's. They're strangers to me.'

'You'll like them. I met them first when they lived in Johannesburg before Jason was transferred to the Cape.'

Jason and Penelope Euclides were an attractive couple, sophisticated and cosmopolitan. Jason represented an Oil Company and Penelope, who had been a ballet dancer, gave dancing lessons to a select class of talented children.

Jason had run lightly down the steps to meet his guests and Vale took to him at once.

'We are having drinks out on the terrace. It's such a gorgeous night.'

'Perfect,' she agreed. 'It was the ideal day for my step-daughter's wedding.'

Jason laughed.

'Your stepdaughter! Incredible. But John told us all about it.'

She smiled at her brother, who was waiting on the terrace at the top of the steps with Penelope Euclides and Maria. But John knew that smile – sweet and false as poisoned honey. He gave her a long ironic look, the stare of a sagacious satyr, triumphant and mocking, and she turned her head away from him in fury. Why had he confronted her with Jef out of the blue when he must have known perfectly well who her escort was to be? It was characteristic – maliciously taking her unawares, and handing her back her lover without a care or twinge of conscience. Impaling the moth alive, watching it flutter on the long pin. Was she the moth? Was Charles? It didn't matter to John.

Jason Euclides had a formidable array of alcoholic drinks set out on a table in the corner of the terrace overlooking the bay.

'You state it, I have it,' he said to Vale, his laughing black eyes glinting with admiration.

'I've been drinking champagne all day,' she said. 'What do you suggest?'

'More champagne. Or perhaps you'd rather have a sidecar?' Suddenly she felt reckless – young and carefree.

'Make it a sidecar.'

'And you, Jef?'

'The same.'

Jason mixed the cocktail in a glass jug and stirred it with an engraved silver spoon with a long pearl handle.

'It's a Turkish salad-spoon,' Penelope explained, seeing Vale's eyes on the decorative spoon. 'My parents are in Athens but they lived in Istanbul for years. They collected some interesting things there. Turkish rugs, icons, chaplets and even jewels. Some wonderful things were brought into Constantinople by the White Russians after the First World War and sold for a song in the Bazaars.'

She picked up a chaplet of amber beads lying on a table near the french doors and handed them to Vale.

'Feel these – the warmth. That's how you know they're real amber, that and the slight dusty deposit where they're threaded. The Turks use these chaplets like an abacus for counting, or they just run the beads through their fingers as a woman plays with her pearls. I have quite a collection – amber, jade, ivory, shagreen. I'll show you some time.'

The dark profile of the Sentinel rose sharp and sheer from the bay and the lights in the lobster-boats bobbed on the water beneath the jagged cliffs and peaks. Stars burned their tiny holes of white fire in the purple summer sky and music throbbed in the night as Penelope put on one of her long-playing records.

They went on later to dine and dance at a nightclub on Chapman's Peak and Jason ordered Moules Marinières and Lobster Thermidor.

Jef asked his hostess to dance, Jason put his hand on Maria's bare brown arm, and Vale found herself being led on to the floor by her brother.

'I'll never forgive you,' she said, under cover of the music.

'Maybe not,' he grinned. 'One day you'll thank me.'

'You're evil,' she said. 'All your life you've played with fire and pulled wings off flies. Nothing matters to you.'

'I had nothing to do with this,' he protested. 'It was fate.'

'You could have given me the red light – instead of letting me meet Jef without dreaming he was in the country.'

'You'd have refused to come.'

'Exactly.'

'What are you so scared of? A little flutter never did a girl much harm.'

'It depends what you call a flutter. Are you having a flutter with Maria?'

'I'm in love with Maria. This is the real thing. I hope to persuade her to marry me.'

'You'll be lucky if you do. She's too good for you.'

'Who isn't – according to you?'

'You're a bad lot. But maybe Maria will reform you. There's room for it.'

'Who's talking?'

She laughed. Her brother was impervious to rebuke.

Jason danced with her next. He danced superbly and she realized that it was a long time since she had been to a party and enjoyed herself like any other young woman. Then she was in Jef's arms and they were dancing together as if they were one person. It was not that he held her tightly, nor that his cheek touched hers. It was simply that every movement and impulse was one. She did not need to follow him because she was part of him.

It was long after midnight when he took her home.

'Where do we stop?' he asked.

'What do you mean?'

'I'm not going to make love to you in the car. Not after all this long time.'

'There's a glade,' she said, rather breathlessly. 'I've often taken Micky there for picnics. It's a very secret sort of place.'

'That'll do.'

It was off the road and in the woods – a grass clearing open to the stars. They left the car.

'Your lovely dress. I don't want to spoil it. Did anyone tell you you looked like a Greek goddess tonight?'

She did not answer and he turned her gently in his arms. She felt his hand on the zip fastener of her dress and heard the faint metallic sound of the tiny teeth disengaging as it gaped and slipped from her shoulders taking her bra with it. She remembered the Transvaal meadow and the Spring Idyll and she knew that Jef would have his way. Her need for him was fire in her veins. Artemis, the huntress, she thought. Moon goddess, maker of spells and love potions. Charles saw her so. But Artemis herself was cold and virginal.

He was standing away from her as if he feared to touch her.

'Persephone,' he said. 'Clothed in starlight. Stay there, love.

Let me look at you. I'd almost forgotten your heart-catching beauty.'

The glade was quiet in the windless night, scented with the resin of the pine and the heavy sweet perfume of wild acacia. A pattern of leaves dappled her alabaster form as she leaned against a keurboom sapling, feeling the smooth trunk against her bare flesh, feeling its life – the sap rising like a strong pale bloodstream to nourish every branch and leaf and honey-fragrant flower. She waited to take her lover.

His clothes, lying beside hers on the ground, were a neat reminder of the conventional world so remote from their pagan glade. The grass beneath them was cool and rough and she heard him say:

'I'll never let you go again. Never.'

If the Voice sought them in Eden that night they heard it not. There was only the whisper of a breeze, cool as a caress, and the cry of a night bird – the forlorn lost cry of the curlew.

Mrs Dupont fussed around the Clifton sea-facing flat with mixed feelings. She was happy for the young pair returning from their honeymoon this afternoon and sad because she had lost her tenant, Claire, who had become like an elder daughter to her. However, the middle-aged widower who had taken on the flatlet was a pleasant and mild-mannered man who was just the type of person she had originally sought. Robert assured her that she would become fond of him.

'You're bound to look after him,' he'd said. 'Because basically you're the mother of all living – thwarted by my economic situation.' Robert could be quite wise sometimes. She would certainly have liked half a dozen children.

She glanced at her watch. Just on noon and the young ones would be back about three this afternoon. She had arranged flowers to welcome them and left a cold supper in the fridge. A bowl of her Mulligatawny and rice soup, a cold boiled chicken and sliced ham, a mixed salad and a selection of cheeses. There'd be nothing for Claire to do except heat the soup. Mrs Dupont had brought in butter and milk, and yesterday she had shown the new char the flat and seen that it was properly cleaned and dusted and the bed made – a large double-bed of which Mrs Dupont heartily approved. It was her experience that most married quarrels could be made up in a comfortable double-bed, though a good deal of nagging could go on in it too, if you weren't careful. That was something to guard against. But, by and large, the pros outweighed the cons.

She left a note on the mantelpiece and stood for a moment looking at the Westhuizen pastel of Claire.

'It's the very essence of youth,' she sighed, half aloud.

Once she too had had that look in her eyes of challenging and beckoning life, of saying, 'Come on, life, I love you!' But she had never had that girlish figure. She'd been plump ever since she could remember, dimpled and cosy, merry, friendly and easy-going, but in her young days nobody had cared about diet, and the right vital statistics hadn't been a fetish. You ate what you liked and if you were the lean kind you stayed that way and if you were not, you got plump. You went along with your nature. Nowadays it was a disaster to go into a shop and run your hand along the rack of forty-fours instead of the thirty-eights. And no wonder. The manufacturers of dresses didn't care tuppence what went into the forty-four racks. That was the dowdy stuff for the over-weight matrons. Oh, well, not to worry. She was as she was and she knew very well that her husband and her friends wouldn't change her for all the willow-wands in the Cape Peninsula.

She took a last look out of the newly-cleaned seascape window. It turned her up to watch that heaving ocean but there was no accounting for tastes. And the noise would drive her up the wall in winter when the sea came raging on to the beaches. No, she wouldn't swop her clifftop home for one of these fancy modern sea-front apartments – not for all the tea in China! But the young ones worshipped sun and sea. No going to church on Sunday mornings for the modern girls and boys, no hats and gloves and prayerbooks, only bikinis and sun-tan oil. Robert said it was a Pagan age, back to Nature. But sometimes it made her anxious for Gene and Kate, as if they had been born into the time of Sodom and Gomorrah. At such times Robert was a comfort, for he just said, 'Ma, you're crazy.' There was nothing she'd rather hear.

She went out into the noonday heat and returned the key to the janitor. Then she crossed the tarmac and plodded up the steep winding wooden steps to her own bungalow on the High Level Road.

'Mrs Dupont's been in,' said the janitor, when he helped Guy with his luggage. 'She borrowed the key – said you knew about it and everything was okay. She brought your new char in yesterday and came along this morning with some stuff for you. She's left a letter.'

'That's fine,' said Guy.

As they closed the door on the crusty old janitor Guy stood against it and put his arms out to Claire.

'I didn't carry you over the threshold.'

He lifted her and carried her into their bedroom as if she were no heavier than Micky. He dropped her on the large bed.

'Now we're home,' he said. 'Whenever we say home this is the place we'll think of.'

She jumped up and flung her arms round his neck.

'It's heaven!'

'Let's make some tea.'

In the kitchen they discovered Mrs Dupont's offerings and in the living-room they exclaimed in delight at the flowers she had arranged with skill and artistry. They read her note of welcome and felt the warmer for it.

'I'm so glad we came back on a Friday. We can organize ourselves tomorrow and spend Sunday at Silverglade,' said Claire.

After they had unpacked and had tea Claire settled herself comfortably at the telephone table to ring Mrs Dupont, Vale, Sarah and Katrina and her Aunt Helen. Mrs Dupont's number was engaged, so she rang Silverglade. Vale answered the telephone.

'How are you both?' Vale asked.

'Wonderful,' said Claire. 'We had a glorious time. Divine weather, everything perfect.'

Vale laughed. 'That's splendid. When are we going to see you?'

'We thought Sunday. Can we come for the day?'

'Why not?' But there was an almost imperceptible hesitation in the words. Claire said quickly:

'Of course if it doesn't suit you —'

'It suits us perfectly. Why shouldn't it?'

'There was something in your tone – a sort of – reservation.'

'Don't be absurd, Claire. It's just that John is bringing Maria over to lunch and we're going to play tennis in the afternoon. Bring your tennis things.'

'Who's your fourth?'

'Claire . . . don't blame me for this . . . our fourth is Jef Broome.'

'Jef Broome!'

Her gasp of dismay brought Guy to her side.

'What's up?' he whispered. She made a gesture of impatience and shook her head.

'What's Jef Broome doing here?' she asked, and saw Guy's eyebrows shoot up.

'Didn't you see the paper – the *Argus* – the one that carried your wedding picture?'

'I'm afraid we didn't read it properly. I just cut out our picture.'

'I don't suppose you were bothering with the news that week-end. Anyway, there was an interview with Jef. He's here to write a novel. He'll be at the Cape some months and John brought him to Silverglade.'

'Did you know Jef was coming to South Africa?'

'Certainly not.'

'Are you alone now? I mean can we talk freely?'

'I'm alone.'

'Why are you asking Jef to Silverglade?'

'I've told you. John brought him here and then your father invited him for Sunday. What could I do?'

'Then Daddy doesn't seem to mind?'

'On the contrary, he made Jef welcome.'

'To test himself – to test you, perhaps. Isn't this a dangerous game you're playing?'

'I'm not playing any game at all. I'm simply accepting a situation I can't avoid.'

'Can you keep it that way? Cool – as if – as if he were just an acquaintance?'

'You'd better come and see for yourself,' she answered tartly. 'Shall we expect you for lunch?'

'You'll have too many for lunch. I suggest we come in the afternoon and stay for supper. By then perhaps John and his party may have left.'

'As you like.'

'Is Daddy there?'

'Not now. He's in the garden.'

'Give him my love, Vale. See you the day after tomorrow. 'Bye for now.'

'Good-bye, Claire.'

Claire put down the receiver with a trembling hand. She turned a flushed angry face to Guy.

'Jef Broome has come back.'

20

SQUALLS

TO CLAIRE THAT SUNDAY AFTERNOON WAS SHEER nightmare. Her father seemed glad to see them and insisted on taking them for a short run in his new manually controlled car. He was obviously pleased with it and with the increased independence it offered him, yet to Claire it had a terrible finality, proving as it did, the hopelessness of his case. She tried not to show how much she hated it but when, at tea in the garden by the tennis court, Jef Broome praised it she was sickened. *He* – with his glowing health and strength – could drive any car at any speed. It was all so unfair, so unequal – this unacknowledged contest between her father and Vale's lover.

After tea John and Guy and Vale and Maria made up a four and Hammond, Mrs Rorke, Claire and Jef sat under the trees watching them. Baby Freya lay in her pram near by, cooing and playing with her bare toes. Suddenly Jef went to the pram and lifted her out and began to dandle her on his lap. She squealed with pleasure, and he laughed and lifted her up so that her little face was close against his own.

'You're a honey chile,' he said. 'I go for you in a very big way.'

'She's a pet,' said Mrs Rorke. She was about to add something when her voice faltered and faded. Then Jef was rocking Freya on his knee again and the moment of truth passed. She was just a baby – any baby – once more. But Claire stole a glance at her father's face. It was pale and stony and

she was sure that he too had observed the uncanny resem-
blance between Jef and the child, both so fair, both laughing,
blunt featured and vital. Micky scampered up from the pool
and jerked at his father's hand.

'Let's go shooting, Daddy! I want Jef to see my bow and
arrows.'

Jef stood up and dumped Freya in Mrs Rorke's lap.

'There's your granddaughter, ma'am, we're going about
men's business now. Archery.'

Hammond extracted a key from his pocket and gave it to
Micky.

'Run on ahead and get the bows from the hut.'

The little boy trotted off happily. Hammond followed
more slowly with Claire and Jef strolling beside his wheel-
chair as they made their way across the lawn to the target
area and the log hut where the bows lay on their racks and
the arrows stood in quivers like miniature golf bags. The
targets, well backed with straw and hessian, were propped
against the trunks of keurbome in a carefully cleared grove.
Katrina had used her imagination in painting Disney type
targets, the silhouettes of various animals, and on each a
bull's eye marked the fatal spot. There were buck in the act
of leaping, birds on the wing, the head of a charging elephant, ears outspread, trunk raised, and the profile of a
shambling polar bear against a black ground. The total effect
was of a glimpse of Disneyland.

'Six shots for you and six for me,' shrilled Micky, who
had already brought out the bows and the long feathered
arrows in their quivers. 'Afterwards Claire and Jef can have
a go. But me first. I want to kill that bear dead!'

The bull's eye was marked in front of the bear's shoulder.

The little boy set down his quiver and took up his stance,
the leather protecting his left forearm and his three bow
fingers. He was sunbronzed and naked, except for his tiny

bathing briefs, and his hair was pale as ripe barley. Hammond watched him with pride and joy as he took up the classic hunter's stance, bow-string drawn into a taut curve, shoulders beautifully strong and open, feet sturdily planted and one eye screwed up as he took careful aim.

'Release!' commanded Hammond, and the silent arrow flew and thudded into the target wide of the mark.

'That's a nice pattern,' said Jef as the next five arrows settled in the area of the bear's shoulder.

'I'm afraid he's only wounded his bear,' smiled Hammond. Jef walked over to the target with Micky to extract the arrows.

Claire said: 'Isn't it rather dangerous – a lethal weapon in the hands of a five year old?'

Hammond's smile had vanished. He was raising his bow, the arrow at the ready, his sights on Jef's back, the muscles rippling under the white tennis vest.

'More dangerous perhaps in the hands of a fifty year old,' he remarked grimly. 'I'd like to try my skill with a moving target.'

Claire shivered. Her father's face was strange to her – a tensed profile, lips drawn unnaturally thin, the three fingers remorselessly ready to draw back the bow-string as Jef moved towards the bear. Suddenly she leaned down and put her hand over his, feeling the leather protection and the warm firm skin. A river of hate ran through her blood. His hate or hers? She withdrew the bow from her father's left hand and waited while Jef cleared the target and gave the arrows to Micky and they strolled back together, the child chattering excitedly.

'Let me have a lesson,' said Claire. 'If Micky can do it, I can.'
'Of course.'

Hammond's features relaxed and Claire sighed, the long indrawn breath slowly leaving her lips. An instant of extreme danger had passed. But it had existed and both she and her father had been aware of it. He's dreadfully unhappy, she thought. He knows – and I know that Jef is Vale's lover. He's guessed that Freya is not his child and he can't take it.

She was in a disturbed and sultry state by the time they returned to their flat after supper. Guy had his arm about her shoulders as they went in to the attractive living-room that they were learning to think of as 'home'.

'Your father's delighted with his new car,' he said. 'I was really impressed by its performance. Let's make some coffee.'

'To hell with coffee! I'm going to have a beer.'

'Well, well. What's eating you?'

She began to unpack and hang up their damp tennis clothes and bathers while he poured a beer for her and one for himself, placidly ignoring her stormy mood.

'To hell with the car too! I hate it. Why should Daddy have this ghastly fight on his hands – against being crippled, against Jef!'

'Aren't you being rather over dramatic?'

'Over dramatic! Today my father nearly killed Jef Broome.'

Guy lit a cigarette.

'How absurd.'

She turned on him and snatched the cigarette from between his lips. She began to smoke it furiously. He raised his eyebrows and quietly lit another.

'I suggest we discuss this matter calmly,' he said. 'What's got you on the raw? Frankly I had the impression that everything went rather smoothly today, all things considered.'

'Go on,' she said coldly. 'Tell me more.'

'Jef is a great friend of John Rorke's – has been for years. John and Maria brought him to lunch and tennis at Silverglade. Vale treated him as she'd have treated any other casual guest, and your father was a good host. Two people were deliberately off-hand. One was you.'

'And the other?'

'Mrs Rorke.'

'Can you guess why?'

'Not really. Vale specifically told us that her mother was ignorant of her run-around with Jef.'

'Not so ignorant she couldn't take a guess at it. She certainly did at one time today – when you were playing your four with Vale and John and Maria.'

'What happened?'

'Fedora had brought Freya into the garden and left her in the pram near us. Jef went to the pram and picked that baby out as if he owned her. What reason could a man have for doing a thing like that?'

Guy was foolish enough to fling back his head and laugh. 'I simply can't imagine any man brave enough to pick a young baby out of its pram – unless that pram was on fire. He must be off his rocker!'

'Jef's not off his rocker,' she said icily. 'If you ask me, he reckoned he did own that baby.'

'What did Freya reckon?'

Claire said irritably: 'Every baby likes being picked up. Freya gurgled and cooed and grabbed at Jef's hair and smiled in her toothless windy way and generally made an ass of herself and him.'

'Which, as you pointed out, proves nothing. And then?'

'Suddenly Jef held her up with her little face right against his and he kept it there long enough for all of us to notice —'

'Notice what?'

'The likeness. I swear he did it as a sort of challenge. On purpose. Mrs Rorke saw it all right. Daddy makes her an allowance. I'll bet that when Jef held Freya like that – their faces together – Mrs Rorke was wondering how long it would be before Vale left Daddy for Jef, and her own useful quarterly cheque went with the wind. As for Daddy, his face was pale as marble.'

'So you think he wants to kill Jef?'

'I know it. After that we went to the target range with Micky. Just Daddy, Jef and I. And after Micky'd shot at his beloved bear he and Jef walked towards the target to retrieve the arrows. Daddy raised his bow and took careful aim at Jef's back. I put my hand over his because I was frightened of what he might do . . .' She shuddered. 'I felt what *he* felt – a wave of hate, a desire to kill.'

'You transfer and attribute your own feelings to other people – to Mrs Rorke and your father. Your father's a disciplined man who's upheld the law all his life. I assure you he wouldn't aim a bow and arrow at another man's back. You've got everything out of drawing. Vale told us she was through with Jef. It's not her fault if John brings him back into her home. Can't you trust her to do the decent thing and stick to her husband?'

'Trust her! Not with Jef around. If you ask me they're lovers again right now.'

Suddenly the whole ugly argument infuriated him.

'Even if they are, is it such a crime? Won't that sort of thing be inevitable in her life from time to time in the circumstances? Jef will go back and it'll be over. But every now and again nature will assert itself and Vale will be vulnerable. It's not easy to sublimate and stifle the sex urge. You and I should know that – and sympathize.'

'Don't compare us with Vale and Jef!'

'Why not? In a way I feel very sorry for Vale. She's like that trapped curlew – caught between the barbed wire of an old infatuation for Jef and the tangled thorn fence of her very great affection for your father. She's going to be injured whatever happens. She has feelings. She'd hate to hurt your father – especially now.'

'You've always been on her side.'

'You're quite incapable of seeing the situation objectively.

You're emotionally involved – partly because of your love for your father . . . and for other reasons too.'

'What do you mean?' She was tense, eyes blazing.

'Well, you've admitted yourself that you were often jealous of Vale – and there was a time when you were in love with Jef Broome yourself.'

Guy was lounging in an easy-chair, his beer beside him, scarcely touched. He had lit another cigarette. Suddenly all the heat and hurt flared up in her and she slapped him smartly across the cheek with the flat of her hand. She saw the cigarette fly out of the corner of his mouth on to the carpet and the red patch flame where she had struck him. He didn't move and it was she who picked up the cigarette and stubbed it out and stamped on the scorched mark on the rug.

'Pull yourself together!' he said sternly.

She slapped him again. He seized her hands and held them in a fierce grip.

'I don't hit women, or I'd retaliate. In any case, I don't think you know what you're doing.'

'I know very well. You deserved that. Marriage is for better for worse – but you don't see it that way. You think infidelity is unimportant, that it doesn't matter if a woman has someone else's baby. You'd condone anything for peace and a quiet life. That's a fine outlook for us!'

He had risen and he looked down at her, the muscles of his jaw taut, a vein throbbing in his forehead.

'I've never compared our marriage with Vale's. How could I? But I'm beginning to think Dr Stern was right when she warned me that you might become excessively irritable. It's a side-effect —'

'Shut up!'

He dropped her hands and turned away in silence. He drained his beer and took the tankard and the empty bottle into the kitchen. She heard him wash the glass and put the bottle into the carton they kept for empties. She felt foolish and deflated. She picked up her own empty tankard and the used ash-tray and followed him into the kitchen.

'I'm going to bed,' he said, coldly, and left her standing at the sink.

She returned to the living-room and plumped up the cushions. Then she drew the curtains wide and stood staring out of the open window at the sea. The night was cool and dark and the vast waters were calm, the waves swelling and breaking rhythmically on the shore. She breathed the strong salt air and felt the elemental murmur of the ocean soothe her. Was it Byron who had said of the sea: 'Dark-heaving – boundless, endless, sublime – the image of Eternity'? She curled up on the wide window-sill and let the sea mesmerize her, but after a time she knew that she was cold and waiting for Guy to fetch her. Surely he wouldn't just leave her sitting there by herself? Surely he'd come and take her to bed? Perhaps the beastly pill *was* making her temperamental. She'd better ditch it. She wanted Guy to put his arms round her and make up this horrid fierce quarrel. It seemed a long while before she realized that he had no intention of doing any such thing. For all he cared she could sit at the open window all night and catch her death of cold. What time was it? Nearly midnight, and tomorrow they both had to go back to work. The honeymoon was over. And how!

She crept into their room and undressed in the dark. Guy lay on his side, quite still, but she knew by his breathing and his rigid back that he was not asleep. She went into the bathroom and brushed her teeth and creamed off her face. It was quite a big bathroom and she kept her cosmetics there. It was more like a dressing-room, rare in a flat.

She slid into bed beside him but he made no sign. Then she put out a tentative hand and touched him.

'I'm cold,' she whispered. 'I'm cold as ice.'

He turned on his back and flung out his arm. She slipped into the warm curve of it and laid her head on his shoulder.

'It's the last night of our honeymoon,' she said.

She put up her hand and stroked his cheek where she had struck it. He felt her creep up like a kitten and lay her face against the mark.

'I'm sorry,' she said.

He still didn't answer.

'You're sulking,' she accused softly.

'I don't sulk.'

'What then?'

'I don't like quarrels.'

'Nor do I. But Daddy frightened me today. He was suffering. I think he was very much afraid of what he might do. There's telepathy between him and me. Forgive me, I was frightened.'

He pulled her close to him.

'I know you were frightened. Perhaps you had reason. Don't let's think about it. Let's just think about us.'

She sighed deeply. The great weight was lifted off her heart and the cold in her limbs ebbed away.

Mrs Rorke, John and Maria returned to Johannesburg and after their departure Guy and Claire seldom met Jef Broome at Silverglade, though they knew he went there frequently. Claire refused to invite him to their flat, but they saw him occasionally at the homes of mutual friends and on those occasions Claire was polite but diffident and Guy was carefully impersonal. If Vale happened to be present her attitude towards him was agreeable but casual. If they saw each other secretly their meetings were conducted with extraordinary discretion.

The weeks slipped by and the heat of February gave way

to the calm fresh brilliance of March and April. The oak leaves were golden in the gutters and the broad plane and elm leaves whirled down the avenues in the changing winds of autumn. The summer south-easters were almost over, and the north-westers began to churn the sea into the preliminary storms heralding the winter gales that had caused the early mariners to name the southernmost tip of Africa the Cape of Storms.

Jef Broome's novel was, in his own opinion, going rather well, and he was also writing articles for the foreign Press that were attracting a good deal of unwelcome attention in South Africa. If Hammond suspected that there was anything between his wife and the young journalist he gave no sign. He had begun to drive himself regularly to Katrina's flat for sittings for the bust. He telephoned her when he left Silverglade, the wheel-chair folded into the boot of his car, and she was invariably there to meet him at the back entrance of the flat, ready to take him upstairs to the penthouse studio.

At first the work had seemed to go well. She had made her usual sketches and rough models before beginning the serious work.

'I'm a slow worker,' she confessed. 'but at least it gives me an excuse for demanding a good deal of your company.'

'Rodin was a slow worker too. Weeks, months, years meant nothing to him.'

'His models were certainly long-suffering,' she agreed.

The studio was restful and pleasant. The overhead light was often broken by scudding clouds or gusty April storms. Hammond liked the sound of rain pattering on the skylight and he enjoyed watching Katrina's strong mobile fingers working the clay.

'You have such small hands,' he said, 'but powerful. My Norwegian masseuse is the same. Wonderful fine-boned hands, strong as iron.'

But as the work progressed he observed that she seemed dissatisfied.

'Can I see what you've done?' he asked once.

'No. You didn't ask me when I was doing the portrait.'

He smiled. 'If you want to know the truth, I took an occasional look. After all, it was there in my library. Did you trust me so implicitly that you thought I'd never steal a glance at it?'

'I liked to think you wouldn't,' she said severely. 'What is trust except hoping for the best?'

She saw his face darken and instinctively she glanced at the skylight but the sun shone and she realized that an inner cloud had settled upon his whole being, shadowing his eyes. It was not the first time that she had observed this sudden greyness overcast his naturally benign expression. It came down upon his features like an attack of pain, and when it happened she made an excuse to stop working and create some sort of diversion.

'A cup of coffee? A drink?'

'Coffee, I think.'

It was more trouble for her to make coffee and she had to go into the kitchen to do so. It gave him a better chance to collect himself. Was she right? Was trust an illusion? A mere 'hoping for the best'? Vale was out a great deal these days and she offered few explanations and made no excuses. On those occasions when he embraced her he could sense her physical revulsion. She was increasingly withdrawn and her old enmity with Claire seemed to have flared up again. She never mentioned Jef Broome and certainly gave him no reason to suppose that she was seeing him, yet he wondered.

'How's the book going?' said Katrina, bringing in the coffee tray.

She did not ask him how he liked his coffee. She simply poured it, rather strong and no sugar.

'Pretty well. I'm working hard. My visits to you are my chief interruptions, I might almost say relaxations.'

She smiled. 'Has any one read any of it yet?'

'Helen has. She gives me no peace. I have to let her see it.'

'Good old Helen. What about letting me have a go at it?'

'When it's finished. Not before.'

'So, you see, we have working methods in common.'

But she found that he was beginning to make excuses not to come to the studio, and on those days when he sat for her the essence of his personality was elusive. Somehow the *rapport* between them had been broken. She spoke to Helen Terblanche about him.

'What's worrying your brother?' she asked, one evening at her friend's flat. 'Is the effort of writing his memoirs too much for him?'

Mrs Terblanche took a sip of her whisky and soda and stared out at the evening light pouring its molten gold over the granite boulders of Lion's Head.

'On the contrary, I sometimes have the feeling it's the one thing he lives for.'

'You've read some of it?'

'As far as it goes, yes. I've seen it.'

'What do you think of it?'

'It's very good indeed. Interesting, exciting, entertaining, better than first-class fiction.'

'Sarah's very interested.'

'I know. But Charles must complete it before he shows it to her.'

'What does Vale think about it?'

'Vale? She's keen. So is that American writer, Jefferson Broome. He's friendly with Charles and Vale and it seems he can find Charles an American publisher with no difficulty.'

'Jefferson Broome? That's the young man who puts South Africa on the map with such a lurid brush?'

'The very one.'

'I've met him at Silverglade once or twice. An attractive personality, if rather pugnacious.'

'Yes,' said Mrs Terblanche, shortly. 'How's the bust coming on?'

'It's not. Charles is dodging our sessions.'

'Too busy with his book?'

'I suppose so. I'll start nagging him soon again.'

Hammond finished his memoirs by the end of May and Jef sent the typescript to his New York publisher who cabled immediate acceptance. There were exciting letters about serial rights and an English publisher who was also interested. South African and foreign rights would follow. Claire was wildly excited.

'You'll make your name as an author, Daddy. There's a whole new career ahead of you.'

They were in the library – Vale, Guy, Claire, Helen Terblanche and the Judge.

'That's quite a thought,' he said.

'You don't sound a bit thrilled,' said Claire. 'You should be right on top of the world!'

'That's a high peak,' said her father, with a twisted smile. 'Quite a ski-lift.'

An awkward silence fell. Mrs Terblanche broke it.

'Josiah brought in the drink tray all of five minutes ago. Isn't it high time we drank to the memoirs?'

'I'm sorry,' said Hammond. 'It was remiss of me not to notice. Please help yourselves. And a whisky for me.'

When they had toasted the book his sister said:

'And now you must give Katrina a chance to finish that bust.'

'I will,' he said. 'Of course I will. Dear Katrina.' But his voice was reluctant.

21

DANGEROUS JOURNEY

VALE SHOWED THE LETTER TO HAMMOND. SHE FOUND him under the trees near the pool, the morning paper open on his lap, but he wasn't looking at it. His glasses were pushed up on to his forehead and his gaze was far away. He took the letter from her and slipped his glasses into position to read it.

'It's from Maria,' she said. 'It seems she and John are going to announce their engagement with a big flourish.'

'Vale dear,' he read. 'This is to ask you to come to Johannesburg to join John and me in celebrating our forthcoming marriage. My parents are coming out from Athens for a few months and arrive next week, so we thought we'd announce the engagement on the first Friday in June and they're giving us a cocktail dance and supper party at their hotel to mark the occasion. I telephoned Jason and Penelope last night and they are going to drive up for it, and so is Jef. You could come with them.

'I can put the Euclides up and Jef can go to John's. I am sure your mother would be overjoyed to have you with her for a few days.'

'How about it? Please say yes.

With love,

Maria.'

'What do you want to do?' he asked, returning the note. She was sitting on the grass beside his wheel-chair. The breeze ruffled her hair and the sun shone on the thick lashes that veiled her eyes. She didn't look up.

'It would be fun to go,' she said. 'As a matter of fact, Penelope rang me this morning. They're driving up on Wednesday week. It would only be for a few days. Fedora goes back to the Transkei at the end of June so it's really my last chance of leaving the children.'

'I thought Angela was perfectly competent to take them on – better than Fedora; and, with me here, you don't have to worry.'

'Oh, yes, Angela's good, and I know you can cope, Charles, but I'll be losing Harmonia too, fairly soon, and I wouldn't dream of going in the middle of such drastic changes in the household. Now is my chance.'

'So you plan to drive up with your new friends, the Euclides . . . and Jef? Is that it? And take two cars?'

'Yes. Jason's and Jef's. I'll be a passenger.'

'You must do as you like.'

'Could you spare me for a week?'

'I must – if you decide to go.'

She had thought he would be more complacent. For the first time she felt resistance building up in him – and resented it.

'How long does Jef propose to stay on in South Africa?' he asked.

'I really don't know. Till the novel's finished, I suppose.'

'When will that be?'

'You can't hustle a writer. You should understand that.'

'I managed to seal, sign and deliver mine by a certain date – a deadline.'

'Yours wasn't creative. A novel is different.' Her voice held a slightly patronizing overtone.

'What do you know about it?' he rasped.

'Jef says it's an entirely different technique. Your type of book needs industry, combined with careful assembling and good editing. The cases are there, cut and dried. A novel is a horse of quite another colour. It requires inspiration – the act of projecting your ego into the characters and behaviour of fictitious people.'

His lips tightened as he tried to control his fear and jealousy. Projecting yourself into somebody else's shoes wasn't too difficult in real life. He could project himself into Jef's easily enough. Was that damned Virginian his wife's accepted lover? The husband was always the last to know, especially when he was in no position to fight back. Yet wasn't this bound to be the pattern of his future? Vale with a lover, and a husband complacent because he was helpless to be otherwise.

He said coolly: 'Has he ever tried a novel before?'

'If he has, it landed in the wastepaper basket. This one he believes in.'

'Let's hope he finishes it – soon.'

At the last minute Jason Euclides was delayed and he and Penelope decided to fly to Johannesburg. Jef and Vale set off alone and she saw no reason to tell Charles of the small but significant change of plan. I'm getting deceitful, she thought. It comes easier and easier. She seemed to be living on two emotional levels, one of increasing delight in her liaison with Jef and the other a corresponding pity for her husband. Exaltation and regret existed cheek by jowl inside her in a state of latent enmity which she accepted along with so much else.

They took the road to the north and the lovely autumnal Cape fell behind them. Up in the Hex River mountains little valleys flamed with the russet of the fall and the dry red leaves of the vineyards hung on the trellissed vines in rags and tatters of vanishing glory. As they ascended the steeply winding Matroosberg Pass, Vale shuddered. Early snow lay on the smooth slopes.

'It was somewhere here – nearly a year ago,' she said. 'That ghastly accident.'

Away to their left lay Leopard Bush and neither of them had any wish to break their journey to visit the farm so dear to Hammond's heart. He had not been near it since the catastrophe that had shattered his life.

'If it hadn't been for that you'd have been in Virginia now – my wife.'

'I sometimes wonder if I would. In the end I might have ratted.'

'Because of Micky, not because of Charles.'

'That still applies.'

'There's Freya now. I want her – and you. She's mine. So are you – more than ever. There's no doubt about Freya any more. You know that. I think Charles knows it too.'

'If he doesn't, it's not your fault.'

She spoke bitterly. Jef and the baby had a natural affinity. She adored him and put out her little arms to him whenever he approached, and the physical likeness between them was growing daily.

'I can't stay on for ever,' he said. 'And I'm not going back without you and Freya. There'll be other babies for us later. If Charles won't give up Micky it's better you should leave him now while he's a little fellow. The longer you delay the harder it'll be for him to forget.'

She knew that it was true, but she said:

'This is such an old argument between us. Let's leave it alone on this journey, Jef. Let's just enjoy ourselves and each other and never mind the future. Please.'

He glanced at her and saw her pleading face turn to him, and suddenly he too wanted to forget the constant tug-of-war that was stretching their pleasure in one another to breaking point.

'Let's call a truce for these few days,' she begged. 'Let's just be happy and live for the day.'

'And the night,' he grinned. 'All right, honey love. It's a pact.'

She smiled her relief. It was as if she could now divest her inmost self of all its warring elements, leaving simply her joy in Jef and her need for him, uncomplicated by the many ties that tangled the whole situation – the ties Jef was so ready to sever, refusing to realize that at least one of them was an artery, her love for Micky. He began to talk of Virginia.

'It's not unlike the Cape, with its forested mountains, its meadows, its great trees and old colonial homesteads. It has the same tradition of hospitality and dignified informality. How I long for you to see the dogwood and laurel in bloom, the azaleas, the great shady Kentucky locusts in the parklands, and the low white paling fences round green fields. You could fall in love with it, Vale. You'd fit in there so wonderfully. I can just picture you riding our spirited thoroughbred horses, and my friends and relations would love you.'

'Would they love me if they knew I'd deserted a crippled husband and a little boy?'

'Hush, you're breaking the pact.'

They were speeding along the broad straight roads of the Karoo now, and the hot afternoon sun was going down. Soon the clear frosty night would fall. They stopped at a small motel in the middle of nowhere and parked the car outside two adjoining single rooms. There was an empty swimming-pool in front of them. To the side was a restaurant and they could hear the metallic music of a juke-box. They signed the register and paid in advance, for they would be on the road again at dawn, and in Johannesburg in time for lunch.

The spectacular sunset burned out of the sky, leaving it flamingo pink with translucent lagoons of pure jade between the herring-bone clouds that feathered the horizon.

'Let's go for a walk before dinner,' Jef said. 'Not a stroll but a real walk to give ourselves some exercise. This scene of semi-desert could be Arizona, especially with the prickly pears and the aloes over there. Your country produces the same fantastic variety of climate and scenery as mine. The lush stormy Cape and then – beyond the coastal mountains – this.'

So they strode out across the low scrub and kept to the roadside, walking briskly in the fresh clean air. As night fell the temperature dropped by the minute and the heat of the sun gave way to the dry cold of the Karoo winter. When they turned back to the motel it was dark. Every star was working overtime in a sky of theatrical madonna blue and the moon poured down, bleaching a scene as desolately lunar as its own far landscape in the wastes of space.

They ate a rather poor dinner but the red Cape wine was bracing and heady.

'Take off your dark glasses,' he said. 'I hate this vogue for dark glasses indoors. It's sinister. Anyway, I must see your eyes to know your moods.'

'I was afraid we might meet someone we knew.'

'It can't be helped if we do. In any case, a pair of glasses is no disguise on a face like yours.'

'One can't get away from it,' she said. 'There's always the guilt.'

'Forget it,' he said roughly. 'The pact was your idea, and you're the one who keeps breaking it.'

She took off the glasses and put them in her bag. Everything was brighter and better. The wine was richer. But suddenly it reminded her of the blood transfusion Charles had had. The bottle and the drip and the way he had shivered. 'It's icy cold going into one's veins. Iced blood!' And he had complained of 'a fullness in his chest' as his system adapted itself to the foreign invasion. His blood pressure had fluctuated and he had felt sick. For all that it had saved his life. But for that timely transfusion he might have slipped away and then everything would have been simplified for her. She passed her hand across her eyes, and Jef knew that she was not free, that part of her was at Silverglade, eluding him. He poured more wine into her glass and saw her shiver. But she drank it and smiled at him in defiance of whatever ghosts were haunting her.

They sat for a while by a roaring fire, and looked at some out-of-date magazines they picked up from a table near the wall. But Vale did not take in a word she read and she doubted if Jef did.

'I'm sleepy,' she said. 'I'm going to bed.'

They strolled across to their rooms and Jef bade her good night in a clear voice intended to be heard if any inquisitive person was interested.

'Good night,' she answered. 'Sleep well.' Her yawn was genuine.

She went into her room and filled her hot-bottle from the near boiling water in the bath-tap. Then she went to bed. The blankets were coarse and heavy but the sheets were clean.

Strange, she thought. No more wondering or trembling as she waited for him. No sharp barbed sense of guilt either. Guilt was still there, but it had long since changed its character. It was no longer fiery but pallid and formless, a phantom dispelled by the touch of a human hand – Jef's hand. Waiting for him now was not anxious and tumultuous as once it had been. It was a confident hiatus filled with happy anticipation. It was almost as if they had been married for many months. She knew how he would knock – a little double knock – and enter on light bare feet, his blue woollen dressing-gown over his pyjamas. She knew how he would come to her and sit for a moment on the edge of her bed, looking at her as if to make sure that she was really there and he was welcome before taking his place beside her, sure of her, wanting her. And if the first shuddering magic of her lover's touch was less acute, the hunger and the habit was more profound. Their love-making was not uncertain and experimental now. It was relaxed and assured, a ritual known and understood, infinitely exciting, infinitely satisfying. How can I ever do without him? she thought. How can I make myself give him up?

His step was soundless, but she heard the familiar knock, and the door opened.

The dry Karoo air flowed into the room and over them with its scent of the bush, the red dust, and of natives burning dried cattle dung some distance away; with it came the silence of the night, accentuated by the occasional barking of a dog or the arrival of a car. So deep was this silence that any slight break in it was instantly healed by its vast elemental quality. It was absolute.

Claire met Penelope Euclides in the Viennese Bakery just round the corner from the S.A.B.C. building.

'I always get rolls here if I happen to be passing,' Penelope said. 'Mrs Graumann has the best bakery in the Peninsula.'

'I thought you were on the way to Johannesburg,' said Claire.

'Didn't Vale tell you? Jason couldn't get away yesterday so we decided to fly tomorrow.'

'I haven't seen her for a few days.'

'We only knew on Tuesday. But it's not important anyway. Vale hasn't missed her lift. She's gone with Jef. What do you think of the engagement?'

Claire made an effort to collect her wits.

'I think John Rorke's a lucky man.'

'And Maria?' smiled Penelope.

'I expect she brings out the best in him.'

'You don't really like him, do you?'

'I hardly know him,' said Claire.

Penelope paid for her croissants and the long crisp French bread Jason loved.

'I s'pose not. You've never lived in Johannesburg, have you? He used to be rather a one for girl-friends, but since Maria appeared on the scene there's been nobody else.'

'I hope he'll make her happy.'

'So do I. She's a darling. I must rush off now. Good-bye, Claire.'

''Bye, Penelope. Enjoy the party.'

'It'll be fun. Anyway I adore an excuse for going back to Johannesburg even for a few days. We loved being there. Your Cape is very beautiful, my dear, but Johannesburg is so much more stimulating. There's nowhere to touch it.'

That evening Claire told Guy of her meeting with Penelope.

'So you see, Vale and Jef went off alone together.'

'But it wasn't planned that way. It evidently just happened. If you must blame anyone, it has to be Jason.'

'Vale could have flown with the Euclides.'

'And paid her fare instead of hitching a ride. That would be pretty silly.'

'I wonder if Daddy knows?'

'Listen, Claire, we're dining at Silverglade tonight and I suggest you say nothing about seeing Penelope in the bakery. It could only worry your father if he doesn't already know of the change of plan. Just leave it alone.'

Surprisingly, she agreed with him. Nothing was said about Vale's journey with Jef, either that night or after Vale's return. It was simply assumed that the Euclides had been with them. Claire held her tongue and asked no awkward questions and Guy was relieved to realize that his young wife was at last learning sense.

The engagement party had evidently been a great success

and the stragglers had left at three in the morning. Mrs Rorke had stayed the course till midnight and reckoned the re-action next day was worth it. To see John in love with, and loved by, a rich and charming young woman had done wonders for her peace of mind.

'Now she reckons both her children are safely settled,' said Vale, smiling at her husband.

'The fish is on the hook,' Hammond said. 'But not yet landed. Wait for the wedding-bells.'

Nobody asked him whether the fish was John or Maria. We're all getting frightfully wary, thought Guy.

'There's something different about Vale since she got back,' said Claire that evening to her husband. 'Do you notice it?'

Guy had indeed noticed a change in Vale and he said so. 'But I can't put my finger on it. It's subtle.'

Claire, for once, was more perceptive than critical where her stepmother was concerned.

'It's as if she's come to some final decision and has no more doubts – as if she'd come to terms with herself. I believe a nun might look like that just before taking her final vows.'

He glanced at her in astonishment. She had, in her own way, described the luminous peace of Vale's expression extraordinarily well. But what were the vows Vale was so calmly prepared to take?

During his wife's brief absence the Judge had gone to Katrina for several sittings.

'How is the bust getting on?' Claire had asked him.

'I wish I knew,' he said. 'Katrina's the most secretive worker I've ever known. The moment the sitting is over she wraps that head up in a wet doek like a mother putting a towel round a baby after its bath, and it's all hidden before I can get a glimpse of it.'

'Are there many more sittings?' put in Vale.

'I don't even know that,' he said. 'I simply turn up and pose for the dear girl.'

'I think she just likes seeing you,' laughed Claire. 'She'll probably smash up that bust and start all over again if it's the only sure way of keeping her sitter!'

Her father smiled. 'I don't flatter myself all that much.'

For the week after Vale's return the weather kept him at home. The north-wester raged across the Peninsula and put up mountainous seas. There were landslides and washaways, trees were blown down, the pondokkie dwellings on the Cape Flats were swamped and CAFDA – the Cape Flats Distress Association – was sorely taxed with an influx of storm refugees in urgent need of shelter, clothing, blankets, warmth and food.

When at last the weather cleared and the fitful sun shone once again Hammond telephoned Katrina.

'Do you want me to come this afternoon?'

'Of course I want you. When can you come? Right now?'

'I can be with you in an hour's time. Say three o'clock.'

'That'll be fine. But don't be later if you can help it. We get the afternoon sun but it doesn't last so long these winter days.'

'I'll leave in less than half an hour,' he promised.

'And I'll meet you downstairs in the parking space as usual.'

Before he hung up he said:

'Isn't it time you told me how the work is going?'

'It's going well, Charles.'

'When will it be finished?'

'A few more sittings.'

'Only a few?'

'Yes. But I could spin them out, of course, and I'd like to. I'll miss you terribly when the work is done.'

'Don't spin them out,' he said abruptly. 'Good-bye, Katrina.'

She put down the receiver with a curious heaviness at her heart. The telephone was in the hall outside the studio so that she could ignore its summons when she did not wish to be disturbed. She rubbed the instrument with her paint-daubed smock for she had a feeling she'd left burnt umber all over it. She put up a hand to smooth her hair and tucked in the usual stray strand that had escaped from the crown of flaxen plaits. She went into the studio and over to the bust of Charles Hammond. She lifted the damp cloth from the clay and stared at it long and reflectively. She could finish it this afternoon, if necessary. In truth, there was little more she could do to it. It was no more now than an excuse to bring Charles here. She had felt of late that he needed comfort, and she had tried to discover in what way she could help him, but, every time it had seemed that he might confide in her, he had retreated – as if such a confidence might involve some form of betrayal.

Dear Charles, she thought. This is the best thing I've done in all my life. But I wonder if it'll ever be cast in bronze? Even today I won't show it to you. You'll ask and I'll refuse, as I've done so often before.

She glanced at her watch. A quarter past two. He'd leave Silverglade at half past. She'd just have time to do something about her face and set a tea-tray. She covered the bust once more and went into the kitchen. She really was going to miss Charles very much when he no longer came for the sittings.

Katrina went down to their usual meeting place at five to three. Hammond was a punctual man and she never had to wait more than a few minutes for the maroon-coloured car he handled so easily and so well. At a quarter-past three she became anxious. At half-past three she went back to the flat and telephoned Silverglade. Josiah answered the phone.

'When did your Master leave?' she asked.

'At half-past two, Miss Katrina.'

'And it's half-past three now. He hasn't arrived, Josiah. He should have been here half an hour ago. Is Madam at home?'

Josiah's voice rose on a nervous note. 'Madam went out just after Master did.'

'Do you know where I could get hold of her?'

There was the merest suggestion of a pause before Josiah replied:

'I couldn't say, Miss Katrina.'

'What shall we do?'

'I have my own car,' said Josiah, with pardonable pride. 'I shall come to Clifton the way Master usually comes – along the coast.'

'Yes,' she said. 'He never goes through the city and he loves the sea. Meanwhile I'll ring Mr Guy and Miss Claire. Be quick, Josiah, he might have had a puncture – or an accident. Take a toolcase with you. And the first aid kit.'

'I'll do that, Miss Katrina. Right now.'

She rang off. Perhaps by now Charles had arrived and was waiting for her, wondering what to do without her help.

She hurried to the lift and cursed the children who were playing in it as usual. Pressing the buttons, riding up and down just for the hell of it. An automatic elevator was a small boy's notion of heaven. It was high time the tenants complained again. At last the lift stopped at the top floor and she got in and pressed the basement button with a trembling finger. Please, Charles, be there, waiting for me, and we can laugh together! You shouldn't scare me like this!

But, when she entered the courtyard, there was no maroon car in its usual place. Nor was it in the road outside. It was nowhere to be seen. It was then that Katrina felt certain that something terrible must have happened.

22

THE CLIFF ROAD

THE LAW COURTS HAD ADJOURNED FOR THE WINTER recess and Guy wanted to take Claire to Natal to stay with his parents at Kloof for a few days and afterwards with his sister and her family in East Griqualand, where his brother-in-law farmed grain and cattle on the high uplands. Claire was equally keen.

'But how can I ask Sarah for three weeks' holiday so soon after our honeymoon?' she had wailed. 'I daren't even mention the idea.'

'Not to her,' he'd agreed. 'But there's a pretty good grapevine in operation if we get your Aunt Helen and Katrina on our side. You never know, something may crop up.'

Something had cropped up. The grapevine had worked, and Sarah had seen interesting possibilities in the proposed jaunt to Natal. The Woman's Hour programme could do with some up-to-the-moment topical slants and Claire had a nose for news features. So it happened that shortly after Judge Hammond had set out to keep his appointment with Katrina Westhuizen, his daughter and her husband were conferring with Sarah Verity in her spacious office at the S.A.B.C.

'Let's see what we can plan,' she said. 'If we consider the matter intelligently, it seems to me you two can have your holiday and provide me with some interesting and original features at the same time. It's a question of give and take.'

'That's fair enough,' said Guy. 'What do you want us to do?'

'Are you going by car?'

'Yes. It's much more fun and we thought we'd go through the Transkei and see how our Bantustan Number One is getting on. Guy speaks Xhosa which'll be a marvellous help. And Josiah has a brother who is a Chief in the territory. I'm sure he'd be useful. As a matter of fact, Guy speaks Zulu as well. We could probably get some entertaining material from Zululand too.'

Sarah nodded and drew a scribble pad towards her.

'Let's work something out. You'd need to – oh, damn, the phone.'

She leaned forward and took the receiver off the hook.

'Sarah Verity speaking . . . Oh, Katrina! What's the matter? You sound worried . . . Claire? Yes, she's right here.'

She pushed the telephone across the broad desk towards Claire. Guy saw Claire's face change and shrink as Katrina spoke to her. He could hear Katrina's voice distinctly.

'Your father was to come to me for a sitting at three o'clock. He hasn't shown up yet.'

Guy glanced at his watch. Ten to four – and Judge Hammond was a meticulously punctual person! He would never have kept Katrina hanging about in the car park waiting to help him up to the penthouse in the wheel-chair.

'He left Silverglade at two-thirty, according to Josiah,' came Katrina's voice. 'I'm sure he took the coast road. He always did.'

'What has been done – if anything?' Claire asked tersely.

'Josiah has taken his own car and is following the cliff road in the direction of our flats. That's all. I don't know what to think —'

Guy took the receiver firmly out of Claire's limp hand.

'Listen, Katrina. This is Guy. Let's get this story straight. The Judge left Silverglade at two-thirty on his way to you. It's now getting on for four and he hasn't turned up yet?'

'That's right. I s'pose it could be just a puncture.'

'It's unlikely with new tyres and a good road, but there might easily be washaways. There were storm landslides on Chapman's Peak over the week-end, and there might well be a slide on some of the curves near Llandudno or Bantry Bay. There was a fire some time ago and there isn't the vegetation to hold the soil.'

'If so, what?'

'He'd have had to turn back, retrace the road and come over Kirstenbosch and Kloof Nek.'

'He wouldn't have done that,' said Katrina. 'He'd have gone back to Silverglade and phoned me. He'd have known I'd be alarmed. Should we get in touch with the police?'

'No, Katrina. We can't notify the police because someone is an hour late for a date. Claire and I will take the Mini and go along the cliff road towards Hout Bay. Then we're bound to meet up with Josiah, and, if the Judge is stranded somewhere, we'll find him. I suggest you take the other alternative road and go to Silverglade via Kloof Nek, the De Waal Drive and Kirstenbosch just as a check. We can be sure of one thing, he'd never go through the city on a busy afternoon. Pick up Helen if you want support. Her flat is right on your way.'

'Thank you, Guy. I'll go that way at once and get hold of Helen if I can. Whatever happens, we'll meet up with you at Silverglade.'

He heard a sigh that might have been relief as she hung up. Her voice had been taut with apprehension.

'Sarah, you heard all that,' said Guy. 'Claire and I must go at once. This could be serious. The Judge seemed so confident in that car of his, but he hasn't driven it very often. He could have met with some mishap.'

'Of course you must go,' Sarah said. 'Let me know as soon as you have any news.'

She sat at her desk tapping her strong white teeth with a

pencil as she watched them hurry from the room. The sun had gone behind a cloud and she was frowning as she recalled an odd incident that had occurred in the studio only last night.

Katrina, usually so cagey about her work, had suddenly stripped the bust for her to see it.

'No one has seen it – least of all Charles,' she'd said. 'What do you think of it? Be frank.'

'Am I ever anything else? Frankness is my besetting sin.'

'I want your honest opinion.'

A long silence had fallen between the two friends while Sarah studied the clay head. At last she had said soberly:

'It's magnificent. Your masterpiece, Katjie. It has everything.'

Katrina had turned away, her fists clenched, her face drawn.

'You're right. It has everything, Sarie. Too much.'

Suddenly now, as she sat in the chill left where the shaft of sunlight had been shining a few moments ago, Sarah Verity felt very much afraid.

Guy headed the Mini towards town in the direction of the Three Anchor Bay flats. There he and Claire checked once more that there was no maroon-coloured car in sight.

'It's five past four,' she said. 'Daddy would never be an hour late for Katrina – especially in the afternoon, when he knows the light goes fast.'

'Of course he wouldn't. He'd never let her hang about this parking-place waiting to help him get the chair out and all that palaver. It's out of the question. Something has happened. But what?'

They turned and headed towards Sea Point, keeping along the Beach Road. They kept a sharp look-out as the miles unfolded.

Presently Camps Bay and Lion's Head lay behind them

and they found themselves on the dramatic drive girdling the flanks of those rugged peaks, the Twelve Apostles. Claire looked down the sheer face of the cliffs to the rocks below – hundreds of feet in places – and slid her hand over Guy's knee.

'I'm getting goose-pimples. Between here and Hout Bay anything could have happened, and he'd have been driving on the outside – the cliff side – of the road. On certain bends he'd have had the sun in his eyes.'

'Darling, he knows this road as well as we do. Is there a curve or a hazard we don't know?'

'What are you expecting to find?'

'A washaway. He may have run into the muck and debris of a small landslide – got stuck – something like that. And he'd be helpless unless someone happened along to help push the car out. Even with a puncture – and a puncture is a possibility, although unlikely – he'd be dependent on outside assistance. You must appreciate that.'

She shuddered violently.

'Oh, my God! I'm so scared, Guy. He can't get out. That's the awful part. If anything happens he can't help himself. I mean if the car has capsized or set on fire —'

'He's very strong. In circumstances like that he could drag himself clear. He can help *himself*, Claire, but he can't mend punctures or use the jacks. He has his limitations.'

They were climbing, the drop beneath them increasing. They could see the great combers curling in and bursting on the rocks below with the force of the week's storms still in them.

'What worries me is that we haven't met Josiah in that old black car of his,' said Claire. 'Surely we should have seen him by now.'

On the slopes above them the ravages of fire had decimated the mountain shrubs; blackened trunks and charred bush clung precariously to ravines worn down by erosion and here and there a spate of earth and rock had spilled over on to the road. Guy said:

'There may be more of this sort of thing farther on where it's steeper – not yet cleared.'

It was as they reached the high curve shortly before Llandudno's shining beach opened out that Guy trod on the brake.

'Josiah's car,' breathed Claire. 'Along there with those others. And no sign of Daddy's.'

Half a dozen cars were parked along the cliff road ahead, including a police van. A little group of people stood staring down at some object caught on a rocky outcrop far below. The angry waves snapped white fangs at it but fell back, failing to touch it, though, with the high tide, they would get at their prey, dislodge and swallow it.

'Stay in the car, darling,' said Guy. 'Let me investigate.'

She shook her head and got out, her knees shaking. He slipped his arm through hers and they went together to the crenellated parapet on the cliff edge. Sharply curving skid marks showed where tyres had braked violently and left the road, going over the cliff through a gap between the crenellations. The bush had been torn and flattened by the headlong tumbling fall of the maroon car that lay on the rocks below reflecting the level rays of the afternoon sun. It was trapped in a fiery glow as if in a casket of flame, but it was not burning. Perhaps the driver could still be saved. Farther down they could see Josiah's heavy figure, still in his white uniform tunic, and that of a wiry young Police Sergeant clambering towards the wrecked vehicle.

'Stay here, please, darling. I'm going down.'

She wanted to go with Guy, but her legs would not hold her and she sat on the parapet feeling faint and sick.

'Are you all right, young lady?'

An elderly man with a kind fox-face was looking down at her. She raised desperate eyes to his.

'What happened?'

'God knows. My name is Vlotman,' he volunteered. 'What's yours?'

'Claire Steele.'

He sat beside her and offered her a cigarette. She held it with trembling fingers while he lit it. He said:

'I was coming from the Camps Bay side, going towards Hout Bay – that's my Jaguar, the green one over there on the left – and suddenly this maroon car comes round the bend at a terrific lick. I think, my God, he's going to strike me! But, at the last minute, he swerves off the road and goes clean over the precipice.' He frowned in puzzlement. 'It was just as if he'd lost control – put his foot on the accelerator instead of the brake.'

But he couldn't do that, she thought. It was manually controlled.

'Did you think you recognized the car down there?' he asked.

'I'm very much afraid so,' she said in a low strained voice.

'Hey, wait a minute!'

He bent and caught her as she fainted. Somebody brought a water-bottle and splashed her face and forehead. The driver of the police van strolled over to find out what the fuss was about. Claire came to herself to see his concerned swarthy face staring down at her.

'Don't take it too much to heart, miss. It's a bad accident, but you never know. We only got here a few minutes ago. The ambulance is on its way. Let's hope they get the man out. It seems there were no passengers – just the driver. This gentleman here says he appeared to lose control. He saw it happen. It was lucky there wasn't a collision.'

'The young lady thinks she may know who owns the

car,' said Mr Vlotman. 'As far as I could see, it was a maroon car – looked new. I didn't notice the make. The driver had no hat but he had grey hair. Or perhaps it was fair. It caught the sun as he went over the cliff. Middle-aged, I should say. There's not much else I can tell you. It all happened so quickly.'

'Does that help you?' the Sergeant asked Claire gently. 'Does that help you to guess who it might be?'

'Yes,' she said. 'It was my father. Judge Hammond.'

She heard the wail of the ambulance siren. As if in a nightmare, she saw the kindly inquisitive faces gather round her and a white-coated man who pushed them aside as he came towards her. He helped her over to the ambulance and wrapped a blanket round her for she had begun to shiver uncontrollably. He made her take some Sal Volatile and she gasped and felt her head begin to clear.

'She's best out here in the fresh air,' he said. 'Keep away and let her be.'

He had seated her on a big flat rock with a pillow under her and one to support her back.

'I'll be all right in a minute,' she said. 'I must go to him – go down there.'

The stretcher-bearers were already on their way, scrambling down the face of the cliff, snaking from ledge to ledge, clinging to the bushes and shrubs through which the car had bounced and ploughed its frantic way.

She struggled shakily to her feet.

'You're not up to it,' said the ambulance driver. 'Better stay put, Mrs Steele.'

But Mr Vlotman, the fox-faced man, took her arm.

'We'll go to the edge,' he said firmly. 'I'll see Mrs Steele is all right.'

The ambulance driver nodded and shrugged.

'I'm going down,' said Claire. 'I must get to my father.'

'I understand,' said Mr Voltman.

He assisted her carefully down the giddy wall of the cliff, the soles of their shoes slipping and slithering as they tried to follow the track of the stretcher-bearers. Then suddenly Claire was aware of a sturdy black figure in the tunic that had once been white advancing up the steep incline towards them.

'Josiah!' she called. 'Josiah . . .'

She put her hand out and grasped his dark one as he clambered within reach.

'Is it Daddy, Josiah?'

He bowed his head and she felt the dust and sweat and heat of his hand as it tightened on hers.

'Tell me . . .' she said.

'Miss Claire, my heart is very sore. This is a heavy thing. My master sleeps and will never wake again. Don't go there, Miss Claire. Don't go down there.'

Mr Vlotman moved aside as if he recognized that she no longer needed him.

Gently Josiah turned her away from the setting sun, the rocks and the hungry waves and helped her climb back up the cliff, her weak leg dragging painfully. The little group on the edge of the precipice made way for them respectfully as he drew her over the parapet. The word had been passed among them that she was the daughter of Judge Hammond, the victim of the catastrophe.

She stood for a long moment to get her breath and her self-control. But when she looked into the stricken eyes of Josiah it was as if she looked into the dark caves of hell. His tunic was torn by thorn bushes, stained with earth and sweat and blood. His face was grey. Without a word she laid her head against his broad shoulder and wept.

The Judge's car had hurtled over the cliff incline and over the first ledge, and then the next, with wildly increasing velocity, and the last sheer plunge had landed it on its nose with the bonnet telescoped and the doors jammed.

It was some time before Guy, the Sergeant, the stretcher-bearers and a makeshift working party of men who had managed to climb down to the scene of the disaster were able to extricate the occupant. But it had been perfectly apparent long before then that the Judge was dead. It had been then that Guy had dispatched Josiah to keep Claire from attempting to reach the car and her father.

'My wife – his daughter – mustn't see him like this,' said Guy, gaunt and appalled, as they finally laid the tragic figure on the stretcher.

The young stretcher-bearer covered what had once been Charles Hammond with a blanket.

'It must have been quick,' he said in an attempt at comfort. 'I'd say there was a whiplash break of the neck, right up there on the lip of the cliff before the car got into its final spin, and the other injuries occurred later.'

His theory was supported by the fact that although Hammond had been strapped into his seat he had evidently made no attempt to unfasten the catch of the safety belt. His ribs had been crushed and his face cruelly cut by violent contact with the driving mirror and the cracked windscreen.

'Man, he never had a hope,' said the Sergeant. 'That's a hell place for skidding, if you take it too fast. He must have lost control, somehow.'

The ascent of the cliff was tortuous and difficult for the bearers with their burden. It was necessary to make hairpin detours to find a track of any sort, and, long before they could reach the summit, Guy had climbed the steep face and was with Claire. She was sitting in the Mini with Josiah standing guard over it like an old watchdog. She looked stunned.

'Darling,' Guy said at the window. 'There's nothing more

we can do here. We'd better get to Silverglade at once. Katrina and Helen will be there with Vale.'

She said vaguely, 'But Daddy —?'

'Darling, there is nothing anyone can do now. We'll receive a telephone call later at Silverglade. The Sergeant is most understanding and he has all the necessary information.'

He turned to Josiah. 'Go on home, Josiah. We'll meet you there.'

The sun had set and the winter evening had turned wet and cold when they arrived at Silverglade. They found Vale in the sitting-room with Helen Terblanche and Katrina. The three women were huddled round a roaring fire and Micky was playing with his bricks near them, making a fort. His tin soldiers, a few outdated cavalrymen and several tanks lay among the scattered bricks. Dart slept with his head practically in the blaze.

'How he has any operative brains left defeats me,' Helen Terblanche was saying. 'They must have been cooked to a frazzle many winters ago.'

Vale sprang up as they entered. Micky was so absorbed in his occupation that he scarcely looked up, while his aunt and Katrina stared at Guy, seeking the information they dreaded in his face.

'Vale,' he said, quietly. 'Come into the library – and Helen, I suggest you get our friend on the floor —'

'Yes,' she put in quickly. 'Leave that to me.'

Vale followed Guy and Claire into the library, her eyes wide and haunted.

'Sit down, my dear.' Guy's voice was gentle. 'I'm afraid the news is bad.'

Claire, who had subsided into the wing chair, broke in suddenly.

'He's dead, Vale. He drove his car over the cliff between Llandudno and Camps Bay.'

'Drove his car?' she echoed faintly. 'What do you mean?'
Guy flashed a look of anger at his wife.

'It was an accident, Vale. He was on his way to Katrina,
as you know, and he took the cliff road and skidded. He must
have been in a hurry, going too fast, because his car left the
road at that bad turn with the crenellated parapet. He went
over through one of the gaps. There was a witness to the
whole thing – a car coming in the opposite direction – a
Mr Vlotman. He says the Judge was driving very fast and
appeared to lose control, he went into a skid on the corner
and – over. Death must have been instantaneous. He was
secured by the safety belt and it seems there was a whiplash
injury to his neck. A break. It must have happened then. In
any case, no one could have survived. The car is a total
wreck.'

Vale sat forward, her face in her hands. 'Why?' she moaned.
'But why?'

'It was an accident, I've said. There's no question about
that. After all, he hasn't had the car very long. He must have
lost his concentration for a moment. You know that road is
dangerous if you're careless. The sun was in his eyes and the
surface was wet and covered with a slide of loose pebbles
brought down by the recent storm. It could have happened
to anybody.'

Claire pushed her hair back off her forehead and stared at
Vale.

'But it didn't happen to anybody, it happened to my
father,' she said. 'He was a careful driver. I feel like Vale does
about it. *Why?*'

Vale was shivering.

'Light the fire, please, Guy. It's icy cold.'

Claire rose and drew the curtains while Guy put a match
to the log fire. Soon the flames were leaping and the fir
cones glowed blue and resinous, crackling and shooting

small sparks that died on the hearth-rug. The last roses of the season were in a vase on the Judge's desk. The flicker of fire-light brought the screen to fantastic life. Guy confronted his wife and her stepmother, his face hard as granite.

'That question – *why?* – is never to be asked again. Your father was the victim of an accident, Claire. How and why it happened is not for us to determine. There will be a great deal to arrange in the next few hours. Let's concentrate on what we have to do.'

'Very well,' said Claire. But her eyes, as she looked at Vale, were empty of sympathy. They were the eyes of an enemy and the look in them chilled Guy. His voice was cold as he spoke to her.

'Please fetch Helen and Katrina, Claire. It's more private here than in the sitting-room. Be sure Micky isn't with them. There's no point in upsetting him. Does he guess anything, Vale?'

'Nothing,' she said. 'Helen told him his Daddy was on the way home. He believed it.'

'Let him go on believing it for tonight.'

As Claire left the room, he added:

'I'm sorry, Vale. Claire's had a terrible shock. She was there. It was very agonizing.'

'I understand,' she said, dry-eyed and calm.

You do, he thought. You really do understand. Why? So there it was again – the forbidden question. Why?

23

REVELATION

A STILL SUNNY WINTER'S DAY IN THE HIGH PEAKS OF
the Cape has a rare ephemeral quality of unpolluted brilliance.
The snow has none of the thick ice-deep grip of the snows
of Europe. It is light and susceptible to the sun that is always
just round the corner, even when it is not shining at full
strength. The dry aroma of herbs and shrubs is as penetrating
as the flower scent of spring, and the sound of bird-song has
the fluted purity of the soloist as compared with the full
symphony of summer. Strong-winged eagles circle the blue
skies slowly in search of their prey and the small creatures of
the bush move furtively between the cool earth and the
sun-warmed foliage.

It was on such a day that Charles Hammond was laid to
rest in the little family cemetery at Leopard Bush.

The inquest had been brief, with Mr Vlotman sole witness
to the catastrophe, and the finding a foregone conclusion.
Accidental death. The Insurance Company had examined the
wreckage of the car but found no fault to account for the
accident. Only the human element could be blamed. The
Judge had driven too fast and had skidded on the fatal bend.

Vale had wondered whether or not to take Micky to the
funeral and had appealed to Guy for advice. Guy had been
in no doubt.

'His father will be buried at Leopard Bush which is now
Micky's property. One day your son must learn the facts of
death. Let him learn them now in a place of great beauty

where only his own family will be present. All his memories of his father are good ones. This, in its own sad way, will be a good one too.'

The only people at the graveside were the Judge's widow, his little son, his daughter with her husband, his sister and his old servants, Josiah and Harmonia, the manager and his wife, Mr and Mrs Steyn, their son, Jaapie, and the coloured farm labourers and their families who regarded Leopard Bush as their home and the Judge as their 'wise father'. They wore their best clothes, all the children had on shoes and the carefully groomed heads of the little girls were adorned by frilly hats.

The brief service was conducted by the vicar of the church in which Guy and Claire had been married. The snow-covered mountains enfolded the fertile valley and the Hex River in spate cascaded over its rocky bed with a sound like music. The birds called to one another in the bright air of the early afternoon. The tremendous words from Revelation were sonorous in the great silence of nature:

'. . . There shall be no more death, neither sorrow, nor crying, neither shall there be any more pain: for the former things are passed away. And he that sat upon the throne said: 'behold, I make all things new . . . I am Alpha and Omega, the beginning and the end . . .'

Claire felt a great peace pervade her as she looked through a mist of tears at the round fair head of the child standing solemn and quiet at his mother's side. 'Behold, I make all things new . . .' My father's broken body and his broken heart, she thought. For him the sorrow and the pain are finished, and perhaps it is best that way. She felt Guy's hand in hers and a deep gratitude that he was beside her.

As the service ended and before the group at the graveside could disperse, the coloured foreman stepped forward.

'We wish to sing a hymn for our Master,' he said reverently.

At once the voices rose in chorus – the children's, high and sweet, threading the deep notes of the men and the sopranoes of the women. Josiah and Harmonia joined in with the full depth and strength of their rich Bantu voices. As the hymn ended in that setting of simple majesty – 'Heaven's morning breaks, and earth's vain shadows flee; In life, in death, O Lord, abide with me' – Claire's tears flowed freely. Here in the winter sunshine, in the place he had loved, his people were offering their tribute, more moving than any formal benediction.

Mrs Steyn had arranged tea for the mourners in the house and then they left Leopard Bush, the farm that now belonged to Micky, and returned to their homes. Helen Terblanche went with Vale and Micky, taking Josiah and Harmonia with them, and Guy and Claire were alone.

'I wonder what will happen to Leopard Bush now?' said Guy some time later. 'The Steyns are wondering too.'

'It'll stay in the family,' said Claire. 'The Steyns will continue there and one day Micky will come back and live there.'

He glanced at her in amazement. 'Who told you? Vale?'

'No one.'

'Yet you say one day Micky will *come back*. Where from?'

'America.'

He was silent – sad and impressed. The implication of her answer was very clear. Her face had a strange fey look though her eyes were hidden by her dark glasses as they drove west into the sunset. She said:

'Young as he is, Micky will remember today always. He's tremendously impressionable and who could forget that hymn, 'Abide with Me', and the way they sang it? He'll never go into a country churchyard without thinking of the family burial place among the mountains. Don't you see that one day he'll have to come home to revisit it?

Leopard Bush is his heritage and has belonged to Hammonds for generations. He can't help loving it.'

'It's a beautiful place. Anybody would love it.'

'Daddy did,' she said. 'It meant more to him than Silverglade. It was his retreat, his sanctuary.'

'It still is,' Guy said gently.

A few days later they went to dinner with Sarah and Katrina. Sarah was engrossed with her plans for Claire's working holiday in Natal and Katrina had excelled herself in the preparation of a simple but satisfying dinner. *Hors d'oeuvres* that were in themselves a feast, luscious *filets mignons*, suitably garnished, Claire's favourite cold *crème caramel* and a tempting cheeseboard. They drank dry sherry and the red wine of Constantia, on the strength of which Claire soon found herself working out fantastic radio features with Sarah that would embrace the Transkei and Zululand, their people and customs.

Guy groaned. 'I can see our holiday whittled down to a day in Durban and a week-end in East Griqualand, and the rest of the time devoted to research in the Bantustans.'

'We can't waste your proficiency in Xhosa and Zulu,' said Sarah.

'The trouble with our country is that it has too much to offer,' added Katrina. 'The material is too rich.'

When they had finished their coffee Claire approached the subject that had secretly been uppermost in her mind all evening.

'Katrina, we want very much to see the bust you've been doing of Daddy.'

A glance passed between Katrina and Sarah. They had been expecting this.

'If you want to see it you have the right,' Katrina said. 'But I must warn you, you may not like it.'

'Go with Katrina, Claire,' said Sarah. 'I will stay here with Guy. He can see it later. You must be alone when Katrina shows it to you.'

Claire followed Katrina along the passage to the studio. The bust, covered by a cloth, was on a table under a standard lamp.

'I'm going to leave you with it,' said Katrina. 'I'll come back in ten minutes.'

She switched on the lamp and took the cloth from the head. The skylight blinds had not been drawn and a faint moonglow filtered through the glass. There was a chair near the bust and Claire sat down. She heard the door close behind Katrina. It was a life-sized head, yet it looked a little smaller, perhaps because the colour of the clay lent it the diminished proportions of death. Cast in bronze it would be impressive. The shoulders were covered with the judicial robe, but this was not the bust of Charles Hammond, the Judge, it was the head of a man who had known for himself the ultimate in human suffering.

Claire found that her hands were cold and trembling and she was glad of the radiator Katrina had turned on before leaving the room. Here was genius and here too was the soul of her father. This was the reverse of the fine but formal portrait. Mr Justice Hammond had looked out of the portrait with penetrating compassion. The lines of the face were those of maturity and experience, enhancing its nobility. It was a portrait of success, of a career brought to a proud climax, of a man in his late prime with the wisdom and the right to pass judgement on his fellows. The sculptured head symbolized a very different mood. It was a thing of planes and shadows, of sightless eyes and mobile suffering lips, of material dimensions and spiritual content, infinitely significant. Here was the man, Charles Hammond, and he was a man of sorrows and humility, strength and mercy.

As she sat before the sculpture Claire was intensely aware of her father. It was as if the face opposite hers expressed all that had never been said between them. The grief and deprivation of her mother's prolonged and painful illness; the responsibility of a teenage daughter; the joy and renewal of youth and vigour that his love for Vale had given him; the secret fear of losing her; the tragedy of his physical destruction and the knowledge that he could no longer fight to hold the woman who was his pride, his life, and the mother of his beloved son. The colourless eyes that looked out of the revealing and faithful mask of her father's soul were no longer blind. They saw the past with its triumphs and tribulations and the empty future, they knew the meaning of defeat and despair but they had passed beyond it into something unfathomable, some mystery of their own.

Claire's breath came short and there was sweat in her palms. It was terribly sad and terribly beautiful. Every man has his Gethsemane, his Cross and his Calvary. This she had not fully known till now.

She heard the door open softly, and she was aware of Katrina standing behind her.

'It isn't quite finished. I was waiting for the flicker of hope to light the eyes. I thought perhaps I could give it back to him.'

Claire turned slowly and looked up at the tall woman with the crown of pale hair.

'You loved him, then?'

Katrina did not answer, but Claire knew that this too was part of the moment of insight.

'It was finished, Katrina. The bust was finished before that last sitting – the one he failed to come for. No one could give him back what you called the flicker of hope.'

That had died when the scales had fallen from his eyes. In the sileece of the studio a memory sprang into Claire's mind.

Jef Broome holding Freya in his arms with her little rosy face close against his own. That day hope had died in her father, and hate had possessed him. She could feel once more the river of revenge flow from his hand into hers as she touched his fingers on the bow-string.

'Do you want Guy to see this bust?' Katrina asked.

'Yes,' said Claire. 'It's a work of genius and love and it's the absolute essence of my father.'

'But is it something you want to own, Claire?'

'I want it in bronze. I want it more than you can believe. It's the most beautiful thing I've ever seen. I don't understand it yet, but one day I will. That face has known despair and come through it to something beyond hope. Resignation . . . sacrifice . . . one day I'll know.'

Katrina put her arms about Claire's shoulders. A strange tender smile was on her lips.

'You've touched a profound truth – even if it's still obscure. Come. We'll send Guy into the studio. This bust is best seen alone for the first time by anyone who cares about your father – and Guy cares very much indeed.'

'Daddy loved Guy too. He was glad about us. In the middle of everything else he could be happy for us. He was truly happy on our wedding day.'

But that, she remembered now, had been before he had known of Jef Broome's return to South Africa.

On the following Saturday Guy was to play in a golf match between the Law and the Medical Profession, so he left Claire with Mrs Terblanche just before noon.

'You girls will have time for a good quack before lunch and I'm sure you'll enjoy your film this afternoon. Shall I fetch Claire, Helen, or will you drop her back to the flat after the picture?'

'I'll drop her back. Then you can take your time at the nineteenth hole while I have a drink with Claire.'

'See you later, then.'

There was plenty to 'quack' about, and Claire could see at a glance that her aunt was in a gossipy mood. That was the nice thing about being with someone of your own family, you could talk a little scandal about your relations without feeling disloyal. Yet, even so, there were certain things Claire had never discussed with her aunt. Neither had hinted to the other that there might be something between Vale and Jef Broome.

Mrs Terblanche poured a gin and tonic for herself and one for Claire. She cut a lemon and dropped two slices into the drinks so that they fizzed invitingly.

'Your father left an interesting will,' she said. 'For someone so scrupulously fair it has some odd discrepancies. It was kind of him to arrange that Mrs Rorke's annuity should continue for her life.'

Claire frowned, ignoring the matter of Mrs Rorke's annuity. 'How do you mean, discrepancies?'

Helen Terblanche raised her eyebrows.

'Take your own position over Silverglade. It's a curious situation. Silverglade is left to you – as it should be, considering it was your mother's family home originally – and yet Charles stipulated that his widow remains in possession for as long as she wishes to live there and be responsible for the upkeep. It means you can't sell until Vale cares to go and live elsewhere.'

'When Vale remarries we can. Daddy made it clear that if Vale remarries or vacates Silverglade, it comes to me at once with no further strings attached.'

'That's a point. I suppose he was assuming she was bound to remarry. After all, she's young and attractive and she won't be poor. She'll have a set income and she has a considerable sum coming to her on the life insurance policy.'

'Yes, Vale gets that, and she'll have the income on Daddy's capital during her lifetime. After that the capital is to be divided between his children.'

'You lose out on that, as you and Vale are so close in age.'

Claire smiled. 'It doesn't matter. My children will benefit. It goes to Daddy's children or their issue, don't forget. Guy and I mean to have a family, now we can afford it.'

'Well, and then there's Leopard Bush. That goes to Micky, so he is really the greatest beneficiary under the will. That's a valuable property but what will become of it till he's old enough to decide for himself? I asked Vale but she hadn't thought about it seriously. She isn't born a Hammond and the place has no sentimental value to her. I doubt if she really cares about it. She's a city girl by birth and inclination.'

'But Daddy protected Micky's rights. Although Vale is his natural guardian she can't sell Leopard Bush on his behalf without the permission of the executors – and you and Guy are executors in Daddy's will.'

'That's so. Actually, if Vale wanted to sell on Micky's behalf I'd be willing to buy myself at a fair price. Klaas Steyn could go on managing the farm and I'd use it as your father did – for holidays and weekends. I've always loved Leopard Bush. But then I'm a sentimentalist where the family is concerned and I adore that farm anyway. I've no children of my own and I could even leave it back to Micky if he turned out well and was a good South African.'

He'll probably 'turn out well' and be a good American, Claire thought, but she didn't say so. She laughed and said: 'You're looking awfully far ahead, Aunt Helen! Don't turn into one of those old ladies who plays wills.'

'Plays wills?'

'It's a sort of game – making and changing your will. My grandmother was always doing that, I'm told.'

Helen Terblanche smiled. 'We aren't really discussing my will, my dear. We were talking about your father's. Now take Freya. Charles made no provision for her to have money of her own.'

'She shares with us – Micky and me – after Vale's death,' said Claire. 'Surely till then it's up to her mother to look after her financially.'

'I suppose so. It just struck me as being a curiously uneven will. It was a very recent one too. I dare say Charles wanted to make certain changes once you were married and off his hands.'

'It seems all right to me,' said Claire loyally. 'I inherited a little from my own mother when she died and Silverglade is worth a great deal.'

'Not as much as Leopard Bush.'

'Maybe not, but Micky is the boy – the Hammond. It was the same for you, remember, when your father died. Daddy got Leopard Bush because he was Hammond. You were already Terblanche. Anyway I don't suppose Vale will stay on at Silverglade very long. It would cost too much – and, in any case —' she broke off, biting her lip.

'In any case – what?'

Suddenly Mrs Terblanche's bird face was sharp and shrewd, and, for the first time, it occurred to Claire that her aunt was not ignorant of the situation that had been developing at Silverglade in the past few months. All this talk about the will had been exploratory. She wanted to discover what Claire knew. They were playing a game of hide-and-seek.

'Aunt Helen,' said Claire. 'What are you really getting at?'

'I think your father knew a great deal more about Vale than any of us ever guessed.'

'Exactly what do you think he knew?' Claire was determined to make her aunt do the talking.

'I think he knew that she was in love with Jefferson Broome.'

Claire caught her breath. Such candour was more than she had bargained for.

'What makes you say that?'

'My dear child, people talk. You've been living in a dream world – in love with Guy, getting married – and you may not realize that our old Cape Peninsula is like a village where we all take in each other's washing and know each other's business. Do you imagine the Euclides didn't notice anything between Vale and Jef? Or that Penelope doesn't like a bit of scandal as well as the next young woman? Gossip reaches me by devious routes, and, when it concerns my brother, it's only hinted at cautiously, and I stamp on it fast, but the seed remains and grows. I've been putting two and two together ever since that young man arrived and went dancing with Vale the night you were married. Oh, I know it was a party, but still it was your wedding night and her place was at home with her husband and her mother and her own family.'

'John Rorke was her family. She went out with him – in his party.'

'Now, Claire, are you defending Vale? Or arguing with me?'

'Aunt Helen, there's something cooking up in you, what is it?'

Suddenly Mrs Terblanche looked old and drawn. The sunlight seemed very strong in the pretty room and very cruel to the lines of her face. She looked more than ever like some heraldic bird. She's like Daddy, Claire thought, but her features are sharper. Her eyes are kind but they haven't got Daddy's compassion in them. He understood people and their sins even if he couldn't forgive them, even when he

was condemning them and demanding a life for a life. Aunt
Helen loved Daddy very dearly. He was all she had really –
Daddy and me – and Micky, of course. She didn't seem very
interested in Freya. Maybe she guessed.

'You've seen the Westhuizen bust?' Mrs Terblanche asked.

'Yes, we want to buy it in bronze. It's wonderful. It's sad
but powerful.'

'It's terribly revealing too. Charles was a very unhappy
man in the weeks before he . . . was killed.'

'You blame Vale?'

'Yes,' said Mrs Terblanche with dreadful honesty.

She turned away from Claire and rang the bell. She put
the gin bottle in the cupboard with a decisive gesture and
locked it and slipped the key into her handbag. When the
maid answered the bell, she said:

'We're ready for lunch, Lena. Serve it right away.'

'We mustn't be late for that film,' she added to Claire.

It was only afterwards that Claire began to wonder
precisely what her aunt had meant when she had said 'yes'
in answer to the question 'Do you blame Vale?'

For what did Helen Terblanche blame Vale? For her
father's unhappiness – or for his death?

24

THE SUMMING UP

THE CHILLING THOUGHT THAT HAD ENTERED HER HEAD that day continued to haunt Claire. Could a woman deliberately drive a man to take his own life – a man as high-principled and well-balanced as her father? Her father had been a careful and capable driver – the more so, if possible, since he had acquired his new car, for he had a keen sense of responsibility to other users of the road. He took no chances and he had known the cliff road like the back of his hand. It was extraordinary that he should have rounded that particular bend at high speed, especially after a stormy week and driving on the precipice side. It just wasn't like him. Was it significant that it was a place where no one else could come to harm if the car left the road?

Claire tried to put the whole thing out of her mind. If, in some way, Vale had taunted her husband or driven him to desperation, nothing could ever be proved. Evil thoughts could only destroy the thinker's peace of mind. Guy had made that clear. He had forbidden the question *why* in connection with the accident.

It was Sarah Verity who unconsciously loosened that curb. When Claire went into Sarah's office to discuss the day's assignments she found her boss reading the morning paper with more than usual interest.

'Have you seen this?' she asked. 'Jefferson Broome has two days in which to leave the country.'

'I haven't read the paper yet. What does it say?'

'It was bound to happen sooner or later,' said Sarah. 'He's been writing some tough stuff about South Africa in the American papers and it's been syndicated all over the world.'

'He feels very strongly about apartheid. You can't expect him to throw away his principles.' Odd that she should be defending Jef, but she could not help admiring the tenacity with which he clung to his creed. He was, in all things, tenacious.

'Well, he's going to have to feel strongly somewhere else. He's had his chips here. Listen to this.' Sarah put on her glasses and took up the paper.

'"U.S. journalist faces deportation. Jefferson Broome has two days in which to leave the Republic. It seems the decision to withdraw Mr Broome's visa was made a fortnight ago. He was immediately advised by the Ministry of the Interior that he would be given two weeks in which to leave South Africa. This period of grace expires the day after tomorrow. If he has not then left of his own accord he will be deported. No reason has been given for the Ministry's decision, but those foreign periodicals carrying Broome's attacks on the Republic's apartheid policy have been banned here. When I went to interview Mr Broome at his Claremont flat he said, 'No comment'. But he appeared to be in the throes of packing."'

'I admit he was asking for it,' said Claire. 'When did you say his visa had been withdrawn?'

'A fortnight ago. I gather he's rather a friend of Vale's.'

'Yes. He was often at Silverglade.'

Sarah put the paper down and opened her diary, thereby closing the subject of Jefferson Broome.

'Let's see, now. What does today bring forth? There's an interview with that New Zealand educationalist – Mrs Downes – have you fixed the time for recording?'

'Yes. Three p.m.'

'And you've arranged about the equipment you and Guy will need when you go on your working holiday next week? Guy's coming in tomorrow to see our technicians, isn't he?'

'Yes. That's all under control.'

'Then I don't think there's anything else for now.'

Claire left Sarah thoughtfully. All that day she did her work automatically. Dates kept chasing each other round and round her mind. A fortnight ago? A fortnight ago Jef Broome had been told he must leave the country – or else. ... And twelve days ago her father had driven over the cliff.

When she arrived home it was raining heavily and growing darker. Guy was already in the flat, for the Law Courts had gone into recess the day before. He had drawn the curtains and switched on the electric radiator. The place looked homely and cosy. Claire kissed him perfunctorily and went into the bathroom and put her open umbrella across the bath and hung up her wet raincoat.

'That's no way to kiss your husband,' Guy called after her. 'What's up?'

She came back into the sitting-room and curled up on the couch near the fire.

'Have you read this morning's paper?'

'Yes, and I see Jef Broome is being kicked out. I'm not surprised. He's let his convictions run away with his common sense. He couldn't really expect to remain here while slating everything South African so vigorously abroad.'

'He was told he'd have to get out two weeks ago. Two weeks ago, Guy.'

'So what?'

The paper was neatly folded in a wicker magazine-holder near the couch. She lifted it out and opened it at the page in question.

'Listen,' she said and quoted:

'"... The decision to withdraw Mr Broome's visa was

made a fortnight ago. He was advised by the Ministry of the Interior that he would be given two weeks in which to leave South Africa. This period of grace expires the day after to-morrow."' She looked up. 'Doesn't that strike you as significant?'

'It strikes me he's leaving things rather late. But he still has a day in hand.'

Guy was smoking a cigarette and watching Claire intently.

'Vale must have known a fortnight ago,' she insisted.

'What of it?'

'That's exactly what I'm going to find out.'

'Claire, you're wearing your hell-raising face. What's in your mind?'

'My father went over that cliff twelve days ago. I'm going to find out why. I'm going up to Silverglade tonight – with or without you.'

'You'll probably find Jef there. His time is short.'

She made a contemptuous gesture. 'Will you come?'

'I think I must. But at least let's warn Vale. And let's have supper here first. I'm famished.'

Claire went to the telephone, her eyes and lips hard. She dialled the number and waited. Josiah answered.

'Josiah, is Madam there?'

'No, Miss Claire. But Madam is coming back to dinner.'

'Tell Madam we are coming to see her after dinner tonight. Mr Guy and I will be at Silverglade at half-past eight.'

Vale seldom used the library now. It held too many memories. There was a little morning-room which she had made her own. She had used it as a study for years and now it had become her sanctum. It was snug with the firelight dancing on ivory walls, on the bookcases and radiogram and on the table where her magazines lay. Vale liked the glossy fashion and house-and-garden magazines. When she was alone she had her evening meals here on a tray. She rang the bell now and looked up from reading the paper as Josiah entered. It was twenty past eight.

'Take the tray, Josiah, and show Mr Guy and Miss Claire in here when they arrive.'

As he left the room she put down the paper and went to the telephone on her desk. She dialled a number.

'Jef? Listen, darling, Claire and Guy are on their way here – I don't know why – but I'll ring you when they've gone. Don't come over before you hear from me. There's the bell, that'll be them now.'

She greeted them with composure. Guy stood with his back to the fire and Claire sat on a stiff-backed chair.

'That's not very comfortable,' said Vale.

'It suits me,' said Claire.

'As you like.'

Vale had relaxed in an easy-chair herself, and Guy observed the new serenity that appeared unruffled by her stepdaughter's hostile manner. She was looking at Claire without animosity, her dark eyes questioning.

'What did you want to see me about?' she asked. 'You seem upset, Claire.'

'There are things I have to get straight,' said Claire. 'Things only you can explain, Vale. I have to know whether my father met with an accident – or . . .'

'Or took his own life,' finished Vale. 'I can give you no answer to that. How can I? I thought we'd decided to leave the subject alone.'

Guy said, 'Charles Hammond wasn't the sort of man to commit suicide. I don't know why Claire persists with these doubts.'

Claire leaned forward, her hands clasped and her knuckles white.

'I've thought and thought what could have driven him

to such an act, and today, when I read the paper, the penny dropped.'

'Tell me what you . . . suspect,' said Vale quietly.

'Jef Broome knew a fortnight ago that he would have to leave the country. He must have told you. And my father drove to his death twelve days ago —'

'Jef told me the moment the Ministry gave him their ultimatum – to get out in two weeks or be thrown out.'

'And then you went to my father. You probably said you were leaving him to go away with Jef?'

Claire's voice was harsh as she flung out the words. Vale did not answer at once. She put up her hand and brushed it across her eyes as if to brush away a mist. Guy said sternly:

'You haven't come here to make accusations, Claire. You've come to try and clear up the facts – and I still say they'd be better left.'

Vale looked at Guy gratefully.

'Maybe I should explain exactly what happened. With these terrible doubts in your mind, Claire, you have the right to know as much as I can tell you. For some reason you seem to hold me responsible for the . . . accident. I hope to God you're wrong.'

'Very well, then, tell us as much as you can,' Guy said. 'It might help.'

She sat forward. She was wearing black slacks and a cherry red pullover and her hands, crossed at the wrists, fell limply between her knees in a relaxed rather boyish attitude. Her chin was up and she spoke slowly as if she were giving her evidence with care, determined to be accurate. She wasn't nervous and Guy felt that she was 'a good witness'. He trusted her. She knew and understood – perhaps even shared – Claire's fears and she seemed half relieved to bring them into the open and dispel them.

Claire said, 'Your *affaire* with Jef – you revived that the

moment he came back to this country. You can't deny it.
And Daddy knew.' She spoke, fiercely remembering the
bust – the man of sorrows Katrina had built up bit by bit as
she added and moulded the cold revealing clay every time
her sitter came to the studio.

'Yes, I admit we've been lovers since Jef got back. I had
no idea he was coming back to the Cape and I certainly
didn't want him to. I was afraid of . . . of waking up again . . .
in that way. I wanted to be loyal to Charles. But it was too
strong for me – my need for Jef. In the circumstances it was
doubly strong. Then, nearly two weeks ago, he told me he
wasn't going to be allowed to remain in South Africa.'

'What happened then?' Guy asked.

She looked up at him and her eyes reflected the pain of
the decision that had been forced upon her.

'There was a scene between us. He insisted that I should go
with him – that I must tell Charles. He was convinced
Charles would give me my freedom to marry him. Charles
was always so selfless where I was concerned – so terribly
conscious of what he called his responsibility towards me.'

She was talking more freely now, more quickly, and her
hands gripped one another and twisted as if she were wringing them in distress.

'Charles couldn't bear being crippled. He didn't talk about
it often but sometimes he was tortured by the way things
had to be between him and me. He'd say it was a crime for
my youth to be allowed to fade – chained to him – to the
wheels of his chair. These moods didn't attack him often,
but, when they did, they were shattering for both of us.'

Claire glanced at Guy and the naked pity on his face
opened up a whole world of agonizing frustration beyond
her comprehension.

'Did he ever offer to release you?' Guy asked.

Vale nodded.

'The day I told him about Jef being forced to leave the country. He looked at me as if I had delivered a death sentence. He just said, "You're trying to tell me that you want to go away with him. If that's what you're trying to say, then my answer is – Go, and take Freya with you and I'll make it easy for you. Divorce is easy in this country – too easy. If you desert me I can divorce you in a matter of weeks. I won't let your mother suffer financially and Freya will share in my will when the time comes." You see, he'd thought it all out long before. He'd anticipated something like this.'

She put out her hand for a cigarette and Guy lit it for her. He said:

'What more could he offer you?'

'There was Micky. I asked if he'd let me have Micky, and he said, "That I cannot do. I cannot and will not give my son to another man to go and be brought up far away in another country. I love Micky more than anything in life."' She half turned to Claire. 'I'm sorry if that hurts you, Claire, but I expect you knew it, anyway. I always did. Micky was everything to him and I hadn't any right to take his son from a man who had already lost so much. We were in the library by the fire, and, when I didn't answer, he said in a desperate sort of way, "That alters everything, doesn't it? You'd like to cut our child in two, like the false mother in the judgement of Solomon?"'

She shook her head as if the wound of those words still pained her. Guy spoke into the silence that fell between them, prompting her.

'So then, Vale, what did you say?'

'What could I say? I told Charles I couldn't leave Micky. That I'd rather give up Jef.'

She paused, seeing again the bitter struggle reflected in her husband's face that day. He had steeled himself to give her her freedom and then he had realized that without Micky she would not take it. She went on steadily:

'After a while he said I could have Micky. It was like cutting out his heart for him to do so. Charles said Jef was an idealist and, although he'd gladly see him dead, he couldn't blame him for loving me.'

Tears filled her eyes as she recalled him, lined and drawn, every nerve strung to breaking point as he forced himself to make the supreme sacrifice.

'My father said that!' Claire exclaimed. 'He left you free to take Micky from him?'

'Yes, he did, but how could I take Micky? Charles and Micky adored each other. Micky loved us both. He was safe and trusting and happy. If I'd taken him from his home and deserted his father he would never have forgiven me. He feels very deeply, child as he is. In time he'd have come to judge me and hate me.'

'So you told Daddy you'd stay with him for Micky's sake.'

'I'm trying to be honest with you, Claire. Many things had to be weighed up. My love for Jef against my relation-ship with my son —'

'Daddy didn't really come into it, did he? As far as you were concerned, he was only an obstacle to your getting Jef, Freya and Micky with no strings attached – no criticism from Micky in later years, or from anybody else.'

Vale sprang up, her eyes blazing.

'You've no right to say a thing like that! What are you trying to do to me? Saddle me with a motive for murder?'

Guy put his hand on her arm.

'Calm down, Vale.'

But Claire cut in.

'Make the cap fit, if you must!'

Vale shook off Guy's restraining hand and stared at Claire, white hot with anger.

'I owed your father the truth, Claire. There are times when one cheats and lies to make life easier, even to spare another person, but in the end the point is reached where only the truth is good enough. I've tried to give it to you as well – the whole truth and nothing but the truth – but you don't want the whole truth – you're incapable of understanding it – all you want are snippets of truth to use against me, to bolster up your dreadful accusation. I didn't know you hated me so much.'

'On your own admission my father offered you everything – but it wasn't enough. There was only one more sacrifice he could make for you —'

'Claire!'

It was Guy's voice that silenced her, and suddenly, as she looked at him, she was ashamed. She had never seen him like this, his eyes hard as steel, cold authority in every line of his face.

'Who do you think you are – the Angel Gabriel? Let's get one thing clear. No one of us three has the slightest right to probe into Charles Hammond's deeds and motives. Whatever happened that fateful day, or why it happened, or whether it was or wasn't an accident, is not for us to decide. We've no business to try to solve the mystery to suit ourselves. Or to make a case against Vale. Vale was honest with her husband, and, the situation being what it was, she could do no more than promise to give up her lover and stand by her son's father. By what right do you, Claire, sit in judgement on anyone? Both Vale and your father were prepared to make great sacrifices. Who are you to assess them?'

Claire looked at the stern face of the man she loved and saw him in a new light. As a judge. A flash of memory flared up in her mind – Guy talking of her father. 'Every judge should have a godlike quality but few of them do. Your father is one of the few. . . . He has wisdom and compassion and he understands the quality of mercy . . .' It was strange how the words came back to her – the place and the time. He had talked of her father by the pool the evening they had rescued the curlew – the evening they had found the letter with the stolen stamps torn off the long foreign envelope. After that everything had changed at Silverglade. Nothing had been the same for any of them any more. Claire looked from Guy to Vale – free now – her head bowed, her face in shadow.

Suddenly she knew that Guy was right. None of them could really fathom the extent of the sacrifice and the suffering life had demanded of her father and his young wife. Nor could they tell for sure whether fate or free will had caused the final crash. She slipped her hand into Guy's and the condemnation in her heart melted away as she accepted its inevitability. She guessed – as the others could not – that her father had lived with the growing fear of being driven to do his wife's lover some mortal injury. Thank God that had never happened.

Vale looked up. She had herself under control once more. She pushed back her hair and made an effort to be practical.

'Claire, you'll want to know how long I mean to stay in Silverglade. I thought that was why you had come here tonight. To find out when it would really be yours.'

'I never thought about it – not tonight.'

'Well, I can tell you. Josiah – like Jef – has been given his marching orders. He was granted an extension of his permit because Charles needed him. That no longer applies. Harmonia and Fedora go back to the Transkei too in ten days time. When they are gone it will be the end of Silverglade for me.'

'For all of us,' said Claire. 'I can't imagine Silverglade without Josiah and Harmonia.'

Her heart sank. This indeed marked the end of an era. Yet this too was inevitable.

'Luckily I have Angela,' said Vale. 'We'll move out at the end of next week. We couldn't afford to stay on here, anyway – even rent free. I've found a cottage in Wynberg. In any case we never really belonged here. It was your mother's home. We were intruders – I and my children.'

'You were part of my father's life – of all our lives,' said Claire. She wished she could take back some of the things she had said, but it was too late. They had made their impact and done their lasting damage.

'For a time, yes,' said Vale. 'But that's over now. I've taken this cottage for six months. After that I don't know what will happen. I just wanted you to realize that you were free to get on with the sale of Silverglade.'

Guy's arm tightened round Claire's shoulders. She turned to him and hid her face against his chest. Now indeed her childhood and girlhood were on the way out. Silverglade would be sold and its ghosts would be laid. But Guy remained – Guy who had been part of it all, and who was part of her now.

Faintness seized her, her hands were cold and clammy, her knees limp. Guy let her gently down on to a chair. Vale brought brandy and water.

'This comes over me from time to time,' Claire said weakly. 'This ghastly feeling. I suppose it's strain.'

'I don't think so,' said Vale. 'You're not the fainting type, never have been.' She smiled with sudden sweetness. 'If you ask me, it's a baby. It's the future, Claire.'

Claire returned her smile.

'Well, I have just wondered lately. I hope you may be right.'